COURAGE to *Love* AGAIN

KIMBERLY BROWN

BLACK ODYSSEY MEDIA

WWW.BLACKODYSSEY.NET

Published by
BLACK ODYSSEY MEDIA

www.blackodyssey.net
Email: info@blackodyssey.net

Library of Congress Control Number: 2023919145

First Trade Paperback Printing: May 2024
ISBN: 978-1-957950-41-9
ISBN: 978-1-957950-42-6 (e-book)

Cover Design by Ashlee Nassar of Designs With Sass

10 9 8 7 6 5 4 3 2 1

Manufactured in the United States of America

Distributed by Kensington Publishing Corp.

Dear Reader,

I want to thank you immensely for supporting Black Odyssey Media authors, and our ongoing efforts to spotlight more minority storytellers. The scariest and most challenging task for many writers is getting the story, or characters, out of our heads and onto the page. Having admitted that, with every manuscript that Kreceda and I acquire, we believe that it took talent, discipline, and remarkable courage to construct that story, flesh out those characters, and prepare it for the world. Debut or seasoned, our authors are the real heroes and heroines in *OUR* story. And for them, we are eternally grateful.

Whether you are new to Kimberly Brown or Black Odyssey Media, we hope that you are here to stay. So please be sure to check out more of Kimberly Brown's array of stories over at our sister and fellow publishing mate B. Love Publications. We also welcome your feedback and kindly ask that you leave a review. For upcoming releases, announcements, submission guidelines, etc., please be sure to visit our website at www.blackodyssey.net or scan the QR code below. We can also be found on social media using @iamblackodyssey. Until next time, take care and enjoy the journey!

Joyfully,

Shawanda Williams

Shawanda "N'Tyse" Williams
Founder/Publisher

AUTHOR'S NOTE

This work of fiction discusses topics of fertility, miscarriage, infant loss, weight, and verbal spousal abuse. This book includes some profanity and descriptive sexual content.

CHARACTER NAME PRONUNCIATIONS
Pasha (Pa-sha)
Callum (Kay-Lum)
Avyn (A-Vin)

CHAPTER ONE
Pasha

I SIGHED HEAVILY AS I pulled into my driveway.

Today had been draining. After my therapy session, I picked up my prescription and headed to the waterfront to self-reflect. My anxiety had been peaking for weeks now. The feeling of impending doom washed over me, and it had yet to leave. I thought some time by the water would mellow me out because it was my favorite place. Sadly, it hadn't. All I wanted to do was climb into my bed, pull the covers over my head, and sleep.

Unfortunately, that wasn't going to be the case. I still needed to cook dinner even though I was not motivated. Part of me just wanted to order takeout and call it a day. However, that would only start an argument with my husband, and I had no energy to argue today. Raymond's annoyance at me seemed to spike whenever I came home from a therapy session. I felt like he was looking to pick a fight when I was the most vulnerable. It was a horrible thing to feel like my husband couldn't stand me at times.

Things weren't always like this. Once upon a time, he was the most loving and caring man. He dated me with purpose and intention. I moved out of my parents' house and into his to fall straight into my role as a housewife. Raymond was ten years older than me. I met him when I was twenty and he was thirty. My parents hadn't been a fan of our age difference. In their mind, a thirty-year-old had nothing in common with a twenty-year-old.

I didn't care.

He wasn't anything like the guys my age. He moved differently. He showed me different, and that made me want him more. He knew he wanted . . . to flourish in his career as a cardiothoracic surgeon and have a beautiful family. I was fine with that. I could handle being a wife and mother. I'd watched my mother do it my entire life. My father took care of the bills, and she took care of the home. That was easy enough . . . until it wasn't. Now, I was barely hanging on by a thread.

Reluctantly, I grabbed my things and stepped out of the car. As I made my way up the driveway, I noticed a pile of suitcases on the front lawn. A frown of confusion settled on my face when I realized that they belonged to me.

"What the hell? . . ."

Briskly, I walked up to the pile. Upon further inspection, I discovered that trash bags filled with my shoes, lotions, hygiene, and beauty products were packed up too. Frantically, I tried to open the front door. It was locked. I stuck my key in . . . only to find that it wasn't working.

"Raymond!" I yelled, banging on the door. "Raymond, it's me!"

His car was here, so I knew he was inside. After a few minutes of knocking like a madwoman, the front door finally opened, and my husband stepped out.

He snapped at me. "Stop banging on this door and yelling like you've lost your damn mind!" He stepped outside and closed the door behind him.

I pointed at my things. "What the hell is this?"

"Look . . . Ain't no easy way to say this, so I'm just gonna put it out there. I want a divorce."

"Raymond!"

"Don't 'Raymond' me. You had to have seen this coming, Pasha. We haven't been happy in a long time, and it's largely in part to you. All you do is mope around here. I'm sick of the depressed act. You barely cook anymore. You don't clean. You haven't fucked me in months, and even before that, it was like watching paint dry. All you've done in the last year is eat and get fat. I'm not even attracted to you anymore."

"I . . . I don't . . ." I struggled to respond. How *could* I respond?

"You *what*? What do you have to say for yourself? Go on, I'm listening." He crossed his arms as he glared down at me.

"I've been in therapy . . . I just need some time—"

"Therapy isn't doing shit. You've been in therapy for almost two years now, and I see no improvement. You can pay for that out of your own pocket now. That means you'll need to get a job. Say it with me, J.O.B."

"How can you do this to me, Raymond?" I was crying profusely at this point. "I'm your wife!"

"You haven't acted in a wife's capacity in so long. When was the last time you felt happy, Pasha? I can't tell you 'cause I don't know myself. I feel like we've been going through the motions, and I'm tired of that. I take care of you, and for the longest, you've been failing miserably to do anything I ask you to when you agreed to marry me."

"You *know* what's going on with me, Raymond."

"What I know is you use your mental health as a crutch. You got a diagnosis and ran with it. Enough is enough. This isn't the life I envisioned as a married man. I'm tired of feeling like I settled. Look at you. Your hair looks a mess, and you're out here looking like a homeless woman instead of the wife of a doctor. I can't take you in public. I can't have people over. It's embarrassing. You can't even bear me a child—"

I jabbed my finger in his face. "That's so hurtful and unfair. You *know* my issues with fertility. I've tried and tried."

"Then something is wrong with you." He scoffed. "I know it ain't me. The more weight you gain, the less likely you are to carry. You haven't even tried to lose it, Pasha."

"I've been depressed, Raymond! Do you know what a struggle it is to get out of bed in the morning? I've had to deal with the death of my parents. I've suffered three miscarriages back-to-back. I dealt with postpartum depression that came back stronger after each one. And then . . . just when I thought my body was finally working with me, I gave birth to a stillborn son—"

"And I get that, I really do. But you just checked out. You checked out of life and out of this marriage. I can't do this anymore, Pasha. You have to go. Get you some real help and move on."

My mouth hung open in disbelief. I couldn't believe this was happening to me. Eight years I'd been with this man. Five of those I'd been a devoted wife. I catered to him and his needs. I put him before myself, and he showed his true colors when I needed him to stand beside me. Last year was the roughest. After giving birth to a stillborn son, my world was shattered.

I developed postpartum, my anxiety was at an all-time high, and I gained a total of forty pounds. I wasn't overweight, but I wasn't the size I used to be. Clearly, I wasn't his preferred size, either. Things changed between us. Raymond wasn't the loving and affectionate man he once was. He turned cold and almost hateful toward me. I kept telling myself once I got it together that things would be better. . . . If I lost the weight, things would go back to the way they used to be.

I was wrong. Things would never be the same, and now they'd never have that chance. I struggled to verbalize my thoughts. My lips were moving, but not a sound came out. Raymond sighed. Just as he went to speak the front door opened.

"How much longer are you going to be dealing with . . . this?"

My eyes settled on a petite woman. Her hair was long and straight, and not a strand was out of place. Her clothes were perfectly pressed and well put together. She was beautiful, and everything about her was the complete opposite of my current self. My eyes left her face and dropped to the prominent bulge in her stomach. They bounced from her to Raymond and back to her again.

"Who is this?" I asked just above a whisper.

She stepped out with one hand rubbing her stomach, and wrapped the other around his arm as she spoke to me.

"Adora . . . Raymond's fiancée and the mother of his child." She flashed a glistening diamond ring at me. "I'm also the new woman of this house, so I'd like you to get your shit off my lawn."

"Raymond . . ." I whispered. "How could you? Eight years—"

"Please don't start that crying shit," Adora said, holding up a hand. "I'm not trying to hear that. It was bad enough I had to listen to it inside."

"Shut up!" I screamed, jumping at her.

Raymond stepped between us and pushed me back. "I'm not about to have you fighting her. You're embarrassing yourself, Pasha."

"I'm embarrassing myself?" I looked around. "Am I being punked? Is this a prank? Are . . . Are there hidden cameras?"

Raymond shrugged. "Look, call yourself a ride, Uber, walk . . . Frankly, I don't care. You're trespassing on private property. You have thirty minutes to get your shit off my lawn, or I will have you forcibly removed. Give me your keys."

Again, I stared at him in disbelief. This was as much my home as it was his. Maybe I didn't work, but I kept this house spotless for years. I kept a hot meal on the table. I made sure our finances were straight. He was the one that made me a housewife. He told me he wanted to care for me as long as I could handle that responsibility. I did that for as long as I could. I was suffering mentally, and he didn't care . . . He just didn't care.

"The keys, Pasha! You know what . . ." He snatched them from my hand. "The clock is ticking."

He and his mistress walked back inside without another word, slamming the door behind them. I couldn't move. My body was riddled with shock and emotion. When I felt my chest begin to tighten, I knew I was having a panic attack. The tightening feeling was soon accompanied by the struggle to breathe. I began to pace, trying to calm myself.

Everything I learned in therapy felt useless at that moment. Part of me wanted this episode to just take me out. I didn't want to feel anything. I just wanted to be numb.

Numb to the pain.

Numb to the bullshit.

Numb to life in general. If I couldn't feel it, maybe it wasn't real. If it wasn't real, it couldn't hurt me. I'd experienced enough hurt . . . I just wanted to feel nothing . . . absolutely nothing.

CHAPTER TWO
Callum

I STARED AT MY computer screen, counting down the minutes until I could go home. Since being down a driver for the last week, I'd been filling in to make things run as smoothly as possible. I was set to end my day in about thirty minutes, and it couldn't be over fast enough. I owned and operated Elite Rides, a car shuttling service. It was something like Uber. I even had a hand in developing an app to run the service through.

In addition to that, I also own a limo/private car service. After seeing how well the car shuttling did, I decided that expanding my services in my local area would be a good idea. I catered to everything from proms to weddings to gala events. A few high-profile clients used me to take them from place to place around the state as well. We are currently booked through the year for various events.

We'd been up and running for about six years now, available in fifteen major cities in the southern states. At thirty-five, I was blessed to be able to make money in my sleep. I honestly could have easily replaced my sick driver temporarily. However, since I lived in the city, it was easier just to cover the shifts myself.

Today, however, was draining. For whatever reason, there was an influx of bookings. I wasn't upset about that. More bookings meant more business, and more business meant more money. I was simply tired. My bed was calling me, and I would answer that call as soon as I left.

The sound of my notifications dinging alerted me to a request.

"I was so close," I muttered.

With a heavy sigh, I looked up the information for this last ride. After claiming it, I grabbed the keys to the last SUV on the lot and headed out. Settled in the driver's seat, I loaded my smooth R&B playlist, rolled down the windows, and started toward my destination. The sun had gone down, and there was a cool breeze blowing. I was thankful for light traffic because this fifteen-minute ride could easily turn into forty-five.

When I pulled into the neighborhood, I turned the music down so I could focus. A minute later, I pulled up to a nice, two-story house. I frowned as I noticed the woman sitting beside a pile of suitcases and trash bags on the sidewalk. When she saw I had come to a stop, she stood slowly. I threw the car in park, climbed out, popped the trunk, and rounded the front to her. At first glance, she looked timid. Her face was beautiful, but aside from that, I could see the puffy red eyes and tear-stained cheeks.

"Ms. Sinclaire? My name is Callum. I'll be your driver this evening."

"Hi . . ." she said just above a whisper. Her voice was raspy like she'd been crying for hours.

I pointed to the pile. "Is all of this yours?"

"Yes."

Asking that seemed to trigger her. She buried her face in her hands, sobbing uncontrollably. I wasn't sure what to do. Did I say something? Should I console her? I stepped forward and rested my hands on her shoulders to guide her to the car. No sooner than I opened the back door of the car did the front door of the house behind us open.

"You still here, Pasha?" a man asked angrily, stalking toward us.

I frowned. "She's leaving."

"Not fast enough."

He started grabbing her suitcases and throwing them into my open trunk.

"I'm leaving, Raymond!" she pleaded helplessly. "Just let me go in peace. You've embarrassed me enough."

"I told you thirty minutes."

He came back for another suitcase, but I snatched it from him.

"I can put her things in my car. Why don't you go back inside? That's as nice as I'm going to ask you."

He scoffed. "As nice as you're going to ask me? You're on *my* property giving demands?"

"It wasn't a demand. It was a very *wise* suggestion."

He poked my chest. "And what are you gonna do if I don't comply with your little 'suggestion'?"

I looked back at Ms. Sinclaire. "Get in the car, baby."

She didn't hesitate to climb into the backseat. I closed the door and turned to see this man standing right up to me.

"Sir . . . I suggest you back up. Allow me to get Ms. Sinclaire's things, and we'll be on our way. If you want her gone, why hinder the process? Make it make sense."

He finally took a step back, glaring at me as he did. His gaze focused on the back window as I put the rest of her things in the trunk. Ms. Sinclaire was crying profusely at this point. This man had to be her husband or at least her boyfriend. Either way, he was a complete asshole, and I couldn't get her away from him quick enough. As I moved to close the trunk, I saw her reaching for the door handle.

"Ms. Sinclaire, he's not worth it," I tried to reason.

"You better not get outta that car, Pasha," he warned her.

She ignored both of our voices. She got out and walked around him and back toward the house.

"Pasha!" he yelled.

Again, she ignored him. Before I knew it, she'd picked up two bricks lining the walkway. She hurled one through the front window of the house and the other through the front window of the costly luxury car sitting in the driveway.

"Oh shit!" I grimaced as she picked up another brick and hurled it through the back window of that same car. At this point, the man I now knew as Raymond was yelling obscenities. He grabbed her, but she jerked away and slapped him.

"Fuck you, Raymond! I gave you eight years of my life! I was nothing but a good wife to you, and you did this to me. Rot in hell, you selfish son of a bitch!"

When a visibly pregnant woman came storming outside, putting two and two together didn't take long. Things were about to take another left.

"You need to leave!" she screamed.

"Oh, I'm leaving!" Mrs. Sinclaire screamed in return. "I wish I could say I feel sorry for you. You think you have one up on me now . . . You'll be just like me as soon as you can't cater to him the way he wants. Enjoy him while you can."

"I'll never be you. Not only do I know how to get and keep my man, but I can give him the one thing you can't."

She rubbed her belly with a satisfied smirk. I anticipated Mrs. Sinclaire's reaction, and before she could charge at the woman, I scooped her up and put her in the backseat. Discreetly, I put the child locks on to keep her from jumping out of the car again.

"Do not move," I said firmly. "Do you understand?"

Her beautiful face held a deep frown. It softened as tears pooled in her eyes. Her bottom lip trembled, and the next thing I knew, she fell against me, releasing a gut-retching cry. I wasn't the biggest fan of physical affection with strangers, yet this woman had an unnerving effect on me in the short time since I arrived.

"Get her away from here," Raymond demanded.

I ignored him as I continued to comfort his wife.

"You have to calm down so we can get outta here. I know this shit hurts, but he ain't worth it. Don't give him that kind of power over you."

"You hear me talking to you?"

Raymond grabbed my arm. Now, why did he do that? I didn't like people touching me, especially in an aggressive manner. I closed the back passenger door. Then with catlike reflexes, I spun around and twisted his arm behind his back, forcing him to the ground. The pregnant woman screamed at me to let him go.

"Let this be a warning . . . Don't *ever* put your hands on me. Now, as I previously stated, Mrs. Sinclaire is leaving. I trust that when I release you, you will show some decorum and take your disrespectful ass inside so she can leave in peace. Are we gonna have a problem?"

"Fuck you!" he seethed.

I twisted his arm tighter. One move, and I could snap it. If he knew what was good for him, he would heed my generous warning.

"I asked if we were going to have a problem," I repeated.

"No! Just let me go!"

I released him and took a step back. "Have a good evening."

Without another word, I retreated into the car and cranked up. As I pulled onto the road, I saw Raymond being consoled by his mistress in my rearview. I shook my head. I didn't know him, yet I could pin him as a weak-ass man with control issues. That woman might have thought she was getting a prize, but I had a feeling she would eventually learn that everything that glittered wasn't gold.

I'd been driving around aimlessly for a good fifteen minutes now, just waiting for Mrs. Sinclaire to calm down enough to tell me where to take her. I didn't want to rush her, especially after that fiasco. Every so often, I glanced at her in the rearview mirror. It gave me a chance to take in her natural beauty. If I had to guess, she was around five foot seven, a little on the thick side, which was absolutely fine by me. I loved a thick woman. A little belly, cellulite, or stretch marks never hurt anybody.

Her skin was cocoa-complexioned and blemish-free. Her full lips and beautiful brown eyes stuck out most to me. I always believed that the eyes were the windows to the soul. When she looked at me back at the house, I saw a soul that was drowning in pain. It was more than what she was going through at that moment. Pain like hers was deep-rooted.

Mrs. Sinclaire cried softly in the backseat. As I pulled to a stop sign, I looked back at her.

"Hey . . ." She slowly wiped her eyes and looked up at me. "Fuck him. I don't know the details, but from the looks of it, leaving is the best thing you could have done."

"I didn't leave . . . He put me out. He packed my things, and he put me out of my home. That . . . woman is his mistress. Excuse me, his fiancée." She began crying again. "How could I not have seen this coming? How could I have been so stupid? All the comments about my depression being too much . . . the constant jabs at my weight and appearance . . . the loneliness I've been feeling in this marriage for the longest. There were so many signs! I'm so embarrassed."

Her cries echoed in the car as I pulled away from the stop sign. The sight of her tears was doing something to me. She looked and felt helpless, and it was stabbing at my soul. Any other time, I would have canceled the service and refunded a client if they had too much drama during a reservation. My heart went out to this woman. Something about her just resonated with my spirit. I knew I couldn't leave her tonight without ensuring she was okay.

Her cries calmed down as I drove aimlessly through the city. Finally, they turned to light sniffles and whimpers. I'd been driving around at this point for thirty minutes.

"Is there anywhere I can take you?" I asked quietly.

She sniffed. "A hotel is fine. Whatever is close. I'm sure you're tired of me. I know this isn't what you signed up for."

I sighed. "It's not, but I'm in it now. I just wanna make sure you have somewhere safe to lay your head tonight."

She nodded. "Thank you. I'm so sorry—"

"Don't be sorry. I can tell you were blindsided. I don't know you or your story, but no woman deserves that from a man, least of all her husband."

"Are you married?"

I chuckled. "No, ma'am. I'm in these single streets."

"Oh."

She turned her head and looked out the window. We drove in silence until she spoke to point out a hotel. I pulled into the parking lot and up to the front entrance. While she went to grab a room, I grabbed a luggage cart and began unpacking the trunk. As I played Tetris, attempting to fit everything, she returned with a distressed look on her face.

"Put it back," she whispered.

"What's wrong?" I asked, confused.

"He canceled my credit cards . . . I can't pay for the room, and I don't have enough cash to cover it."

Her lips trembled as she turned away from me. I felt anger surge through me at that moment. It was enough to make me wish I *had* broken that nigga's arm. What kind of man puts his wife out of their home and then proceeds to cut off her livelihood? Whoever that pregnant woman was must have had his nose wide open. She had to be out of her mind to sit and watch that happen and be okay, let alone feel secure.

Mrs. Sinclaire finally gathered herself. She turned to me with red eyes. Again, my heart broke for her.

"Is there anybody you can call?" I asked. "Parents . . . a friend?"

She shook her head. "My parents died in a car accident a few years ago. I haven't spoken to any friends in so long that I wouldn't feel right asking them for help. You can just take me to a shelter—"

"Absolutely not."

"Please, I'm begging—"

"Let's go inside. I've got you."

"No, no, you can't."

"Mrs. Sinclaire, I'm not leaving until I know you're safe. You don't know me, but I can be annoying as hell. That's the last thing you want. Now, let me help you."

I didn't wait for her to protest. Instead, I grabbed her hand and pulled her and the cart behind me as I headed for the front desk.

"Good evening. My friend here needs a room. What do we need to do to make that happen?"

The receptionist ran me the pricing while Mrs. Sinclaire stood off to the side, looking embarrassed. There was no need for her to feel embarrassed with me, but I understood. If I were in her shoes, I would feel ashamed too. After paying for the room, I led her to the elevator. The ride to the fifth floor was quiet. The walk to the room was quiet, and it was quiet as I unloaded the cart. She seemed to be searching for the right words to say whenever my gaze met hers. Once the last bag hit the floor, she finally approached me.

"Thank you," she whispered.

"You don't have to thank me."

"Yes, I do. You didn't have to do this, yet you did. I promise I will pay you back once I get on my feet." She whipped out her phone. "Give me your number."

"Mrs. Sinclaire."

"Please? Allow me to retain what little dignity I have left."

I sighed as I took her phone and programmed my number in it before handing it back to her.

"The room is yours for two weeks," I said, reaching into my pocket for my wallet. Flipping it open, I pulled out all the cash I had on me, about $600, and handed it to her. "In case you need anything."

"I can't . . . You've done enough."

She wouldn't take the money from me, so I walked over to the nightstand beside the bed and set it there. I would call here in two weeks to see if she checked out. If she hadn't, I would just cover another two weeks. I didn't share that with her, though. She was going through enough. I just wanted to lift a burden from her.

I grabbed her hand and squeezed it. "Get you some rest, Mrs. Sinclaire."

"Please, call me Pasha."

"Pasha . . . take care."

"Thank you." She pulled me into a strong, warm hug. "God bless you."

She kissed my cheek before letting me go, and I walked out the door. I didn't know what it was about her, but I felt I'd be seeing her again. Maybe sooner than I thought.

CHAPTER THREE
Pasha

THE KNOCK ON my door broke me from my zoned-out state on the couch.

Since Callum left, I'd been sitting in this same spot, staring at the wall. He was the only person who knew I was here; surely, he hadn't returned. Who could be knocking at the door? Maybe they had the wrong room. I didn't want to be bothered anyway, so I just let them knock. It wasn't until I heard my name that I paid attention.

"Pasha?"

Immediately, I recognized the voice. It was my best friend, Avyn. Well, I wasn't sure I could call her my best friend anymore. I've been isolating myself from everybody for a while now. I didn't know what was happening with them; all they knew was that I'd been a ghost. Avyn used to be my girl. I knew I'd spill everything to her if I answered this door.

"Pasha, are you in there?"

Again, I remained silent.

"I have a key . . . I'm coming in."

The sound of the door unlocking caused me to groan. I heard the sound of heels clicking across the floor. When I looked up, Avyn was standing there with tears in her eyes. That's when I noticed the hotel uniform and the tag that read General Manager. Of all the hotels to end up at, it would be the one where she worked.

She rushed over and pulled me into a hug.

"Pash . . . God, I've missed you. You just ghosted everybody. We've been worried about you, boo. Tia, Blake, and I have all been worried about you. Every time we called, you wouldn't answer. We'd see your car every time we came by the house, but you wouldn't answer the door. I've even gone to the hospital several times to talk to Ray, and every time, it was the same story: you just didn't want to be bothered by us. We've been friends since we were thirteen, Pasha. How could you just shut us out like that?"

She finally stopped talking long enough to allow me to speak. Looking at her in the face, I felt horrible about abandoning our friendship. I just wasn't in the headspace to deal with myself, much less anybody else. I didn't want to lie to her, but I didn't need her pity right now.

"I'm sorry," I said honestly. "I just needed some time to myself, Avyn. My mental isn't where it needs to be."

"I get that, Pasha. I've seen you go through a lot in the last few years. You've been walking around with your spirit broken, and that son of a bitch has been no help—"

I cut her off. "I don't want to talk about Raymond."

"Did he do something to you?"

"No. I just . . . I just needed a break from life. I promise I'm fine."

"Why are you lying to me?"

She stepped back and took a look around the room. My things were still in the middle of the floor. I hadn't bothered to unpack or move them. Folding her arms, she looked back at me.

"You have a lot of things here for a 'break,' Pasha. I looked at your booking reservation. It said you're here for two weeks. Who is Callum?"

"Avyn, please."

"No!" she yelled, her voice cracking. "You've shut me out long enough. If something is going on, please let me help you. If Raymond is putting his hands on you—"

"He's *not* putting his hands on me."

"Then why else would you be all packed up in here on another man's dime? Are you . . . Are you having an affair? That I could understand."

"No, I'm not having an affair. Raymond isn't physically abusing me. Callum is . . . He was an unexpected blessing. Nothing is going on there."

Avyn shook her head. "I don't like this. You're hiding something from me, and if I have to run down on Raymond to find out what's really going on with my best friend, I will."

Her dislike of Raymond started after the death of our son. She didn't like how he seemingly brushed the whole thing off. He took one day off from work to "grieve." Anytime I caught him looking at me that day, there was no emotion on his face. If it weren't for Avyn being there to ensure I had anything I needed, I would have been left to deal with it alone.

At that point, I didn't know how he was feeling. Maybe he was dealing with it in private. Perhaps he didn't know how to express his mourning. I just didn't know and didn't want to believe he could be so heartless.

"You don't need to do that, Avyn. Please, don't go over there."

I was ready to beg at this point. Avyn frowned as she sighed. Her beautiful face softened a little. My friend liked to fight, and she would have no problem tearing Raymond a new one. I wouldn't have her going to jail over the likes of him.

"I love you, Pasha. You aren't just my best friend; you're my sister. Your hurting hurts me, babe. I wish I could take all of it from you and carry it, but I can't. What I can do is be there for you. You just have to let me. The girls and I would do anything for you, boo. You know that."

I swiped a tear from my eye. "I know . . . I know."

"You have my number. If . . . *When* you need me, call me. I don't care when or where. You call me, and I'll drop everything and come to you."

She pulled me into her arms, hugging me tight. I wanted to break right then, but I held it together. If I really let my emotions go, I would be spilling my guts. The last thing I wanted to do was dig into an open wound by telling her everything that happened just a few hours ago.

"I'll let you get some rest," she said as she pulled away. "I'm about to head home for the night, but I'll be back tomorrow. Maybe you'll let me see you?"

"Maybe."

She offered a light smile. Cupping my face, she placed several kisses on my forehead before walking back to the door.

"Avyn . . ." She turned back to face me. "Thank you. I love you too."

She nodded as she left the room. I fell back onto the couch and curled into a fetal position. I knew I needed to let somebody in. I just didn't know how I was going to come back from this shit. I was on a ledge, and I was likely to jump if one more thing happened.

∞

It was three a.m.

Since Avyn left, I'd been sitting in the same spot on the couch for hours. I'd yet to shower and change my clothes. I was sure I had dark circles around my eyes. I was exhausted, exhausted from the day's events. Exhausted from crying. Just exhausted with life. I'd never contemplated taking my life before, and the fact that it even crossed my mind terrified me.

What did I really have to live for? My parents were gone. I was childless. My husband was divorcing me and having a baby with another woman. I felt like there was nobody left in this world that truly loved me. I didn't like myself very much right now, let alone loved myself. I thought about how different my life could have been.

What if I'd gone to college? What if I had taken up a trade, joined the military, or done something that would make me feel like I had a purpose? I had nothing to show for myself. What money I did have from my parents' death and the sale of their home was tied up in an account that I couldn't touch for the next five years.

Since we didn't need the money, Raymond suggested that I do a certificate of deposit and allow the money to draw interest at a higher rate. That was fine. The problem was my bank didn't allow early withdrawals before the maturity date, so I was shit out of luck. I had about $800 to my name—and six of that came from my driver tonight.

I thought about that kind soul. He'd never know how much I appreciated him and what he did for me. The room he booked me had a kitchen area with a sink, microwave, and a full-sized fridge but no stove. If anything, I could grab a hot plate from the dollar store and pick up a few groceries. I sighed at the thought of having to spend the little money I did have. Eight hundred dollars already wasn't a lot of money. The thought of blowing through it quickly was depressing. What was I going to do when it was gone?

I looked down at the wedding ring on my finger. Raymond paid a good twenty thousand for it. If I pawned it, I could get a few thousand back. That would be enough to get me by for a little while . . . at least until I found a job. I didn't have many skills outside of cleaning and cooking.

I shook the thoughts from my head as I finally stood from the couch. After digging through my suitcases and trash bags, I found my pajamas and body wash. Maybe a shower would soothe me. I'd go through my things in the morning. Right now, I just wanted to cleanse myself of the day and try to get some sleep. In the bathroom, I stripped down and stood in the mirror, staring at the puffy-eyed, pitiful mess looking back at me.

My hands roamed my body and pinched at my skin. Where I was once toned, I now had a little pudge. My breasts didn't sit up quite like they used to. Once upon a time, I could proudly walk around with no bra and be okay. Not so much anymore. It was sad how much my confidence had changed.

I sighed as I pulled a shower cap over my hair. It had been in a bun for the last two weeks. It was a wonder it hadn't matted up too badly. Standing under the steady flow of hot water, I closed my eyes. I thought back to the day my life changed forever . . . the very beginning.

I wandered around the hospital. Avyn's father was having surgery, and I, being a good friend, came along to support her. He was awake and spending time with his family. I didn't want to crowd them, so I told her I'd wait in the cafeteria until she was ready to go. On my journey to the lower-level café, I stopped on every floor just being nosy.

"Are you looking for someone?" asked a deep voice behind me.

I jumped as I spun around, clutching my chest. My eyes widened as I looked up at the most handsome stranger in blue scrubs and a white lab coat. His badge read Raymond Sinclaire, MD. Cardiothoracic Surgeon. He stood roughly six feet even, with honey-colored skin and a neat haircut. His eyes were a deep brown and kind. He was easily everything I loved in older men.

"You scared me."

He chuckled. *"I apologize, Ms. . . . ."*

"Brooks . . . Pasha Brooks."

"Ms. Brooks." He reached for my hand and shook it. *"I apologize for scaring you. You just looked like you were wandering, and I wanted to see if I could be of some assistance."*

"I'm not lost. Just passing time until my friend is ready to leave. I was actually on my way to the cafeteria." I gave him a flirtatious smile. *"Maybe you could show me where it is."*

"I thought you weren't lost?"

"I'm not, but you scared me. The least you could do is walk me."

He gave me that million-dollar smile as he shook his head. *"Lucky for you, I'm on my lunch break."*

"Then you can join me. See how that worked out?"

"Look at that." He offered me his arm. *"Follow me."*

He led me down to the cafeteria. Not only did he join me, but he paid for my meal. For an hour, we sat talking and getting to know each other. By the time he had to leave, I was smitten. Foolishly, I determined that he was everything I dreamed of. I was honest with him about my age, and it didn't deter him from asking for my number. Honestly, at twenty, I could have passed for at least twenty-five. He said he liked how I carried myself and admired my maturity.

I spent the entire ride telling Avyn about the man who swept me off my feet. Just like my parents, she warned me about him. What I thought was a flex, she thought was creepy. They all gave up trying to convince me otherwise once they saw us together. He was sweet, loving, caring, and gentle. He always presented himself as a gentleman. He wined and dined me, bought me expensive gifts, and took me on expensive trips. He opened doors and pulled out chairs. He always treated me like I was the most delicate thing in his world. Those actions were what made me submit to him.

He took care of me. He showed me the type of love I was looking for. It didn't occur to me until this very moment that I had been groomed. I barely knew myself at twenty. All I knew was this fine, older man wanted me, and I wanted him. I was the perfect, unsuspecting candidate; gullible. I was a good girl. I did what I was supposed to. I wasn't out partying and drinking. I went to church every Sunday with my parents.

The furthest I'd gone with a man was allowing an ex to please me orally during my senior year of high school. I was a virgin when I met him. He told me that I was pure and perfect. He loved knowing that when he could touch me, he would be the only man who'd ever done so. When I was no longer perfect in his eyes, he seemed to despise me.

Now, here we were.

Now, here *I* was . . . broken, broken, and touching rock bottom.

CHAPTER FOUR
Callum

TWO DAYS HAD passed since my sad encounter with the beautiful Pasha Sinclaire. I couldn't seem to get her out of my head. I'd never been so affected by what someone else had going on. It wasn't my business, but yet, I'd somehow found myself involved. She was so helpless, and the fixer in me just wanted to do something to help her. Paying for her hotel stay wasn't a second thought.

What I did think about was going back to check on her. That might have been a bit much, though. I just wanted to know how she was coming along. What was her mental state? Was she eating? Was she taking care of herself? Had she reached out to anybody for comfort? Surely, she didn't think she could do this alone. There had to be someone out there that loved her . . . someone that cared.

"Hello! Earth to Callum!"

Perfectly manicured fingers snapped in my face. I playfully slapped her hands away.

"Don't do that."

"I've been talking to you for like five minutes, and you haven't said a word. Have you even been listening?"

"My bad, Bella." I rose from my slouched position in the restaurant's chair, where we had lunch. "What's up?"

She kissed her teeth. "I was just telling you that I got a promotion at work. I made a partner!"

"What! That's dope. I'm hella proud of you, sis."

Bella was my younger sister by five years. When our parents died in a boating accident when I was eighteen, it left me as her sole caregiver. I'd just started my freshman year of college and was thrown into being a full-time parent. I ended up leaving school to get a nine-to-five to make sure we were taken care of. Sure, we had insurance money, but after paying off my parents' house, putting money aside for a rainy day, and for Bella to go to school, there wasn't much left.

I got a job at a power plant and worked there until she went off college. With Bella away at school, I took the time to go back and get my IT degree and my master's in business. Things had been on the up and up for us the last couple of years.

Bella was married and had a four-year-old daughter. With her promotion, she was now the youngest partner at her accounting firm. Not only that, but she was also my accountant for business and personal needs. Even though she made great money on her own, I promised to always take care of her. My business was doing excellent numbers, so if I ate, she would eat too.

"We have to celebrate," I said.

"Martin is taking Precious and me out of town to celebrate this weekend. You're welcome to come."

"Nah, that sounds like a family thing."

"What do you mean? You're my brother. You *are* family."

"I know. I didn't mean it like that. I just meant it's intimate. When you get back, I'll treat you to lunch and maybe some shopping—"

Her eyes were bright. "Shopping!"

"Don't break my pockets, Bella."

"Oh, please! You've got it, and I'm gonna spend it. You know you love spending your money on me, Callum."

I grinned as I shook my head. "I knew it was a mistake to spoil you."

"You created a monster, and Martin feeds the beast. You're both at fault."

"Whatever."

"So, are you gonna tell me what had you in a daze earlier?"

"Oh, that . . ." I glanced down, rubbing my hands against my thighs. "Just thinking."

"About someone or something?"

"I guess you could say it was someone."

"Am I finally gonna get a sister-in-law? Will Precious get the cousins she's been asking for?"

"Martin has six nieces and nephews. She has cousins."

"Not from her favorite uncle! Stop deflecting too. Answer the question."

"The question is absurd."

"Callum!"

I sighed. "It's not like that, Bella. Honestly, I had a customer that left a mark on me. She was just—"

"*She*? A woman has you in your feelings?"

I gave her a brief rundown of my encounter with Mrs. Sinclair. Anger filled her beautiful face as I told her about that bastard of a husband and how shit went down before we left. Talking about it had my blood boiling all over again.

"Oh, he needs his ass beat," Bella said, shaking her head. "You should have fucked him up."

"Everything in me wanted to do more than I did, sis. If it weren't for the neighborhood and the fact that he looked like he'd call the police, I would have."

"I take it you're feeling her? That's gonna be messy, Callum."

"I wouldn't say I'm feeling her, but I am concerned."

"You can't fix everybody."

"I don't wanna fix her. I just . . . I don't know, Bella. Something about her just resonated with my soul. She doesn't have anybody. We know what it's like to feel alone in this world."

She hung her head. Our father grew up in foster care and never knew his family. Mom, on the other hand, had quite a bit of family. She wasn't particularly close to some of them, but there was a handful she dealt with regularly. We assumed somebody would step up to help us when they passed, but that wasn't the case.

After our parents died, nobody in our family wanted to take us in. If a check wasn't involved, most of them said they couldn't afford it. A few even thought I would sign the insurance check over to them, but that wasn't happening. My parents worked hard, and I refused for Bella and me to be left with absolutely nothing. I sacrificed for us, and if I had to, I would do it all again.

"I know," Bella said, reaching for my hand. "But we've always had each other. You were grown, and you could have thrown me to the wolves to go live your life. You never left me behind. I know it wasn't easy. I know you gave up a lot to make sure we could still be a family, and I will always appreciate you, Callum. Your heart is one of the reasons I love you so much."

She came around the table to hug me. Her embrace was warm and loving. Anytime we had these conversations, it made me emotional. I wished that our parents were here to see what we'd become. I wished they'd had a chance to witness every defining moment in our lives. I wished they'd gotten to love on Precious because she was such an amazing, smart, and loving little girl.

I didn't know Pasha's full story, but I could see that she was dealing with years of hurt. My mother always said that the eyes were the windows to the soul. When I looked into her eyes, I saw nothing but pain. *That* was what resonated with me. I didn't know how to stay away from her, but the urge to pull up was real.

∽

After getting out of our feelings, Bella and I had a great lunch. Even though we spoke almost daily, it was always good to see her. I climbed in my car and headed toward the car dealership when we parted ways. Since business had been picking up around here, I was set to purchase five additional vehicles to transport clients. I already had interviews set up for next week to hire a few new drivers.

As I drove, I noticed I was coming to the hotel where I had dropped Pasha off. While my mind was telling me to keep moving, I found myself turning into the parking lot. My feet carried me inside to the receptionist's desk, where a woman with a bubbly personality greeted me.

"Good afternoon. Welcome to Hugo Towers. I'm Avyn. How can I help you?"

"Good afternoon. I, um . . . I was hoping you could tell me if one of your guests is still here."

"I apologize, sir, but I can't give out information like that. I wouldn't want to put any of our guests in danger."

"I understand. The reservation is under my name. Would that be a problem to look up?"

She hesitated for a moment. "What's your name?"

"Callum Ellis."

Her eyes widened. "*You're* Callum?"

"Uh . . . yes. Do I know you?"

"No." She called over one of the other women behind the desk and asked her to take over. "Mr. Ellis, can I have a moment of your time?"

"Um . . . sure."

"Follow me."

She came from behind the desk and led me through the lobby to one of the back rooms I assumed were used for conferences. Once inside, she turned to me with her arms crossed.

"How do you know Pasha?"

"How do *you* know her?" I countered.

"She's my best friend. I went to her room when I saw her name on the reservation with your credit card. What's going on? She won't tell me. I haven't seen or talked to her in months. She shut everybody out, and that son of a bitch she's married to wouldn't tell us anything other than she didn't want to be bothered. I need to know what's going on with my best friend. Pasha wouldn't just pack up and leave her home. For reasons beyond me, she loves that man. I just know he did something to her. Please . . . I'm begging you. Tell me what you know."

I could see the desperation in her eyes, along with the tears threatening to spill. It was clear that she loved Pasha even if Pasha believed she didn't have anyone. I didn't want to be the one to tell her what happened. It wasn't my place, and honestly, it really wasn't my business.

"I think you should try to talk to her again—"

"She won't tell me, okay? Pasha . . . She's delicate. She's always been a good person. She's always tried to see the good in everybody, even when they don't deserve it. Raymond isn't who he pretended to be. I've watched that man turn on her when she couldn't be her best self because of grief. I've had to be the one to hold her when she cried. I've had to pick up the pieces he left scattered, and he's her fucking husband. The fact that you had to pay for her hotel stay tells me something is very wrong here. I'm begging you. I just want to help my friend."

The sincerity in her voice was evident. She wasn't asking because she wanted to get into Pasha's business or gossip. She genuinely wanted to help her. Just from the short amount of time I spent with her, I could tell Pasha would never ask for what she needed. That was the only reason I finally decided to offer up the information.

"He put her out."

"What!"

"She booked a ride. When I pulled up, she was sitting on the curb with all her stuff. He came outside, raising hell about her still being there, and shit just went left. She threw bricks through windows, and I had to put my hands on him for grabbing me." I sighed as I revealed the next part. "There's another woman. She's pregnant."

Avyn's hands went to her mouth, and her eyes widened. "Are you serious?"

"Hand to God."

"I'm gonna kill him."

She began pacing and mumbling to herself. I could tell the news had her livid, and rightfully so. Finally, she stopped and took a deep breath before turning to me.

"Thank you for helping her."

"It was nothing."

"No. God sent you there that night. You were a blessing she didn't know she needed. Thank you for making sure she had a place to lay her head. Why did you come back?"

I shrugged. "She was weighing heavy on my heart. I needed to make sure she was okay."

She nodded. "She's not doing well. She won't open the door for me, and when I use my key, she's just been lying in bed. She won't talk. I don't think she's eaten. I've been sending food to her room, which always comes back untouched. She suffers from depression and anxiety. It started after her parents died in a car accident. Then she had a few miscarriages, and when she lost her son, it just spiraled. Being in that house with that man . . . He just wasn't good for her mental health."

My heart went out to her. So many major losses, one right after the other, and now to be hit with a cheating husband and his pregnant mistress . . . I could see why she wouldn't get out of bed. Part of me wanted to go to her room to comfort her, but that wouldn't be wise. I didn't know her, and she didn't know me. The exchange might have been awkward, and I knew I couldn't stay away from her if I took it that far.

"She's in my prayers," I said. "Can I leave you with my number? She has it, but I know she won't contact me. If she needs anything, please let me know."

"You can leave your number, but why would you go through so much trouble for a stranger?"

"Because I know what it's like to feel helpless. Maybe not in the sense that she does, but I get it. Everybody needs somebody."

She smiled. "I can tell you were raised on love." She grabbed my hands. "Thank you for being a good person."

She pulled me into a hug, and for a moment, I stood frozen. There was the touching thing again. Luckily, it was brief. She handed me her phone, and I programmed my number in. We then headed back up front and said our goodbyes before I left the hotel, praying that Pasha would be receptive to the help her friend would give her.

CHAPTER FIVE

Pasha

"I'M SORRY, MRS. Sinclaire . . . *There's no heartbeat.*"

I stared at the monitor, willing it to move . . . to make a sound . . . something. I needed them to be wrong. My poor, sweet, innocent baby was gone. His life was snatched from him before it could even begin.

"Check it again!" I pleaded.

"I have," the doctor said. "I've checked it three times."

"He can't be . . . He can't be gone. I just felt him moving last night." Tears poured down my face as I tried to come to terms with this heartbreaking reality. "Please . . . Tell me this is a mistake."

She squeezed my hand as she gave me a sympathetic look. "I'm so sorry, sweetheart. We have to induce you."

I began to cry harder. I was eight and a half months pregnant. She just told me my son was dead, and now I had to deliver him. Not only that, but I also had to go home without him. Beside me, Raymond rubbed my back, not muttering a word. I couldn't tell if he was as upset as I was, but he didn't show any emotion. He didn't offer me any further condolences. After three miscarriages, we were finally supposed to have our bundle of joy. Now, that dream was back to what it was . . . a dream.

"Can I hold him?" I asked through my tears.

"Of course. You can take all the time you need. We have a bereavement program where you can take pictures with your baby to

take home. We find sometimes it offers comfort. We're here for whatever
you need, Mrs. Sinclaire."

I nodded, although no source of comfort could ever ease the pain I
was feeling. My child was gone . . .

I sat straight up, gasping for air. My body was covered in
sweat, and I struggled to breathe. I hadn't dreamed of my baby in
a while, and now, the memories came flooding back. Scrambling
from the bed, I ran over to my suitcases and the trash bags,
dumping everything out. I frantically searched until I found the
locked box that housed the only memories I had of my son and my
parents. Using the key I had on a chain around my neck, I opened
it to make sure Raymond left everything inside. I prayed he wasn't
vindictive enough to tamper with it.

I sighed with relief when I found everything as I left it. If
something happened to this, I would have lost it. Closing the box,
I sat back on my haunches, clutching it to my chest. Burying my
face in my hand, I cried for what seemed like the millionth time. I
just wanted to fall apart.

"God give me strength . . ." I whispered. "I don't know if I
can make it through this with my sanity."

Other than getting up to pee, I'd lay in this bed for the
last four days. I hadn't taken my medication. I hadn't showered.
I hadn't brushed my teeth or washed my face. I'd gotten a total
of maybe eight hours of sleep in the last seventy-two hours. My
stomach cramped because I hadn't eaten, and I was beginning to
smell myself. I physically did not have the energy to deal with life.

Avyn had been coming by, and all I wanted her to do was
leave me alone. I understood her concern. I understood she wanted
to be there for me, but I just didn't know how to accept that right
now. I depended on someone for the last twenty-eight years. First,
it was my parents and then my husband. My parents were dead,

and my husband was leaving me. At some point, I had to learn to stand on my own two feet.

The last thing I wanted to do was get out of bed, but I needed to get myself together. If I lay here, my two free weeks would be up, and my situation would only be worse. I was so tired . . . so drained . . . so fucking done. But all I had now was me. I could either sink or swim. After saying a quick prayer, I stood and placed the box beside the dresser to prepare for whatever kind of day I was about to have.

Rummaging through my things, I found something to wear before heading into the bathroom. I turned on the water, then stripped out of the robe I'd been wearing for four days. I avoided the mirror because I didn't want to see the pitiful mess looking back at me. Stepping into the hot shower, I embraced the heat and steam.

I closed my eyes and basked in the soothing stream of water raining down on me. My body was stiff from lying down for so long. I knew I couldn't allow myself to get like this again . . . I couldn't afford to. With my eyes closed, I began praying for strength, clarity, perseverance, and understanding. I had to believe that God had a greater plan for my life than this. There was something better waiting for me. I just had to climb over this stumbling block.

Opening my eyes, I grabbed my washcloth and body wash to give myself a good lather. Once I was done, I thoroughly washed my hair before applying the leave-in conditioner. My natural curls rejoiced at finally getting the TLC they so desperately needed. My depression was crippling. At times, it was a struggle to manage self-care. I knew I needed to get myself together, and I was trying, but damn, it was hard.

Fresh out of the shower, I dried my body and towel-dried my hair before adding moisturizing products to it. Once I was done, I returned to the bedroom to get dressed. I settled on an oversized shirt and leggings, grabbed my phone, and opened the browser to look for a cab. Not so much to my surprise, my service was disconnected. Raymond and I were on the same phone plan. If he would cut off my credit cards, surely he would cut off my phone too.

I sighed as I connected to the hotel's Wi-Fi to book the ride. Someone knocked at my door just as I was about to hit confirm. I knew it was nobody but Avyn. Setting down the phone, I went to answer. When I opened the door, she stood there in her regular clothes. She must have been off today. Her eyes widened as they settled on me.

"You're up . . . and dressed."

"Yeah . . ."

"You look better, Pash."

"Thanks, I guess."

"Can I come in? I want to talk to you."

"Can it wait? I need to take care of some things today, Avyn."

"No, it can't wait."

She brushed past me and came into the room. I closed my eyes, silently cursing as I closed the door. Walking back to the living room area, I found her sitting on the couch. She patted the space beside her. Begrudgingly, I sat.

"So I met Callum."

I swallowed hard. "Oh?"

"Yeah. I had to beg, but he told me what happened. Why didn't you call me, Pasha? Me or Tia or Blake? One of us would have come to you, and you know that."

"I was embarrassed!" I yelled. "That man put my shit on the front lawn for all to see. He put me out of my home to move a new bitch in! She's pregnant, Avyn. He's finally getting what he wanted and has no use for me anymore! Do you know how that felt? I gave everything to that man. I put him above myself time and time again, and this is what he did to me.

"I damn near watched him grow to hate me while I still loved him as best as I could. I put so much blame on myself for how fucked up my mental was, but I'm human. I feel pain just like the next person. I tried to heal and deal with it through therapy, but it was too much, Avyn . . . It was just too much!"

I broke down crying, and she pulled me into her arms, rocking me. I just accepted it. There was no way I could keep fighting against her. Avyn was nothing if not persistent. Now that she knew the truth, she would never leave my side.

"Look at me." She cupped my face. "I love you . . . Don't you know that? There is nothing you can't bring to me, nothing I won't go through with you. Fifteen years of friendship are between us. I've always had your back. If you can't count on another soul in this life, you count on me . . . Every. Single. Time. I got you."

She kissed my forehead and wiped my eyes.

"Come on." She stood to her feet, pulling me along with her. "We're gonna pack your things, and you're coming to stay with me. I've got a spare bedroom, and it's yours for as long as you need it."

"I can't—"

"You can, and you are. I'm not asking, and I'm not fighting with you. You are going to let me help you. Period. Now, come help me pack up this stuff."

She didn't wait for me to protest. As she grabbed my suitcase and started folding my clothes, I shuffled from side to side. Maybe this was part of the journey to starting over. I couldn't do it alone, and she wouldn't let me. Maybe Callum was the blessing I needed to jump-start. Thinking of him made me question how Avyn ran into him in the first place. Slowly, I walked over to the pile of clothes and began picking them up to fold.

"Avyn?"

"Yes?"

"How did you meet Callum?"

"He came in here looking for you."

"What?"

"He wanted to make sure you were okay, Pasha. I could tell he was genuinely concerned about your well-being. His spirit felt genuine."

I looked away. "It did. I probably would have gotten arrested if it weren't for him."

"He said bricks were thrown?"

I shrugged. "Yeah . . . not my proudest moment. I just . . . They taunted me. I was so angry. All I could see was red. They were lucky the windows were the only thing I broke."

"I would have aimed for faces."

"I know you would have. I've never wanted to put my hands on someone so bad, Avyn. I've never been a fighter. You know I don't like confrontation. You know I don't like feeling angry. At that moment, I was so mad. Mad at him, mad at her . . . mad at myself. I felt him loving me less and less. I should have left long before any of this happened. I kept telling myself that if I got my mind right and lost weight, everything would be okay. I was stupid, naïve, and delusional."

"No, baby. You were a woman going through two of the worst types of grief, and you needed support from your husband. It doesn't matter what part you tell yourself you played. He failed you as a husband. That's exactly what I told him."

"Please don't tell me you went to the house."

"Yes, I did. I went over there and cursed both of them out. I was about to pick up a brick and finish the job you started on the rest of the windows. He's lucky the police came."

"Please don't go back over there. I don't need you getting arrested on my behalf."

She giggled. "Well, the responding officer may or may not have been my little boo, so I was okay this time. But you better believe I want all smoke behind this."

I shook my head. "I just need to move on. I don't want revenge. I don't want pity. I don't want a thing from him. This ring . . ." I took off the wedding ring and held it up. "This is bullshit. I don't want anything tying me to him."

"Well, we can sell this and get you a nice chunk of change from it."

I grabbed her hand and placed the ring in it. "Take it. I'll even give you half for letting me stay with you."

"Absolutely not. Whatever comes from that is yours. You know I have a few cousins on my daddy's side who can run in there and grab you a few things. He won't even know they're missing."

"Avyn."

"I'm sorry. I'm just trying to make you smile. You're gonna get through this, Pasha. My granny always said God will make your enemies your footstool . . . of course, when she said that, she was referring to stomping a mudhole in somebody."

I covered my mouth, attempting to hide my smile.

"You know my granny was a thug, right?"

"I remember. I loved your granny."

"She loved you too. If she were still here, she would have pulled up right along with me, and hands definitely would have been thrown. No ifs, ands, or buts about it."

I knew that to be true. Katherine Timmons, affectionately known as Ms. Kat, was nothing to play with. She was a sweet firecracker who treated me like one of her grandchildren. She had the spirit of discernment. If she'd met Raymond, she probably could have told me what it took so long to see.

"Hey," Avyn said, jarring me out of my thoughts. She playfully nudged me. "You're gonna be okay, boo."

I sighed and nodded. I had to believe that.

I couldn't afford to believe anything else.

CHAPTER SIX
Callum

IT WAS FRIDAY morning.

I'd been up since five a.m. because sleep just didn't seem to be my friend. This wasn't the first time it happened to me. It happened every time I had a problem I couldn't fix. This particular problem wasn't mine, but I couldn't tell that to my brain. A whole week had passed since Mrs. Sinclair checked into Hugo Towers. I hadn't been back since the day I ran into her friend.

That didn't mean the urge wasn't real.

Every time I drove past the hotel, I wanted to turn into the parking lot. I'd taken to pressing the gas just a little harder, purposefully missing the turn. Her friend hadn't called me, so I assumed everything was okay. I prayed for her. I prayed for her safety, her healing, and her mind. Depression was a hell of a thing to deal with. I'd never personally dealt with it, but I knew enough to know it was no walk in the park.

Pushing the thoughts from my head, I ended my workout routine. I had time to myself since I wasn't going into the office today. I thought about picking up my niece from day care and spending the day with her. She was such a happy child, and I could use the distraction. As I headed upstairs to my bathroom, I called my sister.

"Yes, dear brother?" she answered.

"Hey, Bells. Precious is at day care, right?"

"She is."

"I'm picking her up early."

"Callum, don't you go giving her a bunch of sweets. I don't need her jumping off the walls when she gets home."

I rolled my eyes. "I won't . . . at least I won't overdo it."

"Callum!"

I laughed at her dramatics. "I hear you, Bella."

"You better. Have fun. I love you."

"I love you too." We disconnected the call, and I undressed for my shower.

Forty-five minutes later, I was pulling up at Charming Oaks Day Care and Learning Center. Since I had my niece often, I kept a booster seat handy. Precious wasn't expecting me, so I knew her little smile would put a smile on my face. Walking inside, I headed to the receptionist area. I was on her approved list of people who could check her out, so they knew my face.

The first person to greet me was Charlotte Gaines, the overly perky receptionist with a bad case of jungle fever. Anytime I came in here, this woman shamelessly flirted with me. She'd even tried to slip me her number, which I promptly put in the trash when she wasn't looking. I didn't want to hurt her feelings, but today might be the day.

"Hey, handsome," she said, leaning across the desk, pushing her cleavage forward in the process.

I gave her a blank expression. "Hey, Ms. Gaines."

"I've told you, call me Charlotte."

"I'd rather call you Ms. Gaines."

"Speaking of calling . . . I haven't heard from you. I know I gave you my number."

"I must have misplaced it. Anyway, I'm here to pick up Precious."

"Well, she's back there. You're free to go."

I started to walk off, but she gently grabbed my arm. Stepping too close into my personal space, she looked up at me. Her hand moved from my arm to my chest.

"Mr. Ellis . . . How long are you going to play hard to get? I'm a beautiful, single woman. You're a handsome, single man. I don't see why we can't enjoy each other's company."

I looked down at her hand and removed it like it was something disgusting.

"Ms. Gaines . . . Would you like me to be honest with you?"

"Yes. Is it because I'm white?"

"It's because you're thirsty, and you make it a habit of pointing out how much you love Black men. You won't fetishize me. I'm not the man you can take home to your parents or show off like a trophy. Simply put, I'm not for you. It has nothing to do with your lack of melanin but everything to do with your agenda. Now, if you'll excuse me, I have to get my niece. Good day."

I left her standing there with her mouth open. As I made my way down the hall to Precious's classroom, I could hear laughter, screaming, and crying coming from various other rooms. One of these days, my home would be filled with all of those. While I wasn't old, I was at the age where I was thinking about marriage and children. My four-bedroom home was too big for just me. I wanted someone to share it and make memories with.

I've been single for a minute now. The only women I entertained were the ones I had a mutual understanding with that it was just sex between us. Even with those parameters, I hadn't had sex in at least three months, and, ironically, I was okay with that. I was, however, beginning to get lonely. Maybe that's what

Ms. Gaines saw in me. I chuckled at the thought of her sniffing me out like a dog in heat.

Walking up to the half door that led to Precious's classroom, I leaned over the bottom half. My niece was in her own little world, playing with the toy grocery store items. She would be a terrible businesswoman. Anytime I played with her, she overcharged me and provided horrible customer service.

"Psst!" I said in her direction.

She looked around and squealed when her eyes landed on me.

"Uncle Cay!"

She ran over to the door as fast as her little legs would carry her. I opened it just in time to catch her running into my arms. She giggled as I smothered her chubby cheeks with kisses.

"Hey, Princess. I missed you."

"I missed you too."

"Guess what?"

"What?"

"I'm here to pick you up. You get to spend the whole afternoon with me. How does that sound?"

"Like fun! Look, Ms. Mary! Uncle Cay came to get me!"

Ms. Mary was an older Black woman with grandmotherly vibes. She walked over with a smile and shook my hand.

"Good afternoon, Mr. Ellis. How are you?"

"Happy to see my favorite person. Has she been behaving?"

"She's been an angel as always."

"Well, I think that deserves a treat."

Precious's eyes lit up. "Can I get ice cream?"

"Just don't tell Mommy." She pretended to zip her lips. "Go get your things, baby."

I set her down on her feet, and she took off to her cubby.

Ms. Mary smiled. "She's always so happy to see you. I hear about you more than anybody else. It's 'Uncle Cay this' and 'Uncle Cay that.' I'd think you were her favorite if I didn't know any better."

"According to her, I am. Probably because I don't have any kids, so she doesn't have to share me with anybody."

"Oh, Lord. What is she gonna do when you finally get married?"

"Give my wife a run for her money."

We shared a laugh as Precious came back over.

"I'm ready! Bye, everybody! Bye, Ms. Mary!"

"Have a good weekend, Precious. I'll see you on Monday."

We waved goodbye and headed back up front. Ms. Gaines avoided eye contact with me as I signed my niece out. It wasn't until Precious said goodbye to her that she spoke. I, on the other hand, didn't say a thing. Maybe our conversation would do something to quench that thirst.

Precious and I sat in Scoops Galore, the local ice cream shop, munching on small waffle bowls of cookies and cream ice cream. We'd grabbed something to eat since I picked her up before lunch. I didn't want to hear anything about me ruining her appetite.

"Here, Uncle Cay," Precious said, holding up a spoonful of her ice cream for me to try.

While I ordered my plain, she wanted chocolate syrup, sprinkles, and whipped cream. I wasn't a fan of toppings, but how could I say no to her? Reluctantly, I opened my mouth and allowed her to feed it to me.

"Is it good?"

"It's amazing," I lied with a straight face.

"You want some more?"

"No, thank you, baby. You enjoy it."

She shrugged her shoulders and went back to eating. Much to my surprise, she ate the whole thing. I just knew I would be dealing with her being hyper the rest of the day. I planned to tire her out so she'd fall asleep by the time she had to go home. After throwing away our trash, I grabbed her hand, and we headed back to my car. She was already hopping and skipping along beside me.

"How about we go to the park?" I said. "I'll see if Uncle Chris can bring Armani to play with you."

Her eyes lit up. Chris was my best friend and one of the codevelopers of my Elite Rides app. Armani was his four-year-old daughter, who was like another niece to me. Quickly, I shot him a text. He responded immediately, saying they would meet us. As Precious and I headed to the car, I spotted a familiar face coming out of a stationary shop. As we got closer, I realized that it was Avyn. She walked toward us, stopping when she recognized who I was.

She offered a smile. "Mr. Ellis? How are you?"

"I'm good. How are you?"

"I can't complain." She looked down at Precious. "Who is this little beauty?"

"This is Precious, my niece. Say 'Hey,' Precious."

"Hi!"

Avyn waved at her. "You must have aggravated her mother her entire pregnancy. She looks just like you."

"I get that all the time. We just have strong genes."

"I see."

"Um . . . Can you wait right here? I want to ask you something. I just need to put her in the car." I pointed out my car, just a few feet away.

"Sure. Go ahead."

I ushered Precious to the car and locked her in her booster seat. After turning on the air and giving her tablet to her, I stepped back to the sidewalk where Avyn patiently waited, tapping on her phone. She tucked it away as I approached her.

"You want to know about Pasha, right?" she asked.

"If it's not too much trouble."

She sighed. "I checked her out of the hotel. You should be getting a partial refund in a few days. She's staying with me now."

"How is she doing?"

"She's . . . She's emotional, but she's trying to pull herself out of it. I just bought her a journal to write in. If she won't talk about it, I, at least, want her to get it out somehow. She was in therapy, but now that Raymond isn't paying for it, we have to figure things out until she can start back."

"Damn . . . I hate that for her."

"Yeah, me too. After you told me what happened, I went over there prepared to rock an orange jumpsuit."

I chuckled. "I don't think orange is your color."

She waved me off. "I look good in everything. For her, I'd do hard time."

"They don't make friends like that. I'm glad she's allowing you to help her."

"I didn't give her a choice. That's my sister. No way was I allowing her to stay in a hotel when I had a whole guest room collecting dust. She can stay as long as she needs to."

I smiled. "I'm glad to hear that."

"I guess we don't need your number now, huh?"

"I guess not." That actually disappointed me a little.

"Well . . . She could always use a friend, Mr. Ellis. You're already good at that." She flashed me a smile and patted my shoulder. "You know how to find me if you ever want to contact her. I have to get going. You and your beautiful niece have a good day."

"You too."

She walked away, and I headed back to my car.

"Who was that?" Precious asked immediately. She was just as nosy as her mama.

"A friend."

"Is she your girlfriend?"

"No, baby."

"Ms. Gaines wants to be your girlfriend, Uncle Cay. She told Ms. Mary you were so fine."

I snorted. Ms. Gaines was out of line and out of her lane.

"You ready to go to the park?"

"I'm ready!"

I backed out of the parking space and headed toward Greenbriar Park. My thoughts drifted back to Pasha. I hoped she was having a decent day.

CHAPTER SEVEN
Pasha

I HADN'T LEFT AVYN'S apartment since moving two weeks ago.

She'd been trying to get me out for some fresh air, but I got plenty of that on her balcony. Most days, I sat out there just looking up at the sky. I talked to my parents as though they could hear me. I prayed. I contemplated life thus far and how I would pull myself out of this slump. Two days ago, while Avyn was at work, Raymond's lawyer officially served me with divorce papers. I guessed that Avyn told him I would be with her.

When the carrier left, I locked myself in my new bedroom and lay in bed, crying my eyes out for an hour. When I finished, I looked over the documents. I knew Raymond *wanted* to give me practically nothing. I was sure it was at the encouragement of his lawyer that he offered anything at all. He was willing to pay for my lawyer and offered a lump sum alimony payment. It was nothing like I deserved, but it was more than I had. I knew this tactic was to get rid of me as soon as possible.

Somehow . . . in between the crying, the feeling of despair, and the cloud of hopelessness . . . I found peace because signing these papers meant I was free from him. I was free of the hatred in his stares. Free of the coldness of his words. Free of the impossible expectations to be perfect at all times. I'd lived in turmoil for so long that freedom that granted me peace of mind was worth more to me than any monetary supplement from him.

The sound of the front door opening broke me from my thoughts. I stood from the patio and walked back inside. Avyn greeted me with a smile.

"Hey! You're up!"

"Yeah, just soaking up some sun. It feels good out."

"It's been a beautiful day."

I noticed the gift bag in her hand. "What's that?"

She looked down. "Oh! I got you something. Nothing big, but I hope it can serve its purpose."

She handed me the bag, and I slowly took it. After sitting on the couch, I opened the bag to find a medium-sized box with a beautiful pink bow on top. When I pulled off the top, there sat a beautiful, black, leather-bound notebook. Gorgeous embroidery spelled my name across the front.

Avyn grabbed my hand. "I know you don't want to talk about things, but I don't want you to keep your feelings inside. I need you to be okay. This is a self-reflection journal. I had it specially made just for you. You can write your feelings, make a goal list, and do daily affirmations in it. It doubles as a planner also. I literally have my entire life in mine. I would lose my head if I lost it."

I smiled softly. "Thank you, Avyn. This was a very thoughtful gift. I promise I'll put it to good use."

I pulled her in for a hug, and she released the biggest breath of relief. I knew she was worried about me, but she never forced me to talk. There'd been a lot of silence here the last two weeks. I was trying my best to stay out of her way and not be a bother. I made sure I cleaned up after myself and kept the place spotless.

"Have you had a good day?" she asked me.

"It's been a better day compared to others." I hung my head for a moment. "I, um . . . I got served two days ago. This is really happening, Avyn."

She gently rubbed my shoulder. "It is."

"This is the first time I've ever been on my own. I don't know what to do with myself. I can't continue to live like a housewife, and I will never have anybody else take care of me again. If I don't take anything else away from this, I'll take away the idea of always being self-sufficient."

"Amen to that," Avyn mumbled. "Sorry, boo."

"No, it's okay. I admire how you've always made your own way in the world. Nobody can ever say they gave you anything. You've always worked hard. That's commendable and respected."

"Thank you, girl. So . . . Is he offering anything?"

"To pay for my lawyer and a lump sum alimony. I'm going to request he be mandated to continue to pay for my therapy for as long as I attend."

"Good for you. You should go after that house too."

"I don't want that house, Avyn. We don't have any children, so there's no reason I should want it. There are too many sad memories there. He and his bad energy can have it. Besides, the taxes are so expensive that I'd lose it anyway. The same with the car."

"I would tell you to sell them both."

"That man would never let me have it in peace. He owned that house before I came along. Even if I didn't want to live there, I'm sure he'd find a way to keep it from selling. I just don't want the hassle. I'm starting over, and I will do this on my own."

She smiled. "Well, I'm glad to see the fighter moving in your spirit. I'm gonna help you help yourself." She reached into her bag and produced a piece of paper.

"What's this?" I asked, taking it from her.

"An application. The hotel is looking for someone new in housekeeping. The application is just a formality since I'm the one doing the hiring. It's a livable wage, and you can ride to work with me. Don't expect any special treatment now just because I like you more than most of them," she added with a giggle.

"Thank you, girl."

"I told you I got you. I've also got some good news!" She reached into her purse and pulled out an envelope.

"What's this?"

"That is an official offer for your wedding ring. I went to seven different jewelry stores, and that was the best offer I got. If you accept it, you only have a week to change your mind."

I opened the envelope to find a tentative offer of $12,000.

"Are you serious?"

"A pawn shop would have never given you that much."

"How did you manage this?"

"I may or may not have shown a little boob."

I playfully smacked her arm. "Avyn!"

She laughed loudly. "I'm playing, girl. You remember Ahmed from high school. His family owned like half of the Palace Plaza."

"I remember. He used to have a crush on you."

"He still has a crush on me. We're supposed to go out tonight."

"So you traded a date for my ring?"

"I secured you an offer for a date. Ahmed isn't the same as we knew. That's a full-grown man now, girl."

"I thought the cop was your boo."

She giggled. "He's one of them."

We talked for a little longer before she headed to her room to nap, and I went into the kitchen to cook dinner. I had to find some way to earn my keep because she refused to take my money. I used her water and electricity, ate her food, and took up space. I needed to show my appreciation somehow. Cooking tonight would be it.

"You have it smelling good in here!"

I looked up to see Avyn standing in the entry of the kitchen. I'd been so focused on preparing the meal that I hadn't seen or heard her come in. She came around to the stove to peek into the pots.

"What are you cooking?"

"A creamy Cajun chicken pasta."

I proceeded to cut a piece of the chicken for her to sample. It was no surprise that she was eager to taste it. She closed her eyes and chewed when I popped it into her mouth. A satisfied moan fell from her lips.

"Mmm . . . That's so good."

"Thank you. *When* I cook, I do a little something."

"Aunt Virginia did keep you in the kitchen growing up."

I chuckled. "She did. She always told me that the way to a man's heart is through his stomach."

My mother told me many things about how to be the perfect housewife. I realized now that that really only applied to my daddy. He was a good man . . . a different breed. She did what was expected of her regarding caring for him, me, and the house. He did what he was supposed to do as the head of the family, but he also wasn't afraid to pick up the slack should she need help. He never complained. He never belittled her if something wasn't done. He simply did it himself. My father was the definition of giving grace. He understood that while they both had duties, my mother was also human, and she got tired like anybody else.

"I guess I must be a man then," Avyn mumbled.

"It's done. I'll fix you a plate—"

"You don't have to serve me, Pasha. I'm fully capable of making my own plate. As a matter of fact, *you* sit down, and I'll make your plate too."

"But—"

"No buts. Sit."

She ushered me over to the dining room table and pulled out a chair. Reluctantly, I sat and waited while she made both of us a plate and drinks. She placed both in front of me, then seated herself and reached for my hands. Bowing our heads, I closed my eyes as she said a prayer.

"Lord, we want to thank you for this meal and bless the hands that prepared it. May we consume it as nourishment for our bodies . . . thank you . . . Thank you for bringing my best friend back to me. I pray that you uncloud her mind and clear her heart to receive all the blessings you have in store for her. In Jesus' name, amen."

"Amen," I whispered. I swiped a tear from my eye before she could see it. "That was beautiful."

"I may act like a heathen at times, but God knows my heart."

We settled into our meal, and she told me about her day. She told me she had lunch with Tia and Black, and they asked to see me. I decided that I was finally ready to have visitors. I did miss them. It wasn't so long ago that the four of us were inseparable. Maybe a little girls' night would lift my spirits. I agreed to see them, and Avyn suggested inviting them over tomorrow night.

"Oh! I meant to tell you something!" She did a little shimmy in her seat.

I giggled. "Why are you dancing?"

"Guess who I saw today?"

"Who?"

"Your angel."

I raised an eyebrow. "My angel?"

"Callum."

"Oh . . . How is he?"

"He's doing good. He asked about you. He wanted to make sure you were doing okay. I think he may be a little smitten with you, girl."

"Avyn, the man saw me on the most embarrassing night of my life. If he feels anything for me, it's pity."

"I don't think so."

"Look at me . . . A man like that would want nothing to do with a woman like me."

"First of all, what you aren't going to do is down yourself. You are a naturally beautiful woman, Pasha. Inside and out. If there are a few things you're unhappy with, change them. But do it for you and you alone."

"I just want to feel like myself again."

"And you will. I have faith in that. This might be the end of something ugly, but it's the beginning of something absolutely beautiful. Just you wait and see."

We continued talking and eating while she told me about her plans for the night. Once we finished eating, we cleaned the kitchen and watched television for a while. When it was time for her to get ready, I retreated to the guest room. I decided on a nice, calming bubble bath to relax and reset. I lit a few tealight candles and played music while the tub filled. After stripping down, I eased my body into the water.

"Mmm . . . That's nice . . ."

Resting my head against the back of the tub, I closed my eyes and allowed the music to soothe me. Once upon a time, this was one of my favorite things to do. My parents had a huge garden tub in their bathroom at our home. I used to lock myself in their bathroom for hours, listening to music and refilling the tub when the water grew cold.

While I soaked, I thought about what my next steps would be when my divorce was final. I knew I didn't want to stay with Avyn for too long. She was a single woman, and I knew she needed her privacy, if for nothing but peace and quiet. The first thing on my list was looking for an apartment and a car.

While I was stuck in my head, Avyn came in and told me she was about to head out. When I looked at the clock, I realized I'd been in the tub for at least an hour. I decided to drain the water and take a shower. Once I finished my hygiene, I changed into my pajamas and climbed into bed. For a moment, I lay there looking up at the ceiling.

The gift bag from earlier caught my attention, causing me to sit up. Removing the journal, I flipped through the pages, landing on a page of aspirations.

What's your aspiration in life?

I thought about it for a moment. What *was* my aspiration? Given everything that life had thrown at me and all I was dealing with, only thing came to mind . . . *to be happy.*

CHAPTER EIGHT
Callum

"LOOK AT ME, Uncle Cay!"

I looked up to see my niece preparing to climb up the mini rock wall of the playhouse with Armani on her heels. She was such a little daredevil at times.

"Be careful, Precious!" I called over to her. She grinned and nodded as she took the first leap. I held my breath until she made it to the top. "That little girl is going to give me a heart attack, man."

Chris chuckled. "Just wait until you have one of your own. I thought having boys was rough, but Armani is no better. She runs right with her brothers. I'm glad she's fearless, but I just want her to be dainty and girly for a little bit. My nerves can only take so much."

"Yeah, well, maybe I'll get to experience fatherhood one day."

"You realize you actually have to date and get to know somebody first, right? Well, not necessarily, but I don't see you having a child with a woman you aren't married to."

"I'm glad you know that."

"When are you gonna get back out there then, man? You can't use Bella as an excuse anymore. She's married and well taken care of. You're financially stable, and you've got everything going for you. Ain't no excuse."

"I'm not making excuses. I believe the woman I'm meant to be with will show up when the time is right."

"The Bible says faith without works is dead. She's not just gonna drop in your lap. You gotta put yourself out there."

"Dating is hard, Chris. Some of these women only see dollar signs when it comes to me. They see a successful, young, Black man with money and think it's a come-up. I struggled to get here. I'll be damned if I let somebody come in and reap the benefits for all the wrong reasons."

"I get it. Hey, Eva has a few single friends. Maybe you should let her hook you up."

"I think not. You know I love Eva, but I've met her friends. They aren't exactly my type."

"Why? Because you can't fix them?"

"Why do you and Bella think I need to fix people?"

"Why do you feel like you need to?"

"I don't."

Chris ran his hand down his face. "I've known you for a minute, Callum. I know you became a full-time parent at eighteen, and while it was the hardest thing you ever had to do, you did it with pride. You put your dreams and education on the back burner to make sure you two were straight when nobody else could or would. I know that even though Belle is married to a good man, you keep her on your payroll, so she is forever good just in case shit doesn't work out. My point is, not only do you like to fix broken things, but you also like to prevent them from being broken again."

I was quiet momentarily when he said that because it was true. Once you make it out of the struggle, you do everything possible never to struggle again. I'd like to say I'd become a bit of an empath. The trauma of losing my parents and being thrown into adult roles early on made me sensitive to others' needs. I didn't have a savior complex or anything like that. I just felt like it was my duty to help those in need if it was within my means.

I understood what it was like not to have anybody and be forced to depend on yourself, even when you may not be your best option. There were times after losing my parents when I was so burned out from having to pour into not only myself but my sister. She needed me, and I needed both of us. I knew that if I gave up, we would both suffer. I could never make Bella suffer. She was only a kid back then. Hell, I was still a kid, my damn self.

I sat back against the bench and blew out my breath. "I guess now would be a bad time to tell you about the woman I met then."

Chris sat up in his seat and leaned forward on his elbows. He chuckled and shook his head.

"Have at it."

For the next twenty minutes, I told him the story of Pasha while we watched the girls play. His face played many of the same expressions mine did as I experienced it myself. When I finished, all he could do was shake his head.

"You know, you see this in movies, but it's always crazy to hear about it happening in real life."

"Tell me about it. This is right out of a Tyler Perry joint."

"You said you've been thinking about her . . . What's up with that?"

I sighed. "I don't know, man. I guess . . . I just want to know how it ends. I want her to be okay, you know?"

"I get that. Seems like you've already become emotionally invested. What are you gonna do if you ever see her again? Pursue that?"

"I wouldn't push it that far, Chris. At least, I don't think that I would. I mean, she's gonna need lots of time and probably more therapy to get through this. She was already dealing with depression and anxiety. This probably set her back."

"I can only imagine." He looked at me curiously. "I feel like this has somehow embedded itself in you. I know you well enough to know that once you get a thought in your mind, you like to see it through. Just be careful. Don't get weird, man."

My brows furrowed. "What do you mean?"

"Don't go looking for her or show up at her job. Coincidently, seeing her in public is one thing, but looking for her will give that woman stalker vibes. Hell, you might even catch a charge. You did your due diligence as a good citizen. The Lord will bless you for that. Just let the cards fall where they may."

"I hear you, Chris."

Even though the urge to check on Pasha was strong, I would fight against it. The last thing I needed was to have my concern misconstrued as something it wasn't. I knew when to leave well enough alone . . . even when I didn't want to. Maybe our interaction was only supposed to be for that one night. Perhaps I had done my good deed, and it was time to go about my business.

"What did you do to my baby?" Bella asked as I carried Precious into her house.

We'd spent a good three hours at the park with Chris and Armani. They played to their hearts' content. When she was good and tired, I took her back to my house and put on her favorite movie. She cuddled up in my arms, and before long, we fell fast asleep.

"I'll never tell," I jested, laying her on the couch. I covered her with a blanket and kissed her forehead before hugging my sister. "How was your day?"

"Ugh! It was a day! Come in the kitchen, and I'll tell you about it."

I followed her into the spacious kitchen. The delectable scent of whatever she was cooking pleased my senses. My lunch was gone, and I knew I'd stay for dinner. Bella retrieved two glasses from the cabinet, then pulled out a bottle of wine from the fridge.

"I don't like how you treat me like one of your girlfriends," I said, gesturing to the items. "You love to wine and gossip with me."

She rolled her eyes. "First of all, you love this wine. I bought it just for you, so you're welcome. Second, you've always been my best friend. If I can't gossip with you, who can I gossip with? So, sit back, sip your wine, and shut up."

"Have you forgotten that I'm the oldest? Don't be talking to me recklessly. I'll come over there and put you in a headlock."

"Remember, you taught me how to fight. I'll kick your ass."

We stared at each other for a moment before breaking into laughter.

"What's up, Bells?"

"So we got this new client today. I think he has this vendetta against women. It's like he thought I was incompetent or something, Callum. Every suggestion I made, he wasn't happy with it. He spoke over me, refused to make eye contact with me, and wouldn't even shake my hand. He only agreed to sign a contract because my male coworker stepped in and finished the pitch. The pitch *I* worked so hard on. He said the exact same thing I did, but it was accepted because it came from a man."

I frowned. My sister was highly competent at her job. She was the youngest partner at her firm, and that, in itself, spoke to her abilities.

"I'm sorry you had to encounter an asshole today, Bells. You know you're a beast with numbers. You could easily start your own firm. I guarantee your clients would follow you."

"I wouldn't want there to be bad blood. That company has done a lot for me, Callum. Days like today, I just wished they'd had my back. I understand not wanting to lose out on a major moneymaking account, but it shouldn't be at my expense. For the first time, I felt undervalued and underappreciated. He made me feel like I wasn't good enough to sit with the big boys at the table."

"You *are* good enough. You're *more* than good. Don't ever let anybody make you feel less than. Look at where we were and where we are. The odds were against us after Mama and Daddy died. All we had in this world was ourselves. We could have fallen by the wayside or run with the wrong crowd because we didn't have parental guidance. We didn't do any of that. You made it through school and college at the top of your class. You climbed the corporate ladder quickly, doing what it took some of those people years to accomplish. You earned and deserved that title as a partner. You wouldn't have been presented with the opportunity if you weren't competent. I'm so proud of you. If nobody else ever tells you that, you'll always hear it from me."

She swiped a tear from her eye. I hated to see her cry. In my eyes, she would always be that little red baby our parents brought home from the hospital. I'd spent my life protecting her and making sure that she was happy, and I would die doing the same thing. Getting up from my seat, I rounded the counter and pulled her into my arms, wrapping her up in a hug.

"I'm glad we've always had each other," she said softly. "You always know how to get my mind right."

"That's what big brothers are for." I kissed her forehead, then released her. "What are you cooking? Your daughter ran me ragged, and now I'm hungry."

She giggled and shook her head as she turned back to the stove. "I'm making gumbo and rice. I already set a place for you at the table."

I looked back at the dining room; sure enough, there were four place settings.

"Can I help with anything?" I asked.

"Nope. Just keep me company since you let my child fall asleep. I would fuss if it weren't a Friday night, and we're going away for the weekend. You're still invited to come."

"As I told you, I don't want to intrude on family time."

"And as I've told you, you are my family. You know, if you'd just get married and have a kid or two, we wouldn't need to have these conversations when I invite you to go on vacation with us. I have a friend or two I could hook you up with."

"Negative. Why would you want me to date your friends?"

She looked over her shoulder at me and smirked. "Because at least I know I like them and won't have to fight anybody. You know I don't play about you."

"I will pass on your friends. Chris tried to slide Eva's friends on me too."

"I like Eva; her friends are cute, but I don't see them as your type."

"That's what I said. I'm good, though. Eventually, my rib will be placed in my path."

"Well, don't go hungry while you're waiting. I'm not saying be a man whore, but you should date. She's not just gonna fall out of the sky, Callum. I want some nieces and nephews to love on, so you need to hop on it."

"I hear you. We'll see what happens."

"Don't just 'see' about it, 'be' about it. Don't play with me like I won't set you up on a blind date."

I shook my head. It wouldn't be the first time she'd done that.

We continued to talk while she cooked. Precious was awake when my brother-in-law came home and wanted to play again. I obliged her while we waited for the food and then ate dinner with them. I returned to my house around eight that evening, and the difference was so noticeable. The silence was deafening, and the house felt too big for me. For the first time in a long time, I truly felt lonely.

But what could I do but wash my body and climb my lonely ass into bed?

CHAPTER NINE

FOUR MONTHS LATER

Pasha

I LOOKED AROUND THE empty space that was to be my little studio apartment. I'd been working, doing overtime, and picked up a second job to save enough money to move into my own place. Living with Avyn had been wonderful. She was encouraging; she was my shoulder to cry on and my voice of reason. There were so many times when I wanted to give up, but she pushed me to keep moving forward.

As great as it had been living with my best friend and rebuilding our friendship every day, I most certainly felt like I was a burden to her. She always assured me she loved having me there, and I was welcomed for as long as I needed to stay. Again, I appreciated that, but I needed to go.

Today was a day I had been anticipating for a while now. I'd been touring apartments for two weeks, and nothing quite felt like me. Then Avyn told me that her building had a vacancy. It was perfect because I'd grown familiar with the area and didn't have to change my routine when getting to and from my second job.

"Does everything look good?" asked Marie from the leasing office.

I turned to her with a smile. "Everything looks perfect."

"Awesome! Well, I have your leasing agreement right here on the iPad. I'll review everything with you, you'll pay your deposit, and then we're good to go!"

We stood at the small bar area while she went over the agreement as thoroughly as possible. Once she was done, I signed it and handed over my money order for the deposit. My excitement peaked when she handed over my keys. This wasn't just an apartment. It was a home that I'd secured all on my own.

Someone had taken care of me my entire life. Someone always had the power to say, *"You wouldn't have that if it weren't for me."* Not anymore. Now, I was taking care of myself. At twenty-eight years old, I felt like I was finally beginning to live for the first time. I had to admit it felt good.

After securing the keys on my key ring, I locked up and headed upstairs to Avyn's apartment. When I walked in, she looked like she was just getting home. She stood at the kitchen counter, sifting through mail.

"Hey, boo," she said, glancing up. "Did you sign your lease?"

"I did! I'll be out of your hair soon."

She dropped the mail and gave me her attention. "Don't do that. You have always been more than welcomed here, Pash."

"I know, I know. I'm joking. I really appreciate you, Avyn. You've been an angel."

"It was nothing, girl. I know if the tables were turned, you would do the same for me. I'm so happy things are looking up for you."

"Yeah . . . me too. It's been a long journey, and it's not over yet."

While I would have liked my divorce to be over and done, it was at the point of things getting nasty. Raymond expected me to be docile about everything. He expected me not to contest the divorce, and he would just be able to ride off into the sunset with his pregnant mistress. That's why he offered to pay for my lawyer.

He and his lawyer had compiled a team of legal representation they were willing to pay for. The problem with that was the fact everybody on the list was someone that he knew and would likely screw me over.

My friend Blake's sister, Sandra, was a divorce attorney. She took my case pro bono. Not only that, but she also was fighting to get me everything she said I deserved. She filed a motion going after Raymond for adultery, abandonment, cruelty, isolation, and emotional distress. She was seeking alimony and was trying to have him continue to pay for my therapy. When my wedding ring was pawned, I took that money to pay for my therapy. Maybe I could have put it off, but I did what I felt was best for me at the time. I needed to maintain that relationship for my sanity.

Raymond was livid the first time we went to court. He couldn't control the narrative, and he couldn't control me. He walked into the courtroom expecting to see his friend standing beside me as my representative. The smile on his face dropped when Sandra appeared at my side. She was one of the top divorce attorneys in the state. If he had made a valid effort to really get to know my friends, he would have known she was Blake's sister.

He managed to get my number from the court documents, and every so often, he called me from a blocked number, harassing me. I'd recorded his rants to present in court per Sandra's advice.

"Hey . . ." Avyn grabbed my hand, causing me to break out of my thoughts. "It may not be over, but I'm so proud of your handling everything."

"I'm trying."

"How about we go do some shopping? Somebody has a new apartment that needs furnishing!"

I smiled. "I can't go overboard now. This is a case of only having enough for the deposit."

"Actually . . ." She reached into her purse and handed me an envelope.

My brows furrowed. "What's this?"

"Just a little love offering from the girls and me. We know you're saving for a car and didn't want you to dip into those funds. We wanted to at least help you get the essentials . . . pots and pans, towels, cleaning supplies . . . stuff like that. Oh, and you can take the bedroom furniture from the guest room. I'm getting a new one for my room and moving the old one in there."

"Avyn . . . That's too much. You've already given me more than I could ask for."

"You didn't ask. I offered, and you'll take it even if I have to drag it downstairs myself. What am I saying? I don't do manual labor. I'll call up Mr. Officer to help move it. He's been asking to see me anyway."

I shook my head. "So you're gonna put him to work?"

"I'll work him out afterward." She winked at me as she slung her purse over her shoulder. "Come on. I'm sending the girls a text. They can meet us for drinks when we're done. You have every reason to celebrate right now. I'm not taking no for an answer."

I rolled my eyes. "Okay, okay. Just let me grab my purse."

I headed to the guest room. After swiping my purse from the dresser, I started for the door. That's when I saw my journal on the dresser. I realized that I hadn't reflected on my daily feelings. Every day, I wrote one word that described how I was feeling. It helped me with keeping track of my moods. Flipping to today's date, I uncapped the pen and wrote the word . . . *grateful*.

That was the first and only thing that came to mind. Today, it was the most befitting.

⌒๑⌒

Avyn and I had been in Splurge, a superstore in town, for almost two hours now.

God was really on my side today. Almost every item I would need was on sale or clearance. Avyn and I had to grab another shopping cart to carry it all. We finally made our way into a checkout line. Because it was Splurge, only a few lanes were open, and they were backed up along with self-checkout.

"I don't know why we love coming to this ghetto-ass place," Avyn said, examining her nails.

"It's a one-stop shop," I answered.

"Yeah, where you can catch a sale, a headache, hands, or a bullet."

I giggled. "Why are you so dramatic?"

"You know I'm extra. It's been that way since we were chaps. Nothing has changed."

Her gaze drifted to the crowd around us. A smirk spread across her face as she nodded to the left of me.

"Speaking of things not changing, your angel still looks as beautiful as ever."

I looked up to see the face of my rescuer. I hadn't seen him since he dropped me off at the hotel four months ago. I'd often thought of him, hoping he was blessed for his kindness. I almost forgot that I needed to pay him back with everything going on. Well, I hadn't forgotten. I just wanted to be in a better position.

He must have felt our eyes on him because he looked in our direction. A smile spread across his face. Avyn waved at him, and immediately, he began walking toward us.

"Why would you wave?" I whisper-yelled.

"Why not? I told you months ago that man wanted to check on you. Act right!" She plastered a smile on her face as he approached us. "Mr. Ellis. How nice to see you."

"Good afternoon."

He extended his hand, and she didn't hesitate to shake it. When he turned to me, his smile brightened.

"Mrs. Sinclaire. It's nice to see you."

"Mr. Ellis. It's nice to see you too."

"How are you? How is everything?"

"Well . . . Things are better than where we left them. I'm still going through the divorce process, but things are looking up. I signed a lease for an apartment today."

He looked at the items in the carts and smiled. "That's great to hear. I'm really happy for you. I, uh . . . I've thought about you."

"You have?"

"Yes." He looked down at his feet. "When I left you, something stuck with me. I guess I worried that you would be okay. Now that I've seen you, maybe my mind will rest."

"If you worried, why didn't you ever reach out? I know Avyn told you where I worked."

He chuckled. "Well, given the circumstances, I wasn't sure how you would take me checking up on you. I didn't want to come off as creepy."

Avyn tapped my arm. "Don't give the man the third degree, Pasha."

"I'm not!" I cleared my throat. "I appreciate your prayers and concern."

"It's no problem. If you need any help moving, I'm available."

"Oh, I don't—"

Avyn cut me off. "That would be wonderful! Is your number still the same?"

"It is."

"Great. I'll text you the address tomorrow morning."

I looked at her like she had two heads. What the hell was she thinking?

"Tomorrow is good. I'll see you then."

He left us with a smile and continued along his merry way. I slapped Avyn's arm.

"What are you doing?!"

"Setting the stage for you to get a good man."

"I don't want a man. Period. Have you forgotten that I'm in the middle of a divorce?"

"I haven't. If Raymond can move on while you two are together, you can move on now. I'm not saying jump in headfirst, but you could always use a friend."

"That's why I have you."

"And I love you. But I can't offer you the kind of friendship he can. You *know* what I'm talking about." She wiggled her eyebrows at me.

I scoffed. "You think I would sleep with that man?"

She snorted. "Shit, I would."

"I can't with you." I folded my arms. "Are you *really* going to give him your address? What happened to you calling Mr. Officer to help us?"

"I'm still calling him. The more manpower we have, the better. You know I don't do that kind of manual labor. I just got my nails done, and I'm not trying to break one."

I rolled my eyes as I turned back to the slowly moving line. I wasn't sure if I wanted this man to know where I lived. What if he showed up unannounced? What if he was really on some creepy shit? He knowing where I laid my head didn't sit right with me. I had enough of a messy situation and didn't know what kind of drama he could have with him. The last thing I needed was some woman to roll up behind him, threatening to fight me over a man that I didn't even want.

"Get out of your head," Avyn whispered in my ear, causing me to jump.

I wish I were able to do that. I'd been in my head for so many years that I didn't know what it was like to live worry and stress free. I knew Avyn meant well, but I got the feeling that this wasn't going to be anything like she was hoping for. I prayed that Mr. Ellis didn't have any ideas about me. He was there to help— nothing more, nothing less.

CHAPTER TEN
Callum

"ARE YOU SURE it's a good idea to go over there?" Chris asked as I made my way over to Pasha's apartment building.

Avyn sent me the address early this morning and told me they would be ready to start moving by eleven.

"It's a fine time to ask, Chris. I'm already on the way."

"I don't know about this. I don't want you to get your feelings hurt. I know you still think about that night, man."

It was true. I did think about that night. Four months had passed, and I still thought about it every time I passed that hotel. I thought about it whenever I went to my contacts and saw Avyn's number. Chris told me months ago that the situation somehow embedded itself inside me.

I wasn't sure why, but it had been my experience that I had to see it through when I felt strongly about something. It never let up on my mental if I ignored it.

"I'm just helping her move, Chris. Nothing more, nothing less."

"If you say so. Are you still coming over for the barbecue later?"

"Yeah, I'll be there. There's not much to move. At least that's what was said this morning."

"All right, well, I'll see you later, man."

"See you later."

The call disconnected, and the music I previously listened to resumed playing through my speaker. This was my Saturday morning cleaning playlist. It was filled with some of my parents' favorite music, an ode to them of sorts.

Every Saturday morning, my mother would have Bella and me up, cleaning the whole house. We knew that time was when Betty Wright's "Clean Up Woman" came blaring through my father's stereo. Even though the song wasn't about cleaning, it was just like a wake-up call. Since I was about to help Pasha move into her place, I needed to get in a cleaning mood like I did when I cleaned my own house.

Ten minutes later, I pulled up in front of the apartment building. It was located in a semi quiet part of town, close to the university. I assumed mostly college students dwelled here since almost every person I saw walking in and out carried a backpack. I climbed out of my truck and headed inside to the tenth floor, where Avyn said she lived. I counted the numbers on the door until I came to ten twenty-one. Taking a deep breath, I knocked. A few seconds later, the door opened, and Avyn greeted me with a smile.

"Hey, Callum. Come on in."

She opened the door wider to allow me entry. Stepping in, I noted how spotless it was. Everything was neat, organized, and color coordinated.

"You have a nice place," I said.

"Thank you."

"Baby, I think we can play Tetris with this furniture—Callum Ellis."

I grinned when I realized the voice belonged to a good friend at the police department.

"Malcolm Holbrook."

He came over and shook my hand. "What the hell are you doing in this neck of the woods?"

"You two know each other?" Avyn asked, folding her arms.

"We go back a few years," Malcolm answered. "How are you, man? How's the family?"

"Bella is good. Precious is growing like a weed and spending all my money."

He chuckled. "Admit it. You love spoiling her."

"I do. That's my lil' baby."

"How do you know my lady?"

"He's actually a friend of Pasha's," Avyn answered. "Say hello to your help for the day."

He shook his head. "I forgot . . . You don't do manual labor."

She smirked. "I'm glad you know this. Anyway, Pash is downstairs doing some last-minute cleaning. She wanted the place spotless before we moved anything."

I raised an eyebrow. "She's moving downstairs?"

"Yes. An apartment became available, so we hopped right on it. It works out since we carpool to work together."

"That makes sense. I'm glad she accepted your help."

"She didn't have much of a choice. I can be quite pushy."

"That's an understatement," Malcolm mumbled with a sly smile.

"I can also be petty," Avyn said firmly.

Malcolm kissed her cheek. "I'm joking, love."

"Mmm-hmm. Why don't you take Callum to the guest room, and you two can figure out how you will move everything." She grabbed two huge rolling suitcases and headed for the door. "She's in apartment eight seventeen. Don't get to chitchatting and take all damn day."

"I hear you, woman. Go on."

She rolled her eyes as she walked out the door.

"I swear she gives me hell sometimes, man. Women."

He shook his head as he led me down the hallway to the guest room. Upon entering, I was surprised to see it so clean since someone was moving out.

"So, how long have you been seeing this friend?" he asked.

"Oh, um, technically, we aren't seeing each other like that. I helped her out a few months back. I saw them at the store yesterday and offered my assistance with moving."

He smirked. "Sounds like somebody is trying to get in where he fits in. I ain't mad at you. Pasha is a beautiful woman; after all she's been through, she could use a good man."

"I'm not—"

"Callum, I know you well enough to know you don't do hookups. You saw something in her. Just know you're gonna need a lot of patience with that one. She's closed off and doesn't say too much. Avyn loves her to death, though. She won't admit it, but she's sad she's moving out. However, she's determined to be a supportive friend. She'll cry about it later."

"How long have you two been seeing each other."

"About a year. Nothing is official . . . but that's my lil' baby. Maybe one of these days, I'll get her to commit to me."

He sighed, and I could tell that was probably an ongoing battle he'd clearly been losing. We made small talk as we followed each other's lead in maneuvering the bedroom furniture out into the living room. We decided it was best to get everything out first to save time. I compared the elevator's size with the furniture's size and figured we could get it all in two trips.

After moving the first load down the hall, we packed it in the elevator and headed down. When we got to Pasha's apartment, the door was slightly ajar.

"Knock, knock!" Malcolm yelled, pushing it open with his foot.

Avyn and Pasha appeared from around the corner. Our eyes briefly met as we maneuvered the heavy dresser through the space to the area designated for the bedroom. It sat behind a floor-to-ceiling bookshelf that served as the partition that separated the living and sleeping quarters. I was just about to ask where she wanted it, but then I noticed the Post-it Notes on the wall labeling the designated furniture spots.

I pointed it out to Malcolm, and we put the dresser in place.

"Good morning," I said, offering her a warm smile.

"Good morning. Thank you again for coming to help. I'm sure you had better things to do today."

"On the contrary, I didn't have any plans. I'm all yours today."

"Well, I'll try not to keep you too long."

I didn't mind. She could keep me all day. She looked cute in her track pants, plain white tee, and a baseball cap with her curls sticking out from under it. In seeing her yesterday, her spirit felt lighter. There wasn't that dark cloud of sadness cast over her. Her eyes weren't red from crying. She had a faint air of happiness.

"It's no problem. How are you feeling about all this?"

She smiled softly. "I'm happy I'm in a position to do better for myself. I've never lived alone, so it'll take some getting used to. But it's mine, and nobody can put me out when they feel like it."

"Amen to that. For what it's worth, I'm proud of you. I don't know you, but you were heavy on my spirit for a long time, Pasha. I don't think I've ever prayed so hard for someone I didn't know."

Again, she smiled. "Well, I've never thanked God so much for a stranger. You blessed me that night. I had no idea where I was going or what I would do. You provided me with a place to rest my head and your kindness . . ."

She paused momentarily to swipe the tear in the corner of her eye. She closed them and took a deep breath before continuing.

"Because of you, I've reconnected with some of the only people who truly love me. I needed them more than I realized."

"I love that for you."

"I know Avyn said the room was partially refunded, but I'd like to pay you back the rest—"

I held up a hand to stop her. "You'll do no such thing. I told you, I'm not worried about the money."

"At least let me pay you for today."

I gently took her hand. "Pasha . . . It's okay. I'm happy to be of service. This is a big step for you. I just want to support you."

She squeezed my hand. "Thank you."

We stared at each other for a moment. Damn, I could get lost in those eyes of hers. She was so beautiful . . . so resilient and deserving, and she didn't even know it. I knew so little about her, yet looking into her eyes, I wanted to know everything. Suddenly, Malcolm cleared his throat, breaking us out of our trance. We looked over to find him and Avyn giving us curious looks. I didn't realize I was still holding her hand until she let mine go.

"You ready to get the rest of this stuff?" Malcolm asked.

"Yeah."

I left Pasha with a smile as we headed back into the hall to grab the items we left beside the elevator.

Malcolm chuckled. "I see why you agreed to come help out."

I feigned ignorance. "I don't know what you mean."

He kissed his teeth. "You're a terrible liar, Callum. Not only that, but you also wear your emotions on your sleeve like a badge of honor. You're attracted to Pasha."

"I mean, she's beautiful; you said that yourself."

"Nah, man. I see her beauty as a woman. You . . . You see it as something you want to experience for yourself. What happened between y'all?"

"Nothing. I just . . . If you'd seen her that night, you'd understand, Malcolm. She was broken. I watched her husband speak to her like some nigga on the street. He kicked her out of her home and moved his pregnant side chick in. The pain and hurt I saw in her face that night was nothing like I'd ever seen. I've thought about that woman so many times over the last couple of months. I've prayed for her heart and her mind. I don't know what it is, but I couldn't seem to shake her."

"Damn, man. That's deep. Who knows. She could be the one. Sometimes, heartbreak is a setup for a hell of a breakthrough. I don't know what or how you're gonna do it, but good luck with that. I mean it."

I didn't say anything as we approached the furniture. I knew it was too soon to pursue anything with this woman. After all, she was in the middle of what I could only assume was a nasty divorce. She didn't need me trying to push up on her, and I would never be that insensitive or disrespectful. However, I did want to offer her friendship. If she was open to that, maybe, just maybe, it was a start.

CHAPTER ELEVEN
Pasha

I LOOKED AROUND AT my little apartment with a smile on my face.

While I still needed a kitchen table and living room furniture, it was already beginning to feel like home. I can admit that when I woke up this morning and came down here to do a little last-minute cleaning, the first thing I did when I walked in the door was cry. But they weren't tears of sadness. They were more like tears of joy. This moment had been a long time coming.

While Avyn said I could stay with her as long as I wanted, I knew I needed to kick-start my independence and get my own place. A place where I could call home. A place where I didn't have to worry about being put out of at the drop of a dime. This was my place of comfort and peace. At the end of a long day, I could come here and leave my burdens at the front door.

"I can't wait to see this place fully decorated," Blake said, throwing herself across my bed.

She and Tia had come over about an hour ago bearing bags of groceries to stock my fridge, freezer, and pantry. I couldn't believe how my friends had blessed me. They made it clear that they would be here for me. All I had to do was let them.

"It'll probably be a while, but the important thing is, I'm in here."

Tia embraced me for the third time. "I'm so happy for you, Pash. Your growth thus far has been beautiful. I know you're gonna come out of this stronger than ever."

I prayed for the same thing. I'd been wallowing in grief for so long that feeling happy was foreign to me. It heightened my anxiety, and the intrusive thoughts of something snatching this happiness away played in my head like a broken record. My therapy sessions were filled with tears, but Dr. Thomas was a godsend. She was as patient with me as she had been for years. She told me that slow progress was still progress, and I needed to believe I deserved my happy ending.

A knock on the wall broke my thoughts. We looked up to see Callum standing there with a smile.

"Pardon my interruption. I was just about to head out and wanted to say goodbye."

"Oh, okay. Well, let me walk you to the elevator."

I didn't miss the smirk on my girls' faces when I stood from the bed and walked out of the space. I followed Callum out of the apartment and down the hall to the elevator. He pressed the button and turned to me while he waited.

"Thank you again for all your help today," I said softly.

"It was no problem. Your place is coming together."

"Slowly but surely."

"You'll get there."

He stared at me for a moment, seemingly contemplating his next words. His hand went to the back of his head, and he took a deep breath.

"I, um . . . I was hoping I could leave you with my number personally. You know, just in case you ever need anything fixed or need a ride to or from work. I know you don't have a car right now, and it's a hassle asking for rides."

"Oh, um . . . Well, I worked my schedule around Avyn's, so a ride is no problem right now. But thank you."

"Okay." He nervously scratched his head. "Can I still leave my number?"

"Callum, you're a nice guy, and I appreciate everything you've done. But I'm just not ready to entertain another man. I don't know when or if I ever will be."

"I just wanted to offer you friendship. No pressure."

I was hesitant. I wasn't sure if having him as a friend was a good idea. Even though I told him I wasn't ready for anything, what was stopping him from pushing for something more? Still, he'd been such a blessing. I didn't want to seem ungrateful.

"Okay," I found myself agreeing.

I reached into my pocket and pulled out my phone. After unlocking it, I handed it to him. He quickly programmed his number and handed it back to me.

"You don't want mine?" I asked.

"I'll let you be comfortable with reaching out to me. Whenever you feel like talking, I'll make time for you."

I nodded as I slipped my phone back into my pocket just as the elevator dinged. "Get home safe."

"I will."

The doors opened, and he stepped inside. I stepped back and watched as they closed on him before returning to my apartment. I walked in to find Avyn and Malcolm kissing in my kitchen. In the four months I had been staying with her, he'd been over weekly. For someone who was openly dating a few different people, he appeared to be her favorite. He seemed nice, and I couldn't fathom why she wouldn't commit to him.

I cleared my throat, causing them to part ways.

"My bad, boo," she said, wiping her mouth. "We got carried away. I guess it's time to take him back upstairs and reward him for a hard day's work."

"Please don't let me stop you."

She giggled. "At least you don't have to hear me anymore."

"I will *not* miss that. You get so loud."

She winked at me. "That's how you know he's doing his job."

"Baby," Malcolm said, elbowing her, "Pasha doesn't want or need to know that." He offered me a handshake. "Congratulations on the new place, Pasha. We're gonna get out of your hair."

Avyn pulled me in for a hug, squeezing me tightly. "I'm so proud of you and love you so much."

"I love you too, Avyn. Thank you for all you've done for me."

"No need to thank me. You're my sister. I'd do anything for you. I'm gonna miss you."

I giggled. "I'm only two floors down, girl."

"I know! But now, I can't just walk across the hall to your room. Don't be surprised if you wake up, and I'm in your bed."

"You're always welcome."

She kissed my cheek, then grabbed Malcolm's hand and left. I headed back into my bedroom space with Blake and Tia. The moment I stepped in, they looked at me with curious faces.

"Sooo . . ." Blake said, dragging out the word, "Where did you find that handsome hunk of man candy?"

"Who, Callum?"

"Um, yes! Girl, he's *beautiful.*"

I rolled my eyes. "He helped me out a while ago. We ran into him in Walmart yesterday, and our big-mouthed friend accepted his offer to come help out today. Low key, she was trying to set me up."

Tia smirked. "Well, our friend has good taste. You deserve a little fun."

"I'll tell you like I told her, I'm not trying to see anyone. I just want to get my life together. He did give me his number and said he wants to be friends."

"Nothing is wrong with being friends," Blake said.

"What if he pushes for more?"

Tia pulled me to sit between them on the bed. She linked her arm through mine.

"There are good men out there, Pasha. Men who would respect a friendship until you feel like you wanted more or even if you didn't. You can't be afraid, boo. I know you don't want to spend the rest of your life alone. You're only twenty-eight. There is plenty of time. I just don't want you to go through the rest of your life being afraid of men and what they might do to you."

"I'm not just afraid of what they would do to me. I'm afraid of what I might allow."

Blake shook her head. "You are so much stronger than you give yourself credit for, Pash. With everything you went through, you are still here, baby. I know you wanted to give up. I know you wanted to end things, but you fought it. You won the battle so many people have lost. I admire you for never taking that route."

They had no idea how many times I wanted to end my life over the years. There were times when I had razor blades to my wrists in the bathtub. There were times when I had a handful of painkillers ready to swallow. There was a time when I had a loaded gun to my head. I'd been so deep in my depression that I couldn't foresee any way out other than ending my life. Then I thought about my parents.

They would be so disappointed in me if I'd done that. I thought about my baby and how he wouldn't want his mommy to die because he didn't get to live. Even when I felt like I didn't have much to live for, I chose to live for the three of them because they couldn't live for themselves. My life as I knew it had ended, and now, I had a chance at a new beginning, and this one would be what *I* made it.

The sun peeked in through my window bright and early Sunday morning. My eyes slowly opened, and I looked around, remembering I wasn't at Avyn's anymore. There wasn't the sound of her gospel music blaring through the speakers. I laughed to myself, thinking of how she used to tell me she attended Bedside Baptist with Reverand Pillow. She maintained the idea that she was a holy hellraiser; she may be a sinner, but she knew God and had a personal relationship with Him.

Tossing back my covers, I stood and headed into the bathroom to relieve myself. When I finished, I washed my face and brushed my teeth. Heading back into the bedroom area, I grabbed my journal and a pen and went into the kitchen to make a cup of coffee. While it was brewing, I threw two slices of bread into the toaster and cut up an avocado to top it. Once everything was done, I grabbed it all and placed it on the floor in front of my living room window. I opened the curtains to let the sunlight in before taking a seat.

After taking a few bites of my toast and a sip of coffee, I opened the journal to today's writing prompt. *Write a letter of encouragement to your mind.* I pondered the sentence. There were so many things I could say to myself. Taking a deep breath, I picked up my pen and began writing.

> *Dear Mind,*
>
> *It's me, your human. I know we've been going through it for a while now, but things are improving. I know I haven't been kind to you. I know I've burdened you with so much, and it's been unfair. It's time we started taking in some of the encouragement*

given to us. We have to believe in ourselves. Take a look around. We aren't where we were four months ago. You need to know that your greatest gift is you. You have resilience that can't be broken, no matter how many times it's been tested.

You are uniquely equipped to carry your burdens. Trust yourself. You will let yourself down. You will make mistakes, but forgive yourself and turn your tragedies and failures into triumphs. Life may knock you down nine times, but you've got to get up ten and keep fighting. Persistence is key. You are not a quitter. You are not weak. You are not unworthy.

You deserve to embrace the fact that you alone control your life. You deserve to allow yourself to feel and be heard. There comes a point in life where self-loathing and self-doubt become torturous and no longer healthy. This is that point. Remember what drives you. Remember what makes life worth living, even in the worst of times. Take a deep break. Inhale. Exhale. You've got this.

Sincerely,
Pasha

I closed the journal and set it aside. That was the kindest I'd spoken to myself in a long time. It felt good and uplifting. I lifted my head toward the sun, allowing it to warm my face. Today was a brand-new day. Today, I would do something just for me because I deserve it and am worthy of having a good day. Pulling out my phone, I booked an Uber for pickup in the next hour. After finishing my toast and coffee, I put my dishes in the sink and returned to my room to find something to wear before hopping in the shower.

I took the time to cleanse my body and complete a makeup routine that I hadn't done in at least a year. I did my lashes and eyebrows and applied a light beat to my face. For my hair, I pulled it up into a sleek, curly puff atop my head and even added earrings. I smiled as I looked in the mirror at the once-familiar reflection of myself. I felt pretty, and that had become foreign to me. Going to my closet, I sifted through my clothes, determined to put on something other than sweats and an oversized T-shirt.

I settled on a pair of khaki joggers that hugged the curves I was trying to embrace, a white T-shirt that I tucked in, and my favorite pair of canvas shoes. Digging through my keepsake box, I pulled out my mother's silver necklace with a small diamond pendant and matching bracelet. I also pulled out my father's favorite wristwatch. They wore these when they passed away, and I hadn't had the heart to touch them since I placed them in the box.

The watch didn't work, but I didn't care. Today, I wanted to feel close to them, so I would proudly wear the pieces. Standing in front of the mirror, I looked myself over with a smile. I even snapped a picture or two because I felt that cute. Then the notification chimed, letting me know that my Uber was waiting outside. Grabbing my crossbody and keys, I headed out the front door to see what adventure awaited me.

CHAPTER TWELVE

Callum

I USUALLY SPEND MY Sundays with Precious and Bella, but since they were out of town again, I decided to leave the house for a little while and enjoy the fresh air. I'd been up since early this morning, getting in my workout routine and meditating. It was something I found calmed my nerves when I was dealing with emotional turmoil after my parents passed away.

Every morning for the last couple of years, I've woken up at sunrise and gone to sit out on my patio. The neighborhood I grew up in was quiet, and there wasn't much movement at six a.m. Out there, it was just me and the sounds of nature. My mother used to meditate all the time. Back then, I'd always ask my father why she was sitting looking up at the sky so early. He said she was centering herself and finding peace and balance. As a kid, I didn't understand, but as an adult, I fully reaped the benefits.

Since it was such a lovely day, I decided to go to the local farmers' market in the town square. Every Sunday, people came to sell fresh produce and handmade goods. It was the perfect opportunity to sow back into the community. Most Sundays as a kid, we ventured here as a family. Some days, I still scooped up Bella and Precious to come out here.

I arrived a little after ten and parked my car. Grabbing my sunglasses, I got out and treaded through the crowded streets. My first stop was always Ms. Carol, an older Black woman who sold homemade treats.

"Callum!" She came from around the table to greet me with a grandmotherly hug. "How are you, baby?"

"I can't complain, Ms. Carol. How are you?"

"Well, the good Lord allowed me to live another day, and I'm just fine with that."

"Amen. What do you have for me today?"

"Oh!" She tipped back around the table and opened the cooler I knew she kept her secret stash in. She pulled out a small bag with about five cookies in it. "Cookie Monster Cookies."

They were crispy, blue chocolate chip cookies loaded with chocolate chips, chopped Oreos, and melted chocolate in the center.

"Ms. Carol, you're trying to make me fat," I said with a light chuckle. "You know I can't eat just one of these."

"That's why there are five in the bag." She pulled out a second bag and handed it to me. "Take that to Precious. Where are she and Bella today?"

"They went out of town. How much do I owe you?"

"It's on me today. I haven't seen you in a while. Consider it a gift."

"Now, Ms. Carol—"

"Aht-aht! Respect your elders." She turned to get a bag, and I slipped a twenty into her tip jar. "You have a good day, and keep cool in this hot sun."

"Yes, ma'am."

I leaned over to kiss her cheek. Bidding her goodbye, I continued through the crowd, stopping at a few tables. After a while, the urge to try one of these cookies got the better of me. I grabbed a bottle of water from a vendor and sat on a nearby bench. The first bite of the cookie caused me to release a deep moan.

"Shit . . ." I mumbled.

I had to hold the cookie away from me and look at it. There was a very strong possibility that Precious wouldn't get her bag if I had to keep them at my house. Before I knew it, I'd scarfed down three cookies.

"Must be good," I heard.

I looked up to see Pasha standing in front of me with a warm smile on her face. I had to do a double take. She looked nothing like she did yesterday. I mean, she was still beautiful yesterday, but today . . . Today, she was radiant. From the hair to the makeup to the way her outfit accentuated her ample curves. She looked like she had a good night's sleep and woke up feeling refreshed.

I swallowed the cookie in my mouth and extended the bag to her.

"Try one."

"Oh, I couldn't. You looked like you were enjoying that, and I don't need a cookie anyway."

I stood and stepped closer to her. Reaching into the bag, I pulled out a cookie and handed it to her. "Taste it," I insisted.

She hesitated momentarily before breaking off a piece and popping it into her mouth. I watched her eyes widen as she chewed.

"Oh my God . . ."

"It's good, right?"

"That's probably the best thing I've ever tasted."

"You want the rest?"

She plucked the remaining cookie from my fingers and took another bite. A few crumbs landed on her lips, and the urge to reach out and swipe them was real. She licked her lips to capture them.

"Thank you," she said softly.

"You're welcome. You look nice. Something about you feels different today."

She blushed. "Well, for one, I woke up happy and well rested. I feel good."

"It shows. What brings you out?"

"Oh, I just wanted to get out for a little while. Soak up the sun. I hadn't planned to come here when the Uber dropped me off in town. I saw the crowd and decided to see what was going on."

"You've never been to the farmers' market?"

She shook her head. "I've been a bit of a hermit the last couple of years. My anxiety has me wanting to run for the hills right now."

"Stay in the moment and work through it. You took a big enough step by coming out here. You deserve to enjoy yourself."

She looked around. "There's just so many people. I wasn't even supposed to come over here. I could feel myself beginning to panic, and you were a familiar face."

"Well, I'm glad my face had a calming effect. I'd be happy to walk around with you if you're comfortable with that."

She was hesitant, but she nodded. I offered her my arm, and she gently wrapped her fingers around it. Something about her touch was practically electrifying. We stared at each other for a moment. She was so damn beautiful. If this was what she looked like before her husband, I could only imagine that she hadn't always been this shy, timid woman who retreated into her shell. I was dying to see her bring that back out.

"Lead the way," I said, motioning in front of me.

She began walking, and I trailed along beside her. For a while, we walked in silence. Every so often, I stole a glance at her, hoping that my staring wasn't coming off as creepy.

"Do you come here often?" she asked.

"On occasion. Usually, I bring my sister and my niece with me."

"Is she your only sibling?"

"Yes. They are really my only family. Well, them and my brother-in-law. His family welcomes me, but Bella and Precious are my heart."

"You don't have *any* other family?"

"I do, but after my parents died when I was eighteen, nobody could or would take us in. I gained custody of my sister, and all we had was each other."

"You lost your parents?"

"They, uh . . . They died in a boating accident. They went on this yacht to celebrate one of their friends' birthday, and the boat capsized. According to those that survived, my mother went under, and my father jumped in to save her, and neither of them came back up."

"Callum . . . I'm so sorry. Were they . . . Were they ever recovered."

"They were. I was able to give them a proper burial. They are resting peacefully in Oakview Cemetery."

Her eyes widened. "My parents are buried there." She swiped a tear from her eye. "I wanted to bury my son next to them, but Raymond didn't think I could handle it."

"Avyn mentioned that you lost a child. She wasn't gossiping. I want you to know that. She was just trying to explain what was going on with you."

"It's okay. I know she meant no harm." She swallowed hard before she spoke again. "It was a year ago. I was almost nine months. One morning, I woke up with terrible cramps. I thought it was normal and would ease up after a while, but it didn't. I was in so much pain, and I could tell that something was wrong. I begged Raymond to take me to the hospital. He insisted that I was probably having Braxton Hicks contractions, but I knew it was something else. By the time we got there, my baby was gone. The cord . . . He got tangled up in the umbilical cord, and there was nothing they could do."

"I'm so sorry, Pasha," I said softly. "You've suffered so much in the last couple of years. First, your parents, then your child . . . now, this. You're stronger than most people. I'm not sure I would have survived everything you've been through."

"Most times, I don't feel strong at all." She shook her head. "But I'm still here. That has to count for something, right?"

"That counts for everything. Don't take that lightly. You may be bruised and bend, but you are not broken."

She smiled softly. "Thank you, Callum. You might be a good friend after all."

I chuckled. "I can be a great friend. So, *friend* . . . How about we focus on having a good day? No more sad talk. You came out of the house, and I'm gonna make sure you make it worth your while. Have you eaten?"

"Just toast and coffee for breakfast. I am a little hungry."

"There's a few food trucks in the back parking area. How about we grab something? My treat."

"I can pay for my own food. You've done enough for me at no cost."

"One thing you'll learn about me is I'm a very generous person. The food is on me. Come along."

She was reluctant to follow me but did so with no further protest. Running into her might turn out to be the highlight of my day. I was on a mission to ensure she left here with nothing but smiles.

⌒つ

Pacha and I ended up grabbing a walking taco from one of the food trucks and cups of lemonade to drink. She seemed a little shy about eating in front of me, and I could tell it came from her husband commenting about her weight. Again, I didn't have a problem with her weight. I loved thicker women. My mama was a thick woman. My sister is a thick woman. There was no way I'd ever disrespect a woman based on her body type when two of the women I loved most shared it.

We'd been walking around for about an hour when we stopped to take a break in the shade. The sun was beating down on us, and we felt the heat. We'd stopped to get some Italian ice to cool us off.

"I should have worn shorts," she mumbled, fanning herself.

"Right. I'm hopping in the shower as soon as I get home."

"Me too."

"How was your first night in the apartment?"

She smiled. "A little lonely, but so peaceful. Avyn came back for a little while after Malcolm left. She said we had to christen the new place by having drinks and a little girls' night. I've missed that."

"She seems like a great friend."

"She is. I've known her since we were kids, and she's always been a good friend. She's always gone out of her way to care for me. I felt bad about shutting all my girls out, but most of all, her. I'm just glad to have them back."

"I'm glad you have that too. We hate to admit we need people, but there is power in support."

"Who supports you, I mean, besides your sister?"

"I have friends that have become like family. They keep my head on straight."

She shoved a spoonful of the Italian ice into her mouth. "I don't see you being too much of a hothead."

I chuckled. "These days, I'm not. It takes a lot to get me out of character, but I will act up over people I care about and the principle of things. Right is right, and wrong is wrong. Ain't no way around that. As my friend, that's extended to you."

"I think I've already gotten a glimpse of that. Since you won't allow me to pay you for your help, I feel I should do something to show my appreciation."

"You spending time with me today is appreciation enough. That is worth more than any monetary gain."

She blushed. "Something tells me you're a smooth talker . . . but you're genuine."

"I'm very genuine. I don't say things that I don't mean, and I don't do anything looking for something in return. My kindness comes from the heart."

"I wish there were more people like that."

"My mother always told me you must be the change you want to see in the world. Who are you, Pasha? Before the hurt and the pain, who were you inside?"

She stabbed at her Italian ice, seemingly pondering the question. Finally, she shrugged.

"I was once a fun-loving, carefree, and happy person. I enjoyed spending time with my friends and family. I loved getting my hair and nails done. I don't know . . . I'm trying to rediscover that part of me."

"Well, this is a good start. I mean, this is the most sincere way. You look beautiful today. I thought you were beautiful the moment I saw you, but today, you look like you feel it too."

Shyly, she looked away. "I felt a boost of confidence this morning."

"Let that continue to work for you. You're glowing, and it has nothing to do with the heat from this hot-ass sun."

She laughed out loud, and I think it was possibly the most beautiful sound I had ever heard. It would be my honor to be the source of that for her. I couldn't put my finger on it, but something about her felt so right with my spirit. I knew God would never send me another man's woman, but that didn't mean I couldn't walk with her on her healing journey until I could make her my own.

CHAPTER THIRTEEN
Pasha

I WAS BEGINNING TO appreciate coming out today. For a while, when I first stepped out of the Uber, my anxiety was on ten. I was feeling out of place. All I wanted to do was get back in the car and go home. When I saw Callum, my feet gravitated toward him, even though my mind told me to go the other way. Even behind his sunglasses, I couldn't mistake him. I'd stolen many a glance at the handsome, six-foot chocolate man yesterday. I watched his muscles flex as he and Malcolm lifted the heavy furniture. I watched him lift his shirt to wipe the sweat from his brow, exposing his toned abs. I noticed the single dimple in his left cheek and the whiteness of his teeth when he smiled.

Even if I didn't want to be attracted to him, he was as beautiful on the outside as he seemed to be inside. His eyes were kind, and he presented himself as a genuine person. But what did I know? My horrible judgment of men began and ended with Raymond. I never wanted to be the type of woman who held all men to the same standard as the one who broke my heart and tried to break my spirit.

We'd been walking around for about two hours now. The sun was blazing, so we took several breaks to find shade and drink water to stay hydrated. We ventured away from the farmers' market and strolled down the Main Street strip. Currently, we were sitting in the courtyard in front of a popular restaurant beside the large fountain. The cool breeze coming off of the water was very refreshing.

"This makes me want to get in the water," I said, leaning back and closing my eyes.

He chuckled. "I can always dip you in there."

My eyes flew open. "You wouldn't dare."

He laughed. "I wouldn't, but I know what you mean. It's a good beach day."

"God, I haven't been to the beach in so long."

"Me either. Maybe we could go one of these days."

I was quiet. Being in town was one thing, but going out of town with him was a different story. Even if I got to know him better, I didn't want him to think this was going further than our friendship. I wasn't sure if I'd be comfortable with him seeing me in a bathing suit anyway. Hell, I wasn't sure if I'd be comfortable seeing *myself* in one. I avoided my naked body in the mirror. How could I put it on display for the world to see?

Just as I went to say something, my eyes landed on the last person I wanted to see while trying to have a good day. There was Raymond and a very pregnant Adora walking hand in hand toward the restaurant.

"Can we go?" I asked, standing.

Callum frowned in confusion. "What's wrong?"

"Please? I don't want him to see—"

"Well, well, well. If it isn't my soon-to-be ex-wife."

I closed my eyes, refusing to look at him, at them. It was enough seeing him in court. I didn't want to see him here.

He chuckled. "You actually look like somebody today."

Callum stood and advanced toward him.

"Callum, please . . ." I begged, only for it to be disregarded.

"Am I gonna have to put my hands on you every time I see you?" he asked, stepping toe-to-toe with Raymond.

"You need to back up."

"And you need to move along. There isn't a reason in the world that you need to stop and talk to her. Are you not standing here with the woman you wanted? Pasha shouldn't bother you like that if you were."

"That fat bitch couldn't bother me if she tried."

Callum had hemmed him up before I knew what was happening and slammed his body against the fountain's seating.

"Let him go!" Adora yelled. "I'm calling the police."

"Go right ahead," Callum said.

He turned to Raymond, who struggled to free himself of his hold. His attempts were useless. Callum leaned into him.

"I can see that my interactions with you will consist of me teaching lessons. The first time, you learned not to put your hands on people. This time, you learned not to be disrespectful. What's it going to be next time? I'm always in the mood to bring you up to speed on shit that you should already know."

He brought his face close to Raymond's and forced him to look at me.

"When you see her, you don't say anything. Don't look in her direction. Don't even breathe hard. If I catch wind that you have been out of pocket with her, things will get very ugly for you the next time I see you. Please don't make me see to it that there *is* a next time."

He yanked Raymond to his feet and shoved him away. Turning to Adora, he shook his head.

"You should be embarrassed and ashamed. Not only are you walking around proud to be pregnant by another woman's husband, but he can't even defend himself. Both of you are pathetic."

Without another word, he grabbed my hand and pulled me away from them. We walked in silence until we were around the corner from where we started. Then Callum pulled me over to a bench and sat me down.

"Are you okay?" he asked softly.

I nodded. "Thank you for defending me."

"I don't play that name-calling or body-shaming."

I shook my head. "He always went out of his way to make me feel bad about the weight I've gained. I carried and lost his child. I could never be that heartless toward someone I claimed to have loved. He always looked at me like he was just disgusted. It was like he took pride in making me hate myself."

Callum grabbed my hand and squeezed it. "That's on him. You are beautiful, Pasha. I have a feeling that deep down, the inside matches the outside. I can see the visible change in you. Four months ago, you had this look like you were broken. Like your mind and spirit were just done with life. I don't see that in you anymore. Your walk is lighter. Your head isn't down. There was joy and happiness in your eyes yesterday. You deserve that. If I have to put hands on that man every time I see him for him to know he doesn't get to break you again, so be it."

I looked at him curiously. He seemed to be a passionate man, a man who always did the right thing and looked out for the underdog. I just wasn't sure why he was being so nice to me. He didn't know me. I'd only been in his presence three times, and each time, he'd looked at me like he saw something I didn't see in myself.

"What's your deal with me?" I asked.

"My deal?"

"Why are you so nice to me?"

"I'm a nice guy."

"And you just want to be my friend?"

"I can offer you friendship until your friendship is what you no longer want."

I raised an eyebrow. "Meaning?"

"I'm on your time."

"And if I said never speak to me again?"

He chuckled. "Well, that would hurt my feelings, but I'd respect it and leave you alone. I'm not here to take anything from you, Pasha."

For some reason, I believed him when he said that. There was nothing for him to gain from lying to me. He didn't seem to be playing with my emotions or cashing in on my vulnerability. There were some people you meet in life that simply had genuine spirits. Callum seemed to be pure, not without flaw, but a man of pure intentions.

I nodded slowly. "I believe you," I said softly. I nervously rubbed my hands together. "I think I've had enough for today. I want to go home now."

"Can I give you a ride or call one of mine to take you?"

Options? He's thoughtful.

"I'm okay with you taking me."

He nodded and stood, reaching for my hand. I slipped my palm in his and stood to my feet. Hand in hand, we walked back to his truck in complete silence. He helped me inside and buckled my seat belt before closing the door. I sat nervously as he rounded the driver's side and climbed in himself. When he cranked up, the smooth sounds of Anita Baker's "Sweet Love" filled the space between us as he pulled out of the parking space. I smiled softly.

"My mother loved this song," I said aloud.

"Mine did too. I have a whole playlist of her and my father's favorites. I usually listen to it while I'm cleaning. You know, that Saturday morning cleaning vibe."

"I remember those days. My mother had me up early every Saturday. Avyn woke me up with gospel music on Sundays. It was a little weird not hearing it this morning. I already miss her."

"Good thing all you have to do is take the elevator up when you want to see her."

"I'm sure I'll see her all the time outside of work."

"You work at the hotel?"

"Yes. I do housekeeping. I also work part time at a grocery store. I wanted to save enough to afford my apartment, and I still have to pay for my therapy."

"How's that going?"

"Well, I had to sell my wedding ring to cover the cost. I knew I couldn't afford not to go, so I paid a year in advance. What I didn't spend, I'm saving up to buy a car. I don't want to keep hounding Avyn to use hers if I need to go out."

"If you need a ride, you can always call me. If I can't make it, I'll send a driver."

"You've already extended your kindness enough, Callum. I can't ask you to do that."

He chuckled. "Good thing you aren't asking."

I shook my head. "I get the feeling that you are the type of friend that doesn't take no for an answer."

"I can accept a no. Sometimes, I may overstep. I'll apologize if I hurt your feelings, but if it's coming from a place of love, I will do it anyway."

"You and Avyn would get along just fine."

"I already like her." He pulled up to my building and in front of the door. "This is your stop."

"Thank you again . . . for everything."

"There's no thanks needed." He grabbed my hand and kissed it. "I hope you have a good rest of your day."

"You too."

I climbed out of his truck and headed up to the door. He waited until I was safely inside before pulling off. Aside from the run-in with Raymond, today had been a good day. Callum had been an unexpected addition, but I couldn't say I didn't enjoy my time with him. I didn't have any male friends. I hadn't had one since I was in high school. He wasn't like any man I'd ever met, and I wasn't sure if that scared or intrigued me. Only time will tell.

⌒∂

I'd been back in my apartment for about an hour.

I busied myself with making Sunday dinner. Growing up, I helped my mother cook in the kitchen, and there was always more than enough food. I never knew how to cook for just one person, so I was sure there would be leftovers I could take to work for the next day. I was knee-deep in cutting up potatoes for my potato salad when I heard the locks of my front door disengage. There was no need to ask who it was because Avyn was the only person with a key.

"Are you decent?" she asked, coming through with her eyes covered.

I giggled. "Like that would have stopped you."

"You're right. I was just being courteous." She hung up her keys and bounced over to me, pulling me in for a hug and a kiss on the cheek. "You look happy today. What's buttered your biscuits?"

"I've just had a good day. It was almost perfect."

"Almost?"

I gave her a quick rundown of my morning out, and she listened intently. She smiled as I told her about Callum, but I could see her fists clenching when I mentioned Raymond.

"See, I like Callum more and more. He should have drowned Raymond in that fountain. He's too damn old to be body-shaming anybody. The nigga is pushing forty, and he's acting childish right now. Didn't Callum hem him up the last time?"

I nodded. "He did. And he said if he has to put his hands on him every time to let him know he doesn't get to break me again, then so be it."

Avyn shuddered. "Whew! That's a *good* man, Savannah," she said, mocking *Waiting to Exhale*. "I'm claiming him for you, boo. That right there is going to be your man."

"He's just my friend, Avyn."

"Please! That man doesn't want *just* to be your friend. What did you think he meant by being your friend until you no longer wanted friendship, Pash? He's leaving the door open. As soon as you give him the green light, he will make you his woman."

"I don't know about all that."

"Well, I do. I see it in his eyes. Malcolm vouched for him. He says he's a good guy with good intentions. He's not one of these men who runs game or tries to sleep with every woman he encounters. He's all about his sister, his niece, and his money. He ain't for the streets."

"How does Malcolm even know him?"

She kissed her teeth. "Girl, that man knows a little of everybody. Apparently, Callum provides car services for the policeman's ball and several other city official events from time to time. They've been friends for years."

"It's a small world."

"I see double dates in our future!"

"You are way too excited about this."

She laughed. "So, what if I am? You deserve a good man, Pasha. You put up with that mess for too long. If you can come out of this marriage with a healthy, loving relationship with a good man, I'm all for it."

"So when are *you* going to get a good man, Avyn? I hear about Malcolm more than any of these other guys you casually date."

She blushed. "I do like him, okay? He's been asking to be official for a while."

"What's stopping you?"

"Full transparency? I'm scared, Pasha. Seeing what you went through . . . I don't think I'd have the mental capacity to handle that. When I love, I love hard. And if you break my heart, I'm gonna end up in jail. He's a cop. Girl, they would throw the book at me. I'm too pretty to be somebody's prison bitch for the rest of my life."

I couldn't help but laugh at her. Although she was making fun, I knew she was serious. I'd seen her heartbroken before, and I even feared for that man's life. We were in our early twenties, and she was dating this guy who had about four years on us. She was so in love, and when she caught him cheating on her, she beat him pretty badly.

I set my knife down and grabbed her hands. "You deserve a good man too, Avyn. You're a good person with an amazing heart. Don't let fear keep you from being happy."

She smiled. "Hi, Pot, I'm Kettle."

I playfully rolled my eyes as I dropped her hands. "I can't with you. Seriously, though. I've watched you with Malcolm over the last couple of months. I could tell you are into him more than you let on. He seems like a good guy."

"Just like Callum."

"I'd feel weird dating while I'm going through a divorce. I mean, it won't be over for a while."

"If Raymond can parade around town with his tramp, so can you. Just tell me . . . Are you attracted to him?"

"I mean . . . He's attractive. Very attractive. And I like his energy. I can't say I'm attracted to him so soon. We'll see how this friendship pans out, and I'll get back to you on that."

I almost regretted that as soon as I said it. The smile on her face was bright and wide. I knew I could expect to be asked for an update after update from her and the girls because she was sure to relay the message.

CHAPTER FOURTEEN
Callum

"READY OR NOT, here I come!"

I crouched down in the dark corner of the closet I was hiding in. I was on uncle duty since Precious's day care was closed for a small renovation this week. So far today, we'd colored, had a tea party, and she had me take her to get a manicure and pedicure. The women in the shop couldn't get over how cute she was. Now, if I had been interested, I would have worked that in my favor too.

Many of them were smiling in my face and telling me what a good uncle I was to babysit. I got compliments on my looks, and a few of them asked if I was single. One even slipped me her number before she left. My niece had unofficially become my wingwoman, and she didn't even know it. Alas, I threw the number away. She was a beautiful woman, but again, I wasn't interested.

After we left the nail shop, we got food and ice cream, a treat I was now regretting. She was hyper, and I had to burn some of that energy off. Or so I thought. Back at my house, we'd jumped rope, roller-skated, and had a dance battle. Currently, she had me playing hide-and-seek. It was the first time I got to sit down since we'd been home, and I was grateful for the break.

"Uncle Cay!" I could hear her little feet running across the hardwood floors. "Where are you, Uncle Cay? I'm gonna get you!"

She giggled as she ran out of the room. I smirked to myself. As a kid, I used to play hide-and-seek for hours with Bella. I moved quietly enough to change spots every time she got too close. Just when she thought she had me, I was gone. When she finally gave up, she would always go get our mother to find me. Every time, she found me in my closet. Eventually, Bella got hip to it and found me with ease.

I heard Precious's footsteps outside of the room again. This time, it sounded like she was talking to someone. I frowned, thinking I know she didn't let someone in my house. Just as I was about to come out of hiding, I heard her loud and clear.

"Mommy, I can't find Uncle Cay. We're playing hide-and-seek, and he got me good."

I waited for a moment, knowing my sister was about to give me up. I heard her laughing on the speakerphone.

"Callum, you will not get my baby like you used to get me!" she yelled, causing me to stifle a laugh. "Check the closet in his office, baby. That's his favorite hiding spot."

I heard the pitter-patter of little feet come back into my childhood bedroom, which was now my office. Then I heard the doorknob rattle and twist until it opened. When Precious's eyes landed on me, she grinned.

"I found you!"

"You cheated, too. How are you gonna call your mama on me? The rules don't say, phone a friend."

She giggled. "Thank you, Mommy."

"Anytime, baby."

"You're a snitch, Bella," I said, climbing out of the closet.

"Why would you torture my baby like that?"

"That was a solid fifteen minutes of rest. She's wearing me out. No more sweets today, Precious."

Bella laughed. "That's what you get. You're trying to tire her out, and she's getting the better of you."

"It's my turn, Uncle Cay. Close your eyes!"

She handed me the phone, and I closed my eyes.

"You ready?"

"Yes!"

"One . . . two . . . three . . ."

She took off running. I opened my eyes and turned my attention back to the phone.

"Is she behaving?" Bella asked.

"You know we don't have those problems."

"Martin is going to pick her up. I have to work late."

"I got you." I pulled the phone from my ear and shouted, "Ten, eleven, twelve!"

"You know she's just going to give herself away, right?"

"Of course, I know. The giggle box can't help herself. I might make her sweat this time."

"Well, you two have fun. Give her kisses for me."

"I will. Love you."

"Love you too." I hung up and shoved the phone in my pocket. "Twenty! Here I come!"

I left the room and began the search for my niece. Within a minute, I knew she was hiding under my bed. I could hear her giggle when I walked into the room. True to my word, I decided to make her sweat a little. I left the room and went into the kitchen to grab us both some water to hydrate once I *found* her. As I turned the corner, someone knocked on my door. I abandoned my original path to answer.

"Who is it?"

"William."

I frowned. My cousin and I hadn't spoken in years. Ever since I cursed out half the family at my parents' will reading, most of them didn't bother with me much. His mother was one of them. She forbade her children from speaking to me again. It was hard at first. Sometimes, we'd see each other, and it would hurt not to say anything. Over the years, it got to the point where we barely acknowledged each other's existence.

My hand lingered on the knob before I twisted it open. William stood on the other side with a pained look on his face.

"You good?" I asked.

He shook his head. "Dad died."

My eyes widened. His father was my mother's youngest brother. William and his father were very close, so I knew this was eating him up.

"I'm sorry to hear that, William. Come in." I stepped aside and allowed him in. "Give me a second."

I headed to my bedroom and located Precious.

"Gotcha!" I said, dropping to the floor. She squealed as she scrambled from under the bed.

"I almost got you!" she declared.

"Yeah, you did. Hey, Precious, I have a visitor. Can you sit in here and watch TV for me for a little bit?"

"Okay."

She climbed onto the bed and relaxed into my pillows. Grabbing the remote, I turned on her favorite movie and left the room. William stood in front of the fireplace, staring at the old family photo perched on the mantle. His head turned slightly as he looked back at me.

"It doesn't seem like it's been seventeen years," he said.

"Yeah . . . It doesn't." I took a seat on the couch.

"This place doesn't look the same as it did when I was a kid."

"I renovated a few years ago. I could never move out, so I made it my own."

"It looks good."

"Thanks. So . . . Was Uncle James sick?"

He slowly turned around with his hands in his pocket. "Lung cancer. I guess all those cigars caught up with him. It's been a quiet three days."

"He died three days ago?"

"Yeah. Nobody was sure if you would have wanted to know, given the parameters of your relationship with the family."

"I guess. Have arrangements been made?"

"The funeral is Saturday at one. Everybody is meeting up at the house around eleven."

"Okay. Well, I'll talk to Bella and make her aware."

He nodded. "You know we miss y'all, Callum. You have to know none of us wanted to cut you off. It's just . . . We were kids, man."

"I don't blame you. I blame the adults involved. William, a lot went down behind the scenes that you don't know. I could understand those who couldn't take us in because they couldn't. I can't hold that against them. What upset me were the people who flat-out said no if they couldn't cash out on it. People were fighting over money they thought my parents had . . . money left to me and my sister . . . money that I refused to sign over. That's what the falling out was about. Bella and I would have been left with nothing if I did that. My parents wouldn't have wanted that any more than they wanted us to split up. Based on those two facts alone, I don't regret anything I did or said."

"I get it, Callum. I know I wished I'd reached out after I left home. Me, Jessa, and Mo talk about that all the time. We've been keeping up with you, though. I see you're doing well for yourself. Bella too. We're proud of you. I know your parents would be proud too."

He stood and headed for the door. His hand lingered on the knob momentarily. Turning, he looked back at me.

"Whether or not you come to the funeral, we'd like to see you and Bella more often. Life is short, and we *are* family."

I nodded as he walked out the door. Then I pulled out my phone to call Bella.

"Princess, Mommy is working—"

"It's me."

"Oh! What's wrong? Why do you sound like that?"

"I just got a visit from our cousin William. Uncle James is dead."

"Oh . . . Well, I'm sorry to hear that."

"The funeral is this Saturday at one. He said everyone is meeting at the house around eleven."

"You thinking about going?"

"I don't know, Bells. He told me he misses us."

"Well, we used to be close to them before Aunt Sheila nipped that in the butt."

"I know . . . How would you feel about going?"

"I'll go if you go, and I want Martin to be there. Somebody has to be able to hold you back if anything happens."

"Maybe you're right. I won't go to the house beforehand, but I'll go to the funeral and burial."

"Okay." She sighed heavily. "This just takes me back to Mama and Daddy dying."

I knew exactly what she was talking about.

It was two weeks after the funeral. My father's lawyer had gathered us together to read his final will and testament. Bella sat beside me on the couch in my father's office with her head resting on my shoulder. She hadn't been herself in days, and I honestly hadn't either. Our house had become a revolving door of relatives coming in and out. Mr. Charles wasn't keen on discussing my father's personal matters in front of everyone, so he brought us in here.

"I'm so sorry for your loss," he said softly. "Your parents were good people. I have known your father for a long time, and he spoke so highly of both of you. He was very proud of you."

"Thank you, Mr. Charles," I said quietly.

"Let's get to it then. Your father had an accountant who kept track of his expenses. He'll be available to help you figure out what you need to do with the money he left you and your sister."

"He left us money?"

"Well, upon his death, everything was supposed to go to your mother had she outlived him. With both of them gone, it defaults to you and Bella. Between his insurance policies at work, retirement benefits, and their personals, there is a total of about $400,000. Since you are of legal age, Callum, that goes to you. This is just my opinion, but that is a lot of money for you to hold on to at such a young age. Maybe it would be better to put it into an account and allow one of your relatives to oversee it until you're older."

I didn't trust that. My relatives were acting suspiciously. They've been over here every day like they were looking for something. I even caught my aunt in my parents' bedroom, searching for something in the closet. She claimed she was looking for something of my mother's that she wanted for a keepsake, but I didn't buy it.

"No. If I did that, Bella and I would have nothing. None of them are willing to take us in without financial compensation. I get that. Taking on an extra mouth is a lot. I can take care of myself, but I have to think about Bella. I have to make sure she's okay, not just for the time being."

I looked down at my sister. Sadness had become a permanent fixture on her face.

"I want to adopt her, Mr. Charles."

"You're eighteen, Callum. You're barely an adult."

"But I'm legally an adult. They have to consider me, right?"

He sighed. "You can be her foster parent at eighteen. There are several requirements, though. You have to have a stable source of income and a place of your own, for example. You can't take Bella on campus with you."

"We can stay here. This is our home."

"Your parents still owe quite a bit on this house, Callum. It would take a chunk of that money to pay it off."

"Then do that. Pay it off and put the house in my name so nobody else can take it or sell it. Put some money aside for Bella and the rest in a savings account. I'll . . . I'll take some time off from school. I'll get a job. I'll do whatever it takes. They just have to give me time. They can give me time, right?"

He gave me a sympathetic look. "There is a grace period. This won't just be on you. This falls on both of you."

I sat up and turned to my sister. Cupping her face, I kissed her forehead.

"Listen to me, Bella. If I do this, you have to work with me. You have to keep up your grades and listen to what I tell you. I want us to stay together, and I know Mama and Daddy would want that too. We can make this work, but you must do your part, you understand?"

She nodded, tears in her eyes. "I understand."

She was only thirteen at the time. It was a lot asking her to help me keep us together, but we had no other option if someone in the family didn't take her. Mr. Charles talked to us a bit more about what we could expect with the process of fostering Bella. When he left, I sent her to her room so I could get everyone out of our house. It was unusually quiet. I searched until I found my two aunts, my uncle, and a few of my mother's cousins in our den. I was about to make myself known when my aunt Sheila spoke.

"James and I have three kids. If we take them, we should get that money. What are any of you gonna do but run through it anyway?"

"*Ha! Like you wouldn't?*" That was my aunt Glenda. "*Your husband has a good job. You don't need the money, Sheila. You're just greedy. I, on the other hand, am raising two kids by myself. I could use that.*"

"*You live in a two-bedroom apartment, Glenda. Where the hell are they gonna sleep?*"

"*We could move in here. Callum's gonna be away at school. He isn't gonna be able to keep up with the mortgage. What does an eighteen-year-old need with that type of money? He's gonna blow it. I say we talk him into signing the checks over. We give him a cut and split the rest.*"

I couldn't believe what I was hearing. My parents were barely dead two weeks, and they were already fighting and plotting on money that wasn't even theirs. I'd entered the room, and before my better judgment could kick in, I cursed out everybody and let them know that none of them would see a dime of that money. They had to listen to my thoughts on how disgusting they were as human beings, let alone a supposed "loving" family. Before I put them out, I told them that Bella and I were better off without them. I guess they took that to heart. In seventeen years, nobody made a move to apologize or make amends.

That was fine by me.

I wasn't wrong. Cutting them off was hard. There were times I needed them, and my pride wouldn't let me go back on my word. I sucked it up and did what I had to do to push through. I refused to touch the money I had set aside for Bella or our rainy-day funds. God forbid anything went wrong with the house and I couldn't fix it. Like I said, it was hard, but we came out of it better than we were—no thanks to my family.

Maybe I would go to the funeral; maybe I wouldn't.

I sighed. "At least we're both grown now."

"And I can fight," Bella tossed in.

I shook my head. "Nobody is fighting anybody. If we go, we'll go to pay our respects, then leave."

She kissed her teeth. "Oh, all right. I guess I can do that."

"I'll let you know what I decide by Friday."

"Okay. Are you gonna be fine? I know how you get when you think about back then."

"I promise I'm good. Besides, I have Precious. How can I be sad around a ball of sunshine?"

"I guess you can't. Please call me if you need me."

"I will."

"You won't, but okay. I love you."

"I love you too."

We disconnected the call, and I stood from the couch. Walking down the hall, I entered my bedroom.

"Okay, Precious. How about—"

I stopped when I saw that she was knocked out in my bed. She had the right idea. I was exhausted, and the old saying was to sleep when the baby slept. Well, Precious wasn't a baby, but she was my baby. I lay my body across the end of the bed and closed my eyes. In no time, I was joining my niece in a peaceful slumber.

CHAPTER FIFTEEN
Pasha

"AYE, MS. P, let me show you this new dance!"

I sat out back in the break area at the grocery store where I worked part time. I'd been here for about two months now, and I was still getting used to working with a bunch of kids who had after-school jobs. They were so different from my girls and me at their age. All they wanted to do was take pictures and videos or dance. I couldn't be annoyed with them because they were just having fun.

Tucking my phone away, I looked up at Marshawn, the bag boy working my line today.

"Go on," I said.

He put on some music I was familiar with and started moving and gyrating. I covered my mouth to stifle a laugh. The song he was listening to was something from my era of music, but the dance was nothing like the original.

"Whatchu laughing at, Ms. P?" he asked, grinning.

"Marshawn, where did you learn this dance?"

"The internet. It's popular. You gotta get with the times, Ms. P."

"First of all, that dance is so far left from the original. I'm not sure what that was, but it wasn't it. Second, exactly how old do you think I am?"

He shrugged. "You ain't no spring chicken, as my grandma would say."

I scoffed. "Whatever. I may not be a spring chicken, but I'm not old enough to be your mother."

"My mama is thirty-five, and I'm sixteen. She was barely old enough to be my mama when she had me."

"Well, that's not my business. Come on, break's over. We only have about an hour left until closing."

He kissed his teeth. "All right. Don't start speed-sliding me those groceries like you do, either," he said, grinning as he opened the back door.

"Well, don't bag so slow."

We headed back to our register. While I had no customers, I took the time to straighten up a little and wipe down so I didn't have too much to do after counting down my register. Marshawn stood in the bagging area, scrolling through videos on his phone and trying to copy dance moves. I shook my head. He was so easily entertained.

"Pasha?"

I heard my name being called. When I looked up, embarrassment flooded my face. Raymond's best friend Carlos and his wife Emily were at my register. We used to have dinner with them at least twice a week. I'd been on vacation with these people. They knew things about me, and seeing them right now was overwhelming. Still, I was at work, and I had a job to do. Pulling back my emotions, I began scanning their items.

"Did you find everything okay?" I asked, avoiding eye contact.

"Yes . . ." Carlos answered slowly.

"Do you have a loyalty card?"

His wife handed hers over, and I scanned it before handing it back to her.

"Um . . . We heard what happened," she said quietly. "I'm so sorry."

"Don't," I said firmly.

"We didn't know," she continued. "It wasn't until he brought her over for dinner that we even had a clue things were over between you two. We've cut contact with him, Pasha."

"Well, I hope you didn't do that on my behalf."

"We did it on principle and morals. He was wrong on all fronts, and we can't condone that type of behavior. You were always such a sweetheart. I'm sure you're no saint, but I do know you didn't deserve that. If we knew, you would have been welcomed in our home."

I paused for a moment, finally able to look at them. Their eyes held pity, but more than that, they were sincere.

"Thank you," I said softly.

"Are things okay for you?" Carlos asked.

"Things are fine. I'm taking care of myself."

"Do you need anything?"

"No. I may not have everything I want, but I have everything I need."

Emily smiled. "Good for you. If you ever need anything, please . . . don't hesitate to reach out."

I knew I would never do that, but I decided to appease them so they could move on out of my line. I didn't feel like talking about my not-so-recent past with them. Not here. Not now. Probably not ever.

"Thank you," I said, sliding the last of their items across the scanner. "Your total is forty-four twenty-three."

He swiped his card, and Marshawn handed them their bags.

"Take care, Pasha."

I nodded, once again avoiding their eyes. It wasn't until they were gone that I could finally breathe again. I expelled a deep breath as I clutched my stomach.

"You okay, Ms. P?" Marshawn asked. I knew he'd been listening.

"I'm fine."

The next thing I knew, he was beside me, wrapping his arms around me in a brief hug.

"What was that for?" I asked, wiping my eyes.

"You just looked like you needed a hug."

"Thank you, Marshawn. That was really sweet."

"No problem. Aye, yo, Ms. P?"

"Yeah?"

"For what it's worth . . . Any man that would leave you is a damn fool. You fly as hell."

I shook my head. "Thank you."

"You know I'll be eighteen in a couple of years—"

I laughed out loud. "Not gonna happen! When you're eighteen, I'll be thirty. That might be grown, but not grown enough."

He grinned as he headed back to the bagging station. "It made you laugh, though. See, I'm useful."

"I guess you are. Get back to work."

We worked with minimal noise for the rest of my shift. Five minutes before it was time for me to go, I shut down my register and counted out. After taking everything to the back, I clocked out and went out front to wait for my ride. Avyn had to work late, so I scheduled a car to pick me up while I was on break. I had only been waiting a few minutes when they rolled around to the front of the grocery store. I quickly climbed into the backseat and strapped on my seat belt. I was set for at least a twenty-minute ride back to my apartment. Soft music played in the background.

I scrolled through my phone, checking messages from the girls. They'd been in our group chat trying to make plans for this weekend. I wasn't sure if I would be in the mood to do much, but if they wanted to go out, I might oblige them. I hadn't gone out with them in so long, but I hadn't forgotten how they liked to party.

These days, I was more of a designated driver. I wouldn't drink excessively but wouldn't ruin their fun.

As I backed out of the message thread, I saw the thread belonging to Callum. I'd texted him so that he could have my number, but we had yet to have a conversation outside of the one we had this past Sunday. I smiled as I thought about that day. I'd really enjoyed his company, and even if it wasn't a good look, I took great satisfaction in watching him hem up Raymond. He could have easily walked away when he saw me, yet he chose to be an asshole—a disrespectful asshole at that. I couldn't feel bad about him continuously getting hands put on him.

I hovered over my keyboard for a moment before typing a short message and pressing send before I chickened out. A few seconds passed before the little bubbles populated on the screen.

Callum: Hey, beautiful. I'm happy to hear from you.

Me: How are you?

Callum: I'm alive. Not in the best headspace, but I'll be okay.

Me: What's wrong?

Instead of responding, he called me. When I answered, I could hear in his voice that something was bothering him.

"Hey, love," he said.

"Hey . . . What's the matter? You don't sound so good."

"I'm just dealing with a situation right now. Um . . . My mother's youngest brother died, and I'm struggling with whether I should go to the funeral."

"I'm so sorry."

"It's okay, really. I haven't seen that man in years. We haven't spoken since I was eighteen."

"Wow. Why not, if you don't mind my asking?"

"There was a big blowup over money my mom's side of the family thought they were entitled to when my parents died. It didn't have to go the way it did, but I overheard some things that had me looking at them sideways."

"That's horrible. Fighting instead of grieving?"

"That was the day I decided that my sister and I would be okay with just us. We didn't need people who weren't genuine with their motives. They would have spent that money and left us with nothing. My dad always told me I had to be cautious of certain family members. He had this discerning spirit about him. I guess growing up the way he did, he had to learn to be extra observant of those around him."

"It's sad that the people you think wouldn't do you like that are the very people that *would* do you like that."

"It is . . . but enough about me. How are you, beautiful? How was your day?"

"It was okay. I'm on my way home from work."

"Any plans for when you get there?"

"Just relaxing. I think I'm gonna light some candles, run me a nice bubble bath, and read a book. I haven't read in a while, and I just bought myself a Kindle. Maybe that will be my escape from reality for a little while."

"Nothing wrong with that. Hell, that sounds like a good idea."

I giggled. "I can't see you as a man who likes bubble baths."

He chuckled. "Maybe not the bubbles per se. But I will put some lavender oil in the water and turn on the jets. All I need after that is some music and a cigar, and I'm in chill mode."

"That's the vibe I'm going for tonight. Maybe not the cigar. I'll take a glass of wine, though."

"Don't get too tipsy by yourself, now."

I giggled. "I know my limit."

He was quiet for a moment. "It's good to hear your voice," he said softly. "I was beginning to think this friendship would be a figment of my imagination."

"Well, you said you were on my time."

"Always. You'll never have to worry about me pressuring you, Pasha. Your voice and feelings will always matter."

I teared up at the sound of that. I sniffled. "Thank you."

"No need to thank me."

"No . . . You don't know how much of a blessing you've been to me, Callum. Even as a stranger, you extended kindness, which is so rare nowadays. I feel in my heart that you are a good person . . . a good soul."

"I just try to put out what I want to get back. Nothing more, nothing less. My sister and my friends think I have this savior complex or something, but it's nothing like that. I just believe in showing the kind of love I wish someone had shown me when I needed it most."

I could tell he harbored a lot of pain from his past. I couldn't imagine losing both my parents as a teenager and then becoming a parent to my sibling. He was still a kid himself. Eighteen was barely an adult. He needed somebody to care for him. Somebody to stand up for him. Somebody to love him. His heart could have hardened after that experience. Instead, it had seemingly bloomed into the beautiful heart it is today.

We continued to talk as the car pulled up to my building. I climbed out and headed up to my floor.

"You're home?" he asked as I jiggled the keys in the lock and pushed the door open.

"Yes. I just walked in."

"I'm glad you made it safe. Do you work tomorrow?"

"No, I'm off all day. You?"

"I'm on uncle duty this week, so no work for me. I mean, I don't do real work anyway. The business basically runs itself, and my team handles the rest."

"Isn't that the best way to work?"

"Most of the time. I do enjoy my time with my niece, though. She keeps me on my toes."

"Do you want children?"

"One of these days. If the good Lord sees fit to send me a wife, I will give her as many as she allows me to. Would you . . . Would you ever want to try again?"

I swallowed hard as I lay back across my bed. "I don't know. I'm afraid. I know what happened to my son wasn't my fault, but that doesn't stop me from wondering if there was anything I could have done differently. I love children and want to be a mother, but having another baby would feel like I'm replacing him. I never really got to say goodbye the way I wanted to." I squeezed my eyes shut, fighting back tears. "I just don't know. Maybe with the right person, I would consider it."

"That's fair." He was quiet for a moment. "I should let you go. I'm sure you want to get out of your work clothes and relax a little."

"Yeah."

"Be good to yourself, Pasha. You aren't where you were. Always remember that. Good night, beautiful."

"Good night."

I disconnected the phone and tossed it on my bed. He was right. I wasn't where I had been. I wasn't there, and I couldn't allow my pain and fears to take me back there. I had to move on eventually, but how?

CHAPTER SIXTEEN

Callum

BELLA, MARTIN, AND I sat outside the church where my uncle's funeral was being held.

It had been against my better judgment to come, but I thought about William and my other two cousins. When I lost my parents, they were there for Bella and me before shit went down. They spent many nights at my house through the whole planning process, offering us comfort. That was the only reason I told Bella that we would go.

"How long are we gonna sit here?" Bella asked from the passenger seat.

"I was waiting on William."

"Are we walking in with the family? Are we sitting with them?"

"I don't particularly want to sit with them, but I want him to know we are here."

Just as I spoke, the family cars pulled up. After coming to a stop, the drivers got out to open the doors. I motioned for Bella and Martin to exit the car. William stepped out of the first car along with Mo, Jessa, and their mother. Dark shades covered their eyes, but I could still see the sadness in their body language. I knew what they were going through all too well.

Slowly, we made our way over to the family. Mo was the first to notice us. He tapped his brother and sister and pointed.

William abandoned his stance beside his mother and came over, pulling Bella and me into a tight hug. Mo and Jessa followed him, and before I knew it, they were surrounding us.

William slapped my back. "Thank you for coming, man."

"We almost didn't."

"I couldn't have blamed you if you hadn't."

"We came for you three. When this was us, you three stuck with us as long as possible."

He nodded.

Jessa smiled at Bella. "You are hardly the same little girl that used to steal my clothes." She looked up at me and cupped my face. Her fingers went to my ears, and she giggled. "You grew into these."

A smile spread across my face. "You grew into that head, Li'l Lollipop."

Mo snickered, and I turned to him. "What about you, boy? Did those braces fix those buck teeth?"

He flashed me a perfect white smile. "It didn't, but my surgeon did."

"Get away from them!" my aunt Sheila snapped as she stormed over.

She pushed her children aside and stepped into my space. My aunt Glenda was right behind her. Both of them glared at me with frowns on their faces. Bella let go of Martin's hand and stood in front of me, giving them the same look right back. It was William who stepped between the three of us.

"Mama—" he started, but she lifted a hand to stop him.

"What right do you have to show up here? You spoke your piece and made your decision seventeen years ago. How dare you come here?"

"I came because your son asked me to."

"Well, I'm telling you to leave. James wouldn't have wanted you here."

Jessa spoke up. "Now, Mama, you know that's a lie. Daddy said a long time ago that he missed these two and wished things were different. He talked about it a lot in his final days. That's why William asked them to come."

"Your father was delirious in his final days. He could have said anything, and he surely never said anything to me about it."

Mo shook his head. "Because he knew you wouldn't listen."

Glenda scoffed as she looked at me. "As disrespectful as he was to both of your parents, you went behind their backs and invited them. If you wanted to make things right, you should have done it when your father was here to get an apology."

I chuckled. "I'm not apologizing for anything. I meant every word that I said."

Bella looked around William. "Listen, Sheila. We came to pay our respects. Nothing more, nothing less. All of this animosity isn't necessary."

"I'm not talking to you, Bella."

"But I'm talking to you. I'm not that thirteen-year-old girl who had to stand back and let my brother argue with you by himself. I'm grown and a mother myself. Nothing is stopping me from whipping your ass right in front of this church if you get out of pocket today."

"Little girl—"

"Hold on there," Martin said, pulling Bella away.

Glenda laughed. "I'm sorry, who are you?"

"That's my wife, and I don't play about her."

"I don't care what you do or don't play about!"

Bella jumped in front of Martin. "Slow your roll talking to him. That's my husband. You know, one of those things you couldn't seem to get?"

Shit. Maybe bringing Bella wasn't the best idea. She didn't bite her tongue, and she never could stand Glenda, even when we were kids. I did not doubt that she would put hands on her in front of this church.

"Can we please just get through the funeral?" Jessa begged, tears sliding down her cheeks. "My father is lying in there. He wasn't perfect, but I loved him, and I just want to give him a proper burial. Please . . . Let's go inside."

Silence fell among us. My aunts glared at us but allowed Mo and William to lead them away. Jessa turned to us. She took off her sunglasses and wiped her eyes.

"I'm sorry," she whispered. "I'm really happy to see you both."

She kissed our cheeks and followed her family back to the rest of them. I stood there for a moment watching. Seventeen years had passed, and nothing had really changed. Maybe we shouldn't have come here. Part of me was hoping to mend things, but it was clear that there was nothing to mend, at least not with Sheila and Glenda. I'd be open to fixing things with our cousins, but that was about it.

"Get back in the car," I said to Bella and Martin.

"You don't want to stay?" he asked.

"Nah, man."

All I wanted to do was get home and away from this suit. I didn't want to think about family. I didn't want to think about death or a funeral. All I wanted right now was peace of mind.

After dropping Bella and Martin off at home, I headed toward my house. I was deep in thought when I came upon the cemetery where my parents were buried. I hadn't been to visit them in a while, and today, I needed to be close to them. All the contemplating I'd done the last few days had them heavy on my mind.

I thought about how I would have retired them both from work now that my business practically ran itself. I thought about sending them on many much-deserved vacations. I thought about them with Precious and how much they would have loved to spoil her. I could see my mother letting her get away with shit we would have been punished for. I could see my father slipping her money when Bella and Martin weren't looking. She would never know them. *My* kids would never know them.

It was sad, and the feeling was very overwhelming.

Pulling into the parking lot, I pulled off my jacket and button-up, leaving me in my undershirt and slacks. I climbed out of the truck and treaded through the gate and the familiar path to their grave sites. We were lucky enough to get them plots right next to each other. Once a month, Bella and I came out to ensure everything was clean. We'd bring fresh flowers and just sit with them for a while. Even if no words were spoken, we just sat there.

I approached the graves slowly. Closing my eyes, I said a quick prayer, then stooped to kiss their headstones. I stepped in between the spaces and took a seat on the ground.

"I know it's been a little while," I said, pulling at a few blades of grass. "I'm sure you were looking down at the mess that took place a little while ago. I went there with good intentions, I swear."

I chuckled. I felt like a kid again, trying to explain myself to avoid getting in trouble. There were a few times that worked in my favor growing up. I must have sat between my parents for a good thirty minutes. I didn't say much. Honestly, I just wanted to be close to them. I could always feel their spirits surrounding me when I came here. I just wanted to bask in that for a little bit. Once I'd gotten my fill, I stood and dusted off my pants. These would probably have to go to the cleaners because I was sure there were grass stains.

I trekked the path back toward the front gate. As I was walking, I saw a woman sitting on a bench in front of two large headstones. With her were flowers and what looked to be party balloons. White bricks sectioned off the plot she occupied. Upon closer inspection, I realized that the woman was Pasha. That's when I remembered she told me her parents were buried out here as well. I guess we both needed to be near our parents today.

I slowly walked over so as not to alarm her. When I stepped on a twig, it cracked, and her head snapped in my direction.

I raised my palms. "It's just me."

"Callum." She quickly wiped her teary, red eyes and sniffled. "You went to the funeral?"

"I went, but I didn't stay. I should have listened to my first mind telling me to stay home."

She stood and walked over to me. "That bad?"

"Bad enough."

She reached out and gently rubbed my arm. "I'm sorry."

"It's okay. If it's meant to be worked out, eventually, it will."

"Were you visiting your parents?" she asked.

"Yeah . . . They've been heavy on my mind since I got the news of my uncle's passing. I figured I'd come see them."

"Are you feeling better?"

"I am." I looked behind her at the balloons and flowers. "What's the occasion?"

"Oh, that? Well, the flowers are for my mom. The balloons are for my dad. Today would have been his birthday. Every year, I bring a cupcake and sing them Happy Birthday. I know it's silly—"

I shook my head. "It's not silly at all. If it gives you comfort, it has a purpose."

"Most days I come out here, it's for comfort. Today, I just needed to talk to my parents."

She sat back on the bench and patted the spot beside her. I sat and wrapped my arm around her shoulder.

"I got a call from my lawyer yesterday," she said softly.

"Oh?"

"Raymond's lawyer subpoenaed my financial records. He's trying to reduce the amount he wants to pay me for alimony. You know the crazy thing, Callum? I never wanted anything from this man. I was willing to leave this marriage with what I came with because none of the material or monetary things would have made me happy. I just want to be free of him. I'm already tired of going to court. I'm tired of him calling and harassing me from blocked numbers. I'm tired of it all."

She dropped her head in her hands. She wore that same look of defeat I'd seen her with the first night, and I didn't like that. I reached out and pulled her hands away. Cupping her chin, I brought her eyes to meet mine.

"In this life, you have to do what brings you peace. You do that for you, not for anyone else. You don't strike me as the type of person that seeks revenge."

"I'm not. I don't have it in me to do people the way they do me. I never have. I've always been unconfrontational. I don't do drama. I like to stay out of the way. I would have gone through this divorce with my head down and my mouth closed. Nothing I gain from it will ease my pain in the end, so what's the use?"

"Then stay true to yourself. Talk to your lawyer. They may have all the training and legal expertise, but you know what's best for you. You know what you can live with."

She nodded. "I will talk to her."

I wiped her eyes and leaned in to kiss her forehead. "Do you need a ride home?"

"Yes, but can we just sit here for a little bit? I'm not ready to go yet."

"Sure."

She picked up the bag next to her and dug through it to produce a cupcake in a plastic container. She also dug out a candle and a lighter. Opening the container, she stuck the candle into the cupcake and lit it.

"Happy Birthday, Daddy. I miss you and Mama so much. I've been struggling, but I'm trying to keep the faith that everything will be okay . . ."

She sniffled, and my immediate response was to pull her close. She rested her head against my shoulder as I gently stroked her arm.

"Please kiss Mama and Jordan for me. Let my baby know that there isn't a day that goes by that I don't miss him or wish he was here. Let him know that I'm . . . I'm sorry. I'm so sorry . . ."

She blew out the candle and set it on the bench beside her. Much to my surprise, she turned to me and wrapped her arms around me. The moment I encased her in my embrace, she broke. Tears stained my shirt, and audible cries echoed in my ears. My heart hurt for her, like hurt to the point where I could physically feel the pain she carried. All I wanted to do was carry it for her.

"I got you," I whispered, stroking her back. "I'm here as long as you need me."

CHAPTER SEVENTEEN
Pasha

TODAY WAS GOING to be a day.

Today, I had a mediation meeting with Blake's sister, Sandra, Raymond, his lawyer, the judge, and me. I wasn't looking forward to this, but I was ready to get it over with. I needed it to be over. Sandra was very disappointed in my decision to forgo everything we had previously decided to go after. Maybe I was stupid. Maybe I was crazy. But this was what I wanted.

What I didn't want was to deal with Raymond ever again. I didn't want to look over my shoulder if I got half of everything because he could be spiteful. I could see him putting sugar in my gas tank if I was granted the car he'd bought me. I could see him hiding money if he was forced to pay me. I could see myself being harassed regularly for simply existing in a world where I had the things I was entitled to.

I didn't want that. I took Callum's advice and decided it was time to protect my peace. Speaking of Callum, God knew what he was doing when he crafted that man. He was making it hard not to be his friend. He was so sweet, understanding, and affirming. My heart could get into serious trouble with him, and I was beginning to think I might enjoy the ride.

"Are you sure you want to do this?" Sandra asked as we waited outside the judge's chambers.

"Yes."

"After what he's done, you deserve everything we asked for. You're walking away from a lot, Pasha."

I shook my head. "I have full faith that I'm walking into something greater, Sandra."

She squeezed my hand. "I was really going to enjoy nailing his smug ass and that lawyer to the cross."

I giggled. "I know you were. That's why I'm requesting he pay your fees."

"I'll take that. I'd never charge you, but he can absolutely run me my money."

We shared a laugh as approaching footsteps caused us to turn our heads. Raymond, Adora, and his lawyer strolled down the hall and took seats across from us. Raymond glared at me as he rubbed Adora's stomach. She looked like she was due any day now, and I couldn't hide my discomfort from seeing her. She was carrying a life with him. While I wished no harm to her innocent baby, I didn't want to see them together.

I took a deep breath and closed my eyes. They remained closed until the bailiff called us into the judge's chambers. We stood until Judge Parker entered the room and motioned for us to sit.

"Good morning," she spoke to the room. "Today, we are here to discuss the mediation for Sinclaire vs. Sinclaire. Mrs. Sinclaire, you filed a motion going forward after citing Mr. Sinclaire for adultery, abandonment, cruelty, isolation, and emotional distress. You were also seeking alimony and to have him pay for your therapy, correct?"

"Yes, Your Honor."

"May I speak, Your Honor?" Sandra asked. "My client has made some decisions I want to present to the court."

Judge Parker raised an eyebrow and sat back in her seat. "You may proceed."

Sandra clasped her hands together as she spoke. "Mrs. Sinclaire has informed me that she wishes to withdraw her petition."

"Do you care to explain, Mrs. Sinclaire?" the judge asked me.

"Yes, ma'am." I stood to my feet and smoothed over my blouse. Taking a deep breath, I turned to face her. "Your Honor, I've spent the last few years of my life in a state of grief and depression. I lost my parents, and I lost my child. I've watched my once-loving husband grow to hate me because those two losses changed me. He made his disdain for me very obvious. There is nothing I want more than to be done with this man and move forward with my life. He can have it all. I only ask that he pay my attorney her fees and my therapy. That's it. He can keep the alimony and have all the assets."

She looked at me and then at Raymond, who held a confused look on his face.

"Are you sure, Mrs. Sinclaire? Once I make the ruling, there is no changing it."

"I'm sure, Your Honor. I've spent my entire life being taken care of. First, by my parents, then by my husband. It's time I stand on my own two feet. I will never give anybody else the power to say I wouldn't have this or that if it weren't for them. I've thought about this. I've prayed about it, and now, it's out of my hands."

She smiled softly. "Very well then. It's so ordered. Mr. Sinclaire, you will pay Mrs. Sinclaire's attorney and therapy fees and retain ownership of all assets. No alimony is ordered. Divorce will be granted upon the signature of both parties after thirty days."

"Thank you, Your Honor," Sandra said.

She nodded as she turned to Raymond. "Mr. Sinclaire, you should count your lucky stars. Any other woman would have taken you for all you are worth. Given the substantial amount of evidence, I would have been inclined to give it to her." She turned to me. "Mrs. Sinclaire, I hope you go on to have a prosperous life. I pray that you find healing and you continue to do the work to better yourself. I pray that you find love in yourself and the courage to allow someone else to love you too."

"Thank you, Your Honor."

She nodded. "Court is adjourned."

She banged her gavel, and we all stood to leave the room. Raymond and his lawyer walked up ahead of us. As Sandra and I stepped into the hallway, his lawyer approached us with a smug look.

"I was prepared to fight you, Ms. James," he said, extending his hand.

She looked down at it, then back up at him stoically. "Mr. Davis, you and I both know you wouldn't have had a chance if things hadn't taken a turn. As the judge said, your client should thank his lucky stars."

Raymond's head snapped around. He started toward us. Adora tried to hold him back, but he snatched away.

"Ms. James, your client was smart to withdraw her petition. Her mental health is her weakness." He glared at me and smirked. "She will *always* be weak."

I smiled. "You know, Raymond . . . I may be a lot of things. But in thirty days, I will no longer be your concern or your problem, and you will be *nothing* to me. *That's* a win in itself."

I spun on my heels and strutted away from him with a smile. I didn't regret my decision. I was stepping into a new era . . . a brand-new Pasha. For once in my life, I was responsible for myself, and gaining my independence felt so . . . damn . . . good.

"Cheers to my girl for being thirty days shy of being a free woman!" Avyn yelled, raising her glass.

I sat in her living room with her, Blake, and Tia, sipping wine. When I called her with the good news after court, she was so happy for me. I'd taken myself out for a predivorce celebratory lunch and eaten to my heart's content. I then did a little shopping and got my nails and feet done. I was feeling pretty good by the time I got home. I'd taken a nap only to be awakened by Avyn calling and telling me to come upstairs.

When I walked in, she and the girls greeted me with confetti cannons and a round of congratulations. There was a banner and balloons, and they even got me a cake. The topper made me laugh. It was a woman in a wedding dress holding her groom's head. Avyn commented that Raymond was lucky it was just the topper and not him.

I smiled brightly. "I really appreciate this, you guys."

Blake waved me off. "Of course, we had to celebrate with you. Sandra said you strutted out of there with your head held high. We are so proud of you, pooh."

"I'm proud of myself."

Tia clapped her hands. "We have gifts!"

"You guys!" I whined. "You didn't have to get me anything!"

Blake rolled her eyes. "We have just a few things to welcome you back to single life. We know you won't jump into a ho phase, so we got you some things to . . . 'alleviate' yourself."

I didn't have to wonder what she meant by that. They all pulled gift bags from behind the couch and handed them to me. I placed my wineglass on the table and reached for them. The first bag was from Blake. Inside was a sexy black lingerie set, warming massage oil, and a black rose vibrator.

I shook my head. "Blake."

She raised a hand to hush me. "I don't want to hear it. This is self-care. By the way, setting number three is my favorite on that one."

I giggled. "I can't with you."

Tia laughed. "Just wait until you see what Avyn got you."

I rolled my eyes as Tia handed me her bag. Inside was this heavenly bottle of pheromone perfume, a sexy lace bra and panty set, and nipple clamps attached to a collar with a chain.

I held the clamps to my breast. "These are gonna hurt."

"That's the point," she said sarcastically. "Combine that with the rose, and you will have to change your sheets!"

"Y'all are some freaks."

"And we are trying to put you up on game," Avyn said, handing over her bag. "How this . . ." She blew a breath. "This right here is almost as good as the real thing."

I opened the bag and fell back laughing. Inside was a ten-inch dildo with a suction cup base. The thing looked so realistic, from the shade of brown to the prominent veins all the way down to the girth.

"Avyn!"

"Girl, I'm telling you! Stick that bad boy to the wall, a chair, or a table, and have the time of your life. It doesn't complain, it doesn't go soft, and it always gets the job done. Now, you combine this, the rose, and the nipple clamps, and you can really have a party. I might just be able to hear you all the way up here."

I had to laugh. "What am I gonna do with y'all? Thank you for this. They made me laugh, but I'm sure they will get some use."

Blake kissed her teeth. "They better."

Tia smirked. "They won't have to get used if she would call that fine-ass Callum."

The mention of his name made me blush, and a smile spread across my face.

"Look at her cheeks!" Blake yelled, pointing at me.

"Stop!" I pleaded.

"You know you think that man is fine, girl."

"I do. He's the reason I decided to let Raymond have everything. He told me to do what would bring me the most peace."

"So you *have* been talking to him?" Blake asked.

"I have. He's a good friend. He listens. He's encouraging and sweet." I smiled. "He's comforting."

"Have you told him about today?" Avyn asked.

"No. I haven't talked to him today."

My phone rang just as I said that. I pulled it from my pocket to see none other than Callum calling me.

"It's him," I said.

"Well, answer it!" Blake urged.

"And put it on speaker!" Tia added.

I shook my head. "Y'all are nosy."

"And is," Avyn boasted. "Answer the phone."

I sighed and took a deep breath. Answering the call, I placed it on speaker.

"Hello?"

His smooth, deep voice came through the speaker. "Hey, beautiful."

I blushed like I did whenever he called me that. "Hey, you."

"I just wanted to check in with you. I know you had a big day today. How did it go?"

"It went well. I let him have everything. All I asked was that he pay for my attorney fees and my therapy."

"How are you feeling about your decision?"

"Like a weight is lifted off my shoulders. In thirty days, I'll be a single woman."

"I love that for you, Pasha. I'm so proud of you, love."

"Thank you. And thank you for being a listening ear. I appreciate you."

"I wouldn't be your bestie if I didn't listen."

I giggled. "My girls won't take too kindly to you calling yourself my bestie."

"Girl, we do not care," Avyn shouted. She immediately covered her mouth. "My bad, boo."

Callum laughed. "Good evening, ladies."

"Heeeey!" they sang.

"I'm sorry. They were just throwing me a little celebratory get-together."

He chuckled. "I hope you're having fun. I didn't mean to interrupt."

I shook my head as though he could see me. "No, you're fine."

"We should have invited you," Blake said.

Avyn leaned into the phone. "Callum, you have to take a celebratory shot for my girl!"

"I can do that. Hold on."

We could hear him shuffling around and then the sound of glasses clinking. I heard him pouring something.

"We wanna see you take it," Tia said, causing my eyes to widen.

Callum chuckled. "I got you."

The phone vibrated with a video call request. The girls eagerly urged me to answer. Gathering myself, I accepted the call. When the video populated, I gasped. There he was in all his shirtless glory. His chest was smooth, and his muscles were toned and defined. Tattoos were etched into the parts of his skin I hadn't been privy to seeing. The girls leaned into the camera to get a look, and their mouths dropped. I don't think I'd ever seen any of them speechless.

Callum raised his shot glass. "Cheers to you, beautiful."

He tossed back the shot, and the slightest bit trickled down his chin to his throat.

Tia fanned herself. "That shouldn't be so erotic," she mumbled. "Whew, chile!"

"When you're officially free, you have to let me take you out to *really* celebrate," Callum said, wiping his chin.

"O-okay."

"I'm gonna let you go. I don't want to intrude on your fun. I just wanted to make sure you were good."

"Thank you. Good night, Callum."

"Good night, baby."

The call ended, and I finally felt like I could breathe again.

Blake slapped my shoulder. "Girl, if you don't get that man, I know something."

Tia agreed. "Right! He would only have to call me baby or beautiful one more time, and it would be a wrap."

"Look at her blushing," Avyn pointed out again. "Ooooh, I can't wait for this to come full circle. I'm putting it in the atmosphere. *That's* gonna be your man, and he will give and show you everything you've been missing."

They started talking over each other. I sat there, still staring at the phone. Was I ready for that? My marriage had been dead for a long time. I simply existed with Raymond for the longest time. I no longer wanted just to exist. I wanted to live. I wanted to live for my parents. I wanted to live for my son . . . I wanted to live for me.

I thought about Judge Parker's words. *"I pray that you find love in yourself and the courage to allow someone else to love you too."*

What if Callum wanted to love me at some point? What if I *wanted* him to love me at some point? Would I be ready for that? Would I accept it? Sabotage it? I wasn't sure about any of that.

CHAPTER EIGHTEEN
Callum

"CALLUM ELLIS! DON'T you go to jail behind some woman!"

I sat beside my niece at Bella's kitchen table as she watched cartoons on her tablet. She insisted I watch with her while her mother cooked. It wasn't doing me any good because she had her headphones on, so I couldn't hear the show if I tried.

"I'm not going to jail."

"If you keep putting your hands on that man, that's *exactly* where you will be. I don't want to have to bail you out."

"But you would."

"Of course, I would. I wouldn't let you sit in jail. You're too pretty for that."

I rolled my eyes. Three weeks had gone by since the incident in town. My friendship with Pasha was making strides. She'd finally texted me to give me her number a few days after our impromptu hangout in town. We texted back and forth sparingly, but since seeing her at the cemetery, it had become a daily thing.

We'd been talking about twenty minutes ago when Bella's nosy self looked over my shoulder. She just had to know who I was talking to, which made me smile. I gave her the rundown on my budding friendship, and while she didn't object to me putting hands on Raymond Sinclair, she knew my temper.

"Are you *sure* you want to get involved with a married woman, Callum? I mean, isn't that like one of the Ten Commandments?"

I sighed. "It is, but hell, he did it first. And technically, she's just my friend."

"A friend you are clearly attracted to."

"Yes, I'm attracted to her. But I'm not doing anything wrong. At least I don't feel like it. I'm acting within the friend capacity."

"For the next month. When she's single, I feel like you will make a move."

I shrugged. I hadn't decided if I was going to put myself out there like that just yet. I wanted her to tell me she wanted more. I told her I was on her time, and I meant that. I'd move however she moved.

"Well, what does she look like?" Bella asked.

I knew she couldn't resist looking for more details. I went to my camera roll to the one picture I'd snuck of Pasha when we were in town. Standing from the table, I went over to show her.

"Oh my! She's gorgeous!"

"She is."

"I don't see this staying a friendship too long. I know you."

"Why does everybody keep saying that? First, Chris, then Malcolm, and now you. Am I that predictable?"

She giggled as she opened the fridge. "You are, dear brother. It's okay, though. It just means people can expect you to be exactly who you are. No surprises, no gimmicks."

She rummaged through the fridge. A frown appeared on her face.

"Shoot. I need heavy cream. Would you mind running to the grocery store around the corner for me?"

"How do you invite me to eat, then send me on errands?" I jested.

"Because if you want this food, you'll go."

I chuckled. "I'm going, I'm going."

I headed out of the kitchen and to the front door.

"Bring back something sweet for dessert too! Ooooh, and some wine!"

"I got you!"

Just as I opened the door, I ran smack into Martin.

"Whoa, there!" he said, dapping me. "Where you running to? I know you aren't leaving before the food is done."

"Never that. Your wife is sending me to the grocery store. I'll be back shortly."

He nodded and continued into the house. As I was leaving, I caught a glimpse of both my sister and my niece going to greet him. I smiled softly. I could only imagine what it felt like to come home to that every day. As kids, we greeted my father the same way. Every day, he came home to hugs, smiles, and kisses from us and our mother. He always said no matter what kind of day he was having, coming home to a warm welcome made all of it worth it.

I made it to the store in five minutes flat. Climbing out of the truck, I headed inside and got a basket with my mental list. I quickly grabbed everything Bella asked for and approached the register. As I was rounding the corner, I collided with someone, damn near knocking them down.

"I'm so sorry, I . . . Pasha?"

She looked up at me, rubbing the arm that had rammed into my chest.

"I'm sorry. I wasn't looking where I was going. I didn't think I would run into a human wall," she added with a smile.

I chuckled. "I apologize. Are you okay?"

"I don't think you knocked anything out of place."

"Good. I'd never forgive myself if I hurt you."

"How are you?"

"I'm good. When you said you worked at a grocery store, I didn't know it was this one."

"Yeah . . . I'm just about to get off."

"Oh? Do you have any plans?"

"Other than finding me something to eat, no."

"Would you like to have dinner with my family?"

"Oh . . . Callum, I don't know. I would hate to impose."

"It's no imposition. I haven't seen you in a while, and I'd love to catch up."

She hesitated for a moment. "Well . . . only if it's okay with your sister."

I shot Bella a quick message, and she immediately responded with eye emojis but told me to bring her.

"It's all good. I'm gonna check out, and then I'll pull my truck up to the door. I'm sorry, did you need a ride?"

"Yes. Avyn is working a double, so I was going to Uber home. Thank you. I'm just gonna go clock out, and I'll meet you."

"Sounds like a plan."

We parted ways, and I headed to the register. Since it was almost closing time, there weren't many people there. I got through the small line rather quickly and returned to my truck. When I pulled around to the front door, Pasha was walking out. She quickly hopped in, buckled up, and we returned to the house.

"How was your day?" I inquired.

"Considering I work with a bunch of teenagers on the weekend, it was okay. Most of them are pretty responsible. They like to ask me what I know about certain music and celebrities they're into. And they like teaching me dances they've learned online." She giggled as she shook her head. "I'm not sure how old they think I am, but they seem like okay kids."

"My niece loves to dance. She's begging my sister to sign her up for it."

"Can she dance?"

"Surprisingly, my baby has a little rhythm. She must get it from me and her daddy because Bella is stiff."

She laughed out loud. "Don't do her like that!"

"Can you dance?" I asked.

"I'm afraid you'd find me stiff too."

"See, we have to get you up to speed. You can't be making me look bad if I ever get you in a position to dance."

She giggled. "I can do my little two-step."

"Nah, baby. You have to move your hips a little." My eyes inadvertently traveled the length of her frame. She wore these fitted khaki pants that hugged every curve in ways that made me envious. When I looked back up at her face, she shook her head, then playfully mushed me.

"Eyes on the road, sir."

"I'm paying attention," I said, my eyes still on her.

"You are no Paul Walker, and I value my life in this car."

I grinned as I refocused my eyes on the road.

"I should warn you, my niece loves people, so she will ask you a million questions. You'll be forced to be her friend by the end of the night."

"I wonder where she gets that from?"

"You got jokes? You don't like being my friend, Pasha?"

She smirked as she shrugged. "Maybe. We'll see."

"Bet."

I pulled into the driveway of my sister's home and shut off the car.

Pasha's eyes widened. "Wow . . . This is beautiful. What does your sister do?"

"She's an accountant. She made a partner a few months ago. Her husband is an oral surgeon. Don't be surprised if he compliments your teeth. It's his thing . . . Well, one of them."

"Duly noted."

We climbed out of the truck, and I grabbed the bags from the backseat. Before we reached the front door, Bella opened it with a smile.

"Hi!" she said excitedly, pulling Pasha in for a hug.

It seemed to take her by surprise, but she hugged her back.

"I'm Bella, Callum's sister. It's nice to meet you."

"I'm Pasha. It's nice to meet you too. Thank you for having me at the last minute. I told Callum I didn't want to impose."

"Oh, girl, it's okay. There's plenty to share. Now I don't have to worry about greedy here eating me out of house and home."

I rolled my eyes and mushed her forehead with my finger. "Don't act like you don't like not having to store leftovers. You see how she does me?" I said to Pasha, who simply smiled.

"You stick around long enough, and you'll see what a disposal system he is, Pasha."

"Oh, I've seen him put away cookies like it was nothing."

Bella laughed as she opened the door wider to let us in.

"You have a beautiful home," Pasha complimented as we stepped inside.

"Thank you. Precious!"

My niece came running around the corner, her head full of beads bouncing around. She stood at my sister's side, gripping her leg as she looked up at Pasha with wide eyes and a smile.

"Precious, this is Uncle Cay's friend, Ms. Pasha. Say hello."

"Hi! She's so pretty, Uncle Cay. Is she your friend *friend* or your girlfriend?"

Pasha giggled. "I'm just his friend. And thank you. You're so pretty yourself. I like your beads."

"Thank you. My mommy did my hair. She could do your hair like this."

I chuckled. "Baby girl, I think she's a little too old for that hairstyle."

"Huh-uh! Ms. Caresha at my school has beads on her braids." She motioned for Pasha to come close, then whispered very loudly, "Ms. Caresha thinks Uncle Cay is cute."

Pasha laughed. "Does she?"

"Precious, what have I told you about gossiping?" Bella asked, shaking her head. She looked up at me. "This is *your* fault for always picking her up early. Got those women lusting after you in front of my baby."

"How is it *my* fault that one of the teachers thinks I'm cute?"

"Because I'm sure you walk in there looking like a S.L.U.T."

Pasha stifled a laugh.

"Mommy, what's that spell?" Precious asked.

"Nothing, baby." She took the bag from me. "Pasha, would you like to help Precious and me in the kitchen?"

"Sure."

Precious grabbed her hand and pulled her away, already talking her ears off. Bella turned to me, catching me staring at Pasha as she talked away.

"She's even prettier in person. And she's thick like you like them. I saw you staring at her ass."

"Say what now?"

She playfully punched me. "Don't act dumb." Her face turned serious. "Promise me you'll be careful in this friendship, Callum. I know your heart, and I don't want you getting hurt."

"I promise I will be careful. Scout's honor."

She smirked. "You know I do have that one picture of you in your Boy Scouts uniform with those ashy-ass knees. Maybe I'll show it to her."

"Please don't make me disown you."

She laughed out loud. "Martin is in the den. Go join him, and don't come interrupting us."

"I might listen."

She playfully slapped my arm before running off. I headed into the den, where Martin was sitting nursing a beer.

"What's up, man?" I said, dapping him.

"Not much. Who is this you brought into my house?"

"A friend, man. Just a friend."

"That ain't what my wife said."

"I was gone all of fifteen minutes, and she's already gossiping with you?"

He chuckled. "You know that woman can't hold water. I'm expecting pillow talk about this tonight. If I don't get any sleep, I'm beating your ass."

"Fair enough."

He took a sip of his beer. "So? Who is she?"

"Her name is Pasha."

"And are you into this Pasha?"

"I might be, but friendship is all I can offer right now."

"Bella told me about her situation. Who's her husband?"

"Raymond Sinclaire."

"You kidding me? I know him. I work with him from time to time when I pick up shifts at the hospital. Damn, man. I didn't know he was like that. I'm definitely giving him the side eye the next time I see him."

"You can side-eye him. I might just have to put hands on him again."

"All right, Tyson."

"I got bail money."

He chuckled. "I know you do. He's not worth it, though. I can't be bringing my baby to see her favorite uncle in an orange jumpsuit."

"I *would* miss Precious and our middle-of-the-day uncle and niece dates."

"Right. Who else will hype her up on sweets and then drop her off to us? I'm sure she's in there vetting her potential auntie right now."

"Potential auntie?"

"You don't bring women around, Callum. If you brought her, you feel something. Even if it's soon. One thing I've learned about you is you are very sure of yourself, and you are intentional. I respect that. So, if you're bringing her around, we'll make sure to treat her like family. Come on and introduce me."

"Your wife said to stay out of her kitchen."

"I'm not afraid of my wife," he said, standing. "She's only five foot two."

I laughed as I got up to follow him into the kitchen. Bella was short, but he and I both knew she wore the pants in the family.

CHAPTER NINETEEN

Pasha

I COULD TELL CALLUM had been talking to Bella about me because she was being super friendly. It made me wonder what he'd said. It wasn't that she was trying to be in my business; more so, she knew something I didn't. Precious, however, was just as friendly as he told me she would be. Right now, I was following her instructions on how to set the table. It was the cutest thing because she was so serious.

"Uncle Cay's plate goes right here," she said. "He always sits next to me, but you can have my spot tonight."

I smiled. "Are you sure? I hear he's your favorite uncle."

She giggled. "He is. But I can share him tonight."

"Well, thank you, Precious."

"Ms. Pasha, do you have kids?"

"Precious, that's personal," Bella immediately interjected. She offered me a sympathetic look, and I knew Callum had mentioned me losing my son.

"It's okay," I said quietly. I turned back to Precious, stooping down to eye level with her. "I had a baby a year ago, but he didn't make it."

"So he's in heaven?"

"Yes."

She looked sad for a moment. "I'm sorry."

"You have nothing to be sorry about."

"Mommy and Uncle Cay's mommy and daddy are in heaven too. I bet they look out for him."

Her innocence made me smile.

"That would be nice. I'm sure between them and my mom and dad, he has a lot of people caring for him."

Her eyes widened. "You lost your mommy and daddy too?"

"I did."

She looked back at Bella, tears brimming in her eyes. "Mommy, that's so sad. She's all alone." She turned to me and threw her arms around my neck. "I don't want you to be alone."

I picked her up and gave her a reassuring hug.

"I'm not alone. I have some really great friends that are my family."

She pulled back and looked at me. I swiped the tears from her eyes.

"Like Uncle Cay?"

"Well, your uncle is a different kind of friend. I'm still getting to know him."

"He's my best friend. He can be a real good friend to you too."

I smiled. "You think so?"

"Yeah! He can take you for ice cream, and you can have sleepovers and watch movies and go to the park! All kinds of stuff!"

Her excitement was infectious, and I couldn't help but laugh.

"Sounds like you two have a lot of fun together," I said.

"So much fun!"

"Okay, Precious," Bella said. "Don't talk Ms. Pasha's ear off. Why don't you go in the living room and watch TV for a little bit?"

"Okay, Mommy."

She kissed my cheek before I put her down, then ran off.

"She's the sweetest thing," I commented.

"She's like her daddy when it comes to meeting new people. He's very friendly. Just don't be alarmed if he looks at your teeth. It's kinda his thing as an oral surgeon."

I snickered. "Callum has warned me."

"Soooo . . ." She dragged the word out as she stirred her pot. "You and my brother?"

"He's just a friend."

"Callum doesn't *have* female friends. You must be pretty special."

"Well, I wouldn't say that."

"If you saw how he was smiling while talking to you earlier, you would." She smirked as she looked at me. "You two would make a beautiful couple. And I'm not just saying that because that's my ugly-ass brother."

I laughed. "He's quite handsome."

She pretended to gag. "He's okay."

"Well, Precious's teachers seem to think so."

"I'm learning that her teachers are thirsty. He pays them no mind, though. Precious is all he sees when he has her. They make me sick sometimes, girl. She'll literally forget about me when she's with his big-head ass."

"Isn't that what uncles and aunties are for?"

She kissed her teeth. "I guess."

The sound of approaching footsteps caused her gaze to shift. When Callum and, who I assumed to be her husband, walked in, she stopped stirring the pot and placed her hands on her hips. Callum raised his palms in surrender.

"I told him," he stated. "He said he wasn't afraid of you."

His brother-in-law slapped his arm. "Bruh!" He glared at him for a moment before smiling, walking over to his wife, and sliding his arms around her. He placed a kiss on her lips.

"I didn't say that, baby."

Callum smirked. "Punk ass. Pasha, this is Martin. Martin, this is Pasha."

"It's nice to meet you," I said, smiling warmly.

"Nice to meet you . . . You have nice teeth."

Both Callum and Bella laughed.

"Told you," they both said.

Martin looked around, confused. "What?"

Bella pecked his lips. "Nothing, my love. Why are you in my kitchen?"

"I just came to speak since neither you nor your brother introduced me to our guest."

"Well, you've met her. Now get out."

Martin shook his head. "You see how she does me? I'm going. Give me a kiss."

He pulled her closer, pressed his lips to hers, and then kissed her all over her face. She broke into a fit of giggles that ended with her snorting and covering her mouth. She playfully slapped his chest.

"Stop making me ugly laugh!" she exclaimed. "Get out of my kitchen."

"Yes, ma'am."

He grabbed two beers from the fridge. Then he and Callum headed back in the direction they came from.

"Are you two like this all the time?" I asked.

"Yes, girl. He makes me feel like a teenager again . . . hopelessly in love."

"That's beautiful. You make a nice couple."

"Thank you. He's my college sweetheart. Callum wasn't happy when I brought him home, but he loves him now."

She went back to stirring her pot. I took a seat on the stool in front of the island. I could see that she and her brother were as close as he said they were.

"Can I ask you something?" I said.

"Sure."

"How was he as a parental figure? He said he raised you after you lost your parents."

She smiled softly. "He was strict, but at the same time, he was very loving, understanding, and hands-on. He never missed any of my big moments. He was always right there encouraging me and being my biggest cheerleader. He put his life on hold to make sure we could stay together. When everyone backed out of taking us in, he stepped up. He left school and got a nine to five. Sometimes, I could hear him crying and praying to God that things would get better and easier, and that broke me, Pasha. The love I have for him goes past him being my big brother. He took care of me when he was still a kid himself, and I have so much respect for him."

She reached across the counter and took my hands.

"He told me about your situation. And it wasn't to tell me your business. It was to make me aware of the parameters of your friendship. I say that to say this. If you ever find yourself catching feelings for him or no longer wanting just a friendship, you will have a good man. He's not perfect, but he's one of the best men I know. I stand ten toes down behind that."

"I hear you."

"So . . . Tell me a little about you."

I gave her a short rundown. I found that she was really easy to talk to. She, like her brother, had a genuine spirit. I could tell that she was a good person and probably someone I would enjoy being around. About fifteen minutes later, dinner was done. I helped her plate everything, and then she called the household to eat. As we made our way to the table, Callum pulled up my chair and allowed me to sit. I offered him a grateful smile. He grabbed my hand as we bowed our heads to pray. While Martin led the table in prayer, I snuck a glance at Callum. I just couldn't get over how handsome he was and how good he had been to me. I knew that if I kept being around him, it would make just being his friend very hard.

Dinner was great.

Callum's family was very welcoming and gave me all-around good vibes. Precious quickly became my little friend, just as her uncle said she would. I couldn't help but love her sweetness and innocence. She asked me questions like she was conducting an interview. It was amazing how articulate she was for a four-year-old. By the night's end, she'd fallen asleep in my arms.

"I'll take her," Martin said, standing from the couch. "It's way past her bedtime anyway. Thank you for joining us, Pasha. You're welcome anytime."

"Thank you for having me."

He smiled as he scooped Precious up and carried her upstairs.

"Are you ready to go?" Callum asked from beside me.

"Yes. The food was good, and I enjoyed the company, but the 'itis' is kicking in. My bed is calling me."

He stood and reached for my hand, pulling me to my feet. Bella stood and walked us to the door.

"It was so nice to meet you, boo," she said, pulling me in for a hug.

"It was nice meeting you too. I appreciate your hospitality."

"We have to get together without this one." She gestured to her brother, and he looked at her offended.

"How are you gonna steal my friend?"

"'Cause I can. You take care, Pasha. You have my number. Don't be a stranger. I'll see you this week, Callum."

"You will. Love you, sis."

"I love you too."

They shared a brief embrace, and he kissed her forehead. Then he grabbed my hand and led me out to his truck. After helping me in, he rounded the driver's side and climbed in himself. I settled into the comfort of his leather seat with a smile. He looked over at me when he closed his door.

"You good?" he asked.

"I'm great. Thank you for tonight. I haven't felt a genuine family vibe in a long time. I mean, I have my girls, but that's different. This was . . . I don't know. It made me feel all warm inside. I needed that."

"I'm glad I could provide that for you."

He cranked up and backed out of the driveway. The ride back to my apartment was made in comfortable silence, aside from the smooth R&B playing through the speakers. I glanced at Callum, and thoughts of his sister's words ran through my mind. I didn't feel she was trying to cover up for him. As she spoke about him, the look in her eyes was one of love and adoration. There was no way to fake that. On the outside, maybe, but not inside.

We pulled up to my apartment building about twenty minutes later. Much to my surprise, he pulled into a parking spot instead of in front of the door.

"Can I walk you up?" he asked.

"Sure."

We climbed out of the truck, and he walked around to offer me his arm. I accepted, and we headed into the building. We spent the ride up to my floor, stealing glances at each other and smiling. I couldn't seem to get myself together. Why was I acting like a schoolgirl with this man? We stepped off the elevator and made our way down the hall to my door.

"This is me," I said, pressing my back against it.

"It is."

"Thank you again for tonight."

"Pasha, if you thank me one more time, you're gonna know something."

"Well, I don't know what else to say!" My cheeks were heating up because I was blushing so hard.

"Say you'll spend some time with me this Friday."

"Are you asking me on a date?"

"I'm asking you to let your *friend* take you out and show you a good time."

"Just as friends?"

"Just as friends."

I pondered his request. I had nothing to do once I got off from the hotel. The girls hadn't mentioned making any plans, so my evening was wide open. I found myself nodding.

"Okay. I get off at six."

"Dress comfortably. We're gonna do something fun."

"Something fun like what?"

"I guess you'll have to wait and see."

"I don't know if I like surprises."

He chuckled. "Just trust me. You're in good hands." He lifted my fingers to his lips and kissed them. "Can you do that for me?"

"O-okay."

He smiled. "Good. I'll see you Friday. Be ready at seven thirty."

"Okay."

He leaned in and kissed my cheek. "Good night, Pasha."

"Good night."

I unlocked the door and stepped inside as he made his way back down the hall. I couldn't stop smiling as I sauntered into my bedroom. I almost jumped out of my skin when I saw Avyn sitting on my bed, grinning like a Cheshire Cat.

"You scared the hell out of me!" I exclaimed.

"I bet I did."

"What are you doing here?"

"I *was* waiting for you. But I see you were *preoccupied*."

"Were you . . . Were you at the door?"

Her smile widened. "I may have seen him kiss you, and you let him."

"It was on my cheek!"

"It didn't look like that. You walked in here blushing and whatnot. Let me find out!"

I rolled my eyes. "It's not that serious."

"So, enlighten me on *what* it is. Where have you been?"

"He asked me to have dinner with him and his family."

"Oooooh!" She patted the space beside her on the bed, and I climbed up. "How did it go? Wait, first, how did that even happen?"

"I was getting off work, and I literally bumped into him when he came to pick up some things for his sister. Everything went well. She's super nice, and so is her husband. And their daughter is just the most adorable little girl I have ever seen. She's so sweet and well mannered."

"Awww, sounds like you had a really good time."

"I did."

"That's twice you've been in his company since moving in here."

"He asked to take me out on Friday."

Her eyes widened, and her mouth dropped. She scrambled to her knees and tackled me on the bed.

"You have a date!"

"It's not a date! Just two friends hanging out and enjoying each other's company."

"Bullshit. Y'all can call it what you want. Friend date. Date date. That's a date, pooh. Please let me help you get ready. The girls can come over, and we can get you all glammed up."

"Pump your brakes. It's not that kind of party. He said to wear something comfortable."

"Comfortable can still be cute, and cute you will be. I'm so excited for you, Pash. I like Callum for you. Whether this stays a friendship or branches into something more, I'm happy that somebody is making you smile these days."

She threw her arms around me and hugged me. It wasn't until I felt the tears seeping through my shirt that I realized she was crying. I held back and looked at her.

"What's wrong?"

"To see you living a little after being down for so long . . . It's beautiful to watch. When Raymond isolated you from us, I worried about you so much, Pasha. I cried for you. I prayed for you. I wanted so bad just to come and snatch you up out of that house. You could have stayed with me forever, and I wouldn't have cared. That's how much I love you and want you to be happy."

"I love you too, Avyn. I'm grateful every day that I ended up at your hotel. I'm not sure where I would be right now without you."

We embraced each other in a loving hug. I could feel the emotions running through her. Avyn wasn't the most emotionally expressive person with everybody. Even Blake and Tia didn't get to see her the way I did. For her to express full-out emotion, she had to be feeling it heavily. At this moment, I realized just how much my traumas impacted her too. I never wanted to cause her distress, and I didn't want that for myself ever again.

CHAPTER TWENTY
Callum

"WHAT DO WE have on the upcoming books?" I asked, surveying my small meeting room.

Angela, my booking manager, scrolled through her tablet. "Friday, the fifth, is a dinner at the mayor's mansion. Saturday is the charity gala. Then, for two weeks after that, we have four weddings."

I nodded. "That's solid income for the month."

Chris cleared his throat. "I've made a few changes to the app to help it run a little smoother and faster. They should take effect by tonight."

Palmer, my lead supervisor, spoke up. "We may need to task a few more drivers for the weddings. I was looking for the forms, and two of them are on the same day."

I nodded. "Whatever you need to do to make it work. Anything else?"

Angela shook her head. "Not on my end."

Chris shook his head. "Nah, but let me rap to you right quick."

"See you later, gentlemen." Angela excused herself, leaving Chris and I alone.

"You seem like you're in a good mood," he stated.

"I'm in a great mood."

"Would this have anything to do with Pasha?"

I smirked. "Maybe."

"I take it things are going well?"

"They are moving along. She had dinner with the fam a few nights ago."

"Oh really? How was that?"

"Good. She and Bella got along great, and Precious fell in love just that quickly. She ended up falling asleep in her arms."

He chuckled. "I swear, if baby girl doesn't do anything else, she's gonna make her a friend."

"Facts."

"You still on this friend bid, too?"

I sat back in my chair and locked my fingers behind my head. "I'm still offering friendship. I'm not gonna push up on her like that. I really just want to enjoy her company. We have good chemistry, man."

"You seem sure of yourself. I hope it works out for you in the end. Just be careful. I don't want things to get messy for you. That is still somebody's wife until the ink is dried on those divorce papers."

I heard what he was saying, but the last thing I was worried about was things getting messy for me. Raymond Sinclaire had proven himself to be a weak man. He took more pride in trying to bring down his soon-to-be ex-wife than trying to defend himself against me. I would, however, be careful with Pasha. I would hate for any of the backlash to fall on her for my actions against that bastard.

"I hear you, man," I said, sitting up.

"Well, since you're determined to see this through, you can bring her to our game night next week."

"I almost forgot about that."

"I invited Malcolm too. He supposed to bring somebody."

"Would you believe that he's dating Pasha's friend? I forgot to tell you that. I learned that when I helped her move."

"Well, damn. It's a small world. Shit, maybe you two *were* meant to cross paths after all."

I hadn't thought about that, but maybe he was right. I firmly believe in people coming into your life when they are supposed to. It could be for a season, or it could be for a lifetime. I wanted to know what it was about this woman who grabbed ahold of me and wouldn't let go. The night we met was supposed to stay just that. My concern should have remained my concern. But something about her embedded itself in me. It was more than worry that filled me when I looked into those pretty brown eyes for the first time.

Chris and I talked for a little while longer before he had to leave for another meeting. I was pretty much done for the day, and it was only around noon. After locking up my office, I said goodbye to everyone and headed out to my car. Settled in the driver's seat, I unlocked my phone. The first thing I saw was the text thread between Pasha and me. Our most recent conversation was from yesterday. I'd sent her a picture of Precious and me together after I picked her up from day care.

We'd gone shopping, and she asked me about Pasha, so I suggested we send her a picture. That birthed an hour-long video call with her because Precious kept asking me questions about her. She was her mother's child through and through because she was nosy too. By the time we got back to my house, I decided just to let her ask them herself.

We camped out on my couch while Pasha rested comfortably in her bed. Since she'd been off from work, she said she was just lounging around reading a book. Precious loved books and insisted on showing her favorite one at my house. She was learning to read, and what she couldn't read, she made up a story using the pictures.

It was adorable to watch. Pasha listened attentively as she read her the book, using different voices for the characters. The child reminded me so much of her mother that it was crazy. Bella had a wild imagination as a kid, and so did Precious. Sometimes, I had to look at her and wonder where she was learning some of the things she said.

I chuckled at the memory as I went to her contact and pressed the call button. She answered on the third ring. I could hear the sound of her shuffling about before I heard her voice.

"Hello?"

"Hey, beautiful. How are you?"

"Hey, I'm okay. I'm at work right now, but I go to lunch in about fifteen minutes."

"I was on my way to grab something to eat. You wanna join me?"

"Um . . . sure. Lunch would be okay. I'll meet you outside."

"Okay. See you soon."

"See you soon."

We disconnected that call, and I pulled out of the parking lot. I headed over after stopping to get gas and run my car through the wash. I pulled up just as Pasha was walking outside. Throwing the car in park, I got out to open her door.

"Thank you," she said, offering me a smile as she climbed in.

I nodded and closed the door before returning to the driver's seat.

"Do you have a taste for anything in particular?"

"I could go for some tacos."

"Tacos it is."

"I mean, if you want something else, I'm open. I just really love tacos."

I merged into traffic as I responded. "You'll learn that I'm not a picky eater. If I don't do anything else, I'm going to eat. Bella can vouch for that."

"I watched you inhale that food the other night. I believe you."

I chuckled. "Don't play me like that."

"You played yourself."

"Whatever. How's your day been?"

"It's been decent. Nothing is fascinating about cleaning hotel rooms. However, you would be surprised by the things people leave behind. Just this morning, I found vibrators, butt plugs, and nipple clamps . . . all in one room."

"Have you found anything that makes you want to be a fly on the wall in that room?"

She giggled. "Not yet, but I'm sure it's coming. Some of my coworkers have been there so long they say nothing shocks them anymore. I like the job, though. It's quiet. I can work independently, and it's simple. For my first job, I didn't think I'd like it."

"If you could do anything else, what would it be?"

She shrugged. "I don't know. I've always imagined my life as a homemaker. Most of the women in my family stay at home and take care of the house and the kids. I've never pictured being anything else before now."

"And now?"

"I can admit, I like earning my own money. I like not having to ask for permission to spend it. Nobody is clocking my pockets. Now, I don't think I will ever like paying bills."

I laughed. "I promise you won't. But I'm glad you're looking at the positives in life right now. Starting over can be hard, but it can also be beautiful."

She plucked at her fingernails. "It can. I'm learning a lot about myself. I don't think I'll come out of this the same woman, and I'm okay with that."

I nodded as I pulled into the parking lot of Mexi Grill, a spot that serves some of the best tacos in the city and the surrounding area.

"I think different versions of yourself are needed to survive life. Life will humble the hell out of you."

"You can say that again."

I shut off the car and got out to open her door. When I offered her my arm, she wrapped her fingers around my bicep and followed me inside. The place wasn't busy, so we were seated relatively quickly. I ordered a shot of tequila, and she ordered a margarita to start us off with. While the waitress went to put the order in, Pasha and I chitchatted.

"Are you going to give me a hint about what we are doing tomorrow night?" she asked.

"Nope. I think I'm gonna let you suffer until we get where we are going."

"Maybe I should just stay home them," she jested.

"I know where you live. I can always pull up on you. How can you stand up a face like this?" I gave her a playful pout and sad eyes. "You wanna break my heart, Pash? I thought we were friends, baby."

I didn't miss the subtle biting of her bottom lip and the moment she caught herself doing so. She playfully elbowed me.

"We *are* friends."

"Best friends?"

She giggled. "I think Avyn would fight you for that title."

"I think I could take her."

We laughed as the waitress returned with our drinks and took the order for our food. We both decided on the five-taco platter with Cajun fries. As the waitress left, Pasha sipped her margarita and did a little happy dance.

"Are you good to drink that before you return to work?" I asked.

"Yes. I made sure to order the mocktail version. I won't be getting fired today."

She took another sip before setting down the glass. We talked a bit while waiting for our food to be delivered. Ten minutes later, the food arrived and was placed in front of us. After a quick prayer, we dug in. The sounds of Pasha moaning after every bite were doing me in.

"Did you eat breakfast this morning?" I asked.

"I didn't, and I'm starving. These are so good."

She eyeballed my plate, and I knew what was coming next. Just like most women, she wanted to "try" mine, and she made it known in the most innocent way.

"What's that one?"

"A fish taco."

"Ooooh. I've never had a fish taco."

I chuckled. "Would you like to try it?"

"Just a little bite."

I wiped my hands, then cupped her chin. Picking up the fish taco, I held it to her lips.

"Open."

She gasped for a moment, her eyes widening at my request. She swallowed hard before her lips parted, and she allowed me to feed her a bite of the taco. Watching her plump lips wrap around the tasty morsel was so sexy . . . She was so sexy. The scrubs she wore hugged her curves in all the right places. She was simply the type of woman who was beautiful no matter what she was doing or wearing. At least in my eyes, she was. I had it bad for her . . . real bad.

"How's that?" I asked, grabbing my napkin to dab the avocado ranch dressing that fell on her chin.

"It's good . . . real good. You should try my birria."

She dipped it into the sauce. Grabbing the napkin, she held it under my chin and fed me a taco bite. Our gaze never wavered as I chewed the same taco that was on my plate. For some reason, hers tasted so much better than that one. I would say she was flirting with me if I didn't know any better.

"How's that?" she asked, dabbing the corners of my mouth.

I grabbed her hand and held it tight. "Perfect."

My eyes dropped to her lips. It took everything in me to fight the urge to lean in for a kiss. I promised myself and her that I wouldn't push up on her. That I would let her come to me when she felt like she wanted more, but damn, it was hard. She was right here in front of me, but still so far out of my reach.

We continued eating and conversing, neither of us bringing attention to the obvious. Our plates were clean when we got ready to leave, and I had a nice little buzz from the shots I'd consumed. Hand in hand, we walked back to my truck like it was the most normal thing for us. I helped her in, then climbed in myself. The drive back was quiet, but not an awkward type of quiet. It was a quiet lie . . . We both knew something was brewing, yet we didn't dare speak on it. Back at the hotel, she directed me to pull around to the employee parking.

"I'm sure Avyn is being nosy because she's already texted me. I don't want her to make this more than it is like she already has. I just want to enjoy your company."

"Well, I hope I'm at least making this worth your while."

She palmed my face. "You are . . . You're seemingly perfect, Callum. The part of me that's afraid is just waiting on you to cut me so I can see how bad it hurts."

"What's the rational part of you saying?"

She dropped her hand and looked down at her fingernails. "That you're the person you portray yourself to be, and I have no reason to be afraid."

"Stick with that one. I respect whatever you feel. Just know I'm not out to cause you harm or distress." I tucked a stray curl behind her ear and leaned closer. "I want to know you, Pasha. Every single thing that makes you who you are."

"I'm bruised . . . slightly broken."

"So am I."

"What are two bruised, slightly broken people supposed to do together?"

"Heal." I kissed her cheek and sat back in my seat. "I hope you have a good rest of your day, Pasha."

"Y-you t-too," she stammered.

She quickly climbed out of the truck and sprinted inside, looking back momentarily at me before closing the door.

CHAPTER TWENTY-ONE

Pasha

"I CAN'T MISS THIS air of happiness surrounding you," Dr. Thomas said with a light smile.

Today, I had a therapy session before I headed in to work. I'd mentioned it to Callum while we were at lunch yesterday, and much to my surprise this morning, I woke up to a message from him, letting me know that a car would be waiting to take me to my appointment, so I didn't have to bother Avyn. Not only that, but the driver was also available to me all day—that man.

He made me smile more than I had in years, and all he was doing was being himself. I couldn't pretend that I didn't like him because I did. Way more than I should have. That was the part that scared me. Here I was a few weeks shy of being a free, single woman, and I was already attracted to another man. It terrified me too.

"I, um . . . I met someone," I said quietly.

"Oh! Well, tell me about him."

"You remember the driver I told you about? The one that picked me up the night Raymond put me out?"

"The one that paid for your hotel stay . . . Yes, I remember."

"Well, Avyn and I ran into him at Walmart a few weeks ago. He offered to help me move into my apartment, and we've been building a friendship."

"How does that make you feel?"

"Nervous. I've had the same friends for as long as I can remember. And then the part of me that's afraid is screaming at me to cut him off before I fall, and he hurts me too. The thing is . . . I don't think he's like that. He's been so genuine, so sweet, patient, and caring. I just . . . I feel like it's too soon."

"How does this gentleman make you feel?"

I pondered the question. "Seen . . . heard . . . beautiful. He calls me 'beautiful' every time I talk to him. He compliments me. He just . . . He looks at me like I'm the most beautiful thing in the world to him. I feel like I can just be myself when I'm with him. I can be vulnerable, and he doesn't judge me for having a moment. It's . . . nice."

She smiled. "He sounds like a wonderful addition to your circle."

"He is."

"How are divorce proceedings going?"

I sighed. "Well, I'll be a single woman again in a few weeks. I'm excited about the next chapter in my life. I haven't decided what I want to do yet. I don't want to work at the hotel and grocery store forever. I was thinking about going back to school."

A smile spread across her face. "That's great! Have you been looking at any programs? Areas of study?"

"Last night, I was looking up this phlebotomy program. Of all the ones I looked at, that one was the most interesting to me."

"That's a quick program, and you can get hired pretty easily."

"I'm a little nervous about stepping out there. I'm sure I'll be one of the oldest people in class."

"You're never too old to learn something new. My mother earned her bachelor's degree at forty-five. I'm sure she never imagined becoming friends with a bunch of twenty-somethings, but they loved her. To this day, they still come to her home for dinner, and she's well into her sixties. Sometimes, you just click with people."

That was an understatement, and the thought brought me back to Callum. We clicked, and at times, it scared me. But every time I talk to him, every time I'm in his presence, every time he touched me, whether it was a hug, or a forehead kiss, or whatever . . . I felt a chill crawl up my spine. Comfort and more spread throughout my body. And when I looked into his beautiful brown eyes, I saw nothing but genuineness and sincerity.

We were set to go out this weekend, and I was a little nervous about that. My girls kept telling me that this was a date date, and I kept trying to convince them it was not. They weren't having that, though. They liked him, and they liked him for me. I was trying to figure out how they came to that conclusion when they hadn't really been around him. They said that they could see the difference in me since he and I became friends. I couldn't see where I was different, but who was I to say they didn't see something in me that I couldn't see in myself?

I continued to talk with Dr. Thomas for another forty-five minutes before our time ended. After scheduling my next appointment, I headed out front. The driver that picked me up was waiting beside the SUV. I smiled and thanked him as I climbed into the truck. When I spoke to Callum last night, I told him about the therapy appointment I had today. The last thing I was expecting was for him to send a car to make sure I got to work afterward.

I immediately pulled out my phone to send Callum a thank-you once again.

Me: Thank you again for the ride. You didn't have to do that.

Callum: I know I didn't, but I wanted to. I know you don't like to ask for help, but I'm the type of friend who will provide it any way I can. I would have picked you up myself, but I am on a play date with Precious and my friend's s daughter.

Me: Tell my little friend I said hi.

Callum: I will. She's only asked about you fifty times today. I guess you're gonna have to come back over for dinner, huh?

Me: Lol. I might be able to make that happen.

We continued to talk as his driver took me back to work. When he pulled up, he got out and opened my door for me. I tried to tip him, but he assured me that it was all taken care of. I left him with a smile as I headed into the building.

Callum: You made it okay?

Me: Yes. I just walked in. Thank you again.

Callum: No problem, love.

"Hold it right there!" Avyn said, stopping me as I was walking to clock in.

I paused. "Is something wrong? Am I late? Did I do something wrong?"

A smile spread across her face. "You have a delivery."

My brows furrowed. "Of what?"

She stooped down, and when she stood again, she held the most beautiful crystal vase of red roses. My eyes widened, and my smile mimicked hers as I took the arrangement. I put them to my nose, inhaling deeply.

"Somebody was thinking about you, friend," Avyn said. "Read the card."

"Have you already read the card, Avyn?"

"I . . . might have snuck a peek."

I shook my head as I placed the vase on the counter and pulled the card out.

Hey, Beautiful,

I just wanted to brighten your day a little. I hope these make you smile that beautiful smile. I look forward to seeing you tomorrow.

Callum

I couldn't stop blushing and smiling. He really sent me flowers just because.

Avyn giggled. "Look at you! That man really likes you, boo. And was that one of his people dropping you off?"

"It was. I mentioned I had a therapy appointment to him last night. I didn't expect him to send me transportation. He's so thoughtful."

"I know you better make the most of this date tomorrow."

"It's not a date!" I protested.

"Is he picking you up? Did he plan it? Is he paying?"

I avoided her eyes. "Yes, yes, and yes."

"Then it's a date. Embrace it. You can put these in my office until you get off."

She left me with a smile. I picked up the vase, carried it to her office, and then headed to clock in. Before I did so, however, I took a moment to call Callum. His thank-you deserved to be heard, not read through a text message.

"Hey, beautiful." I could hear the smile in his voice.

"Mr. Ellis, you are something else."

"What did I do?"

"You know what you did." I giggled. "Thank you for the flowers. They are beautiful and my favorite. Nobody has sent me flowers in forever, let alone 'just because.' You trying to make me feel special or something?"

"You *are* special to me, Pasha. I don't know what it is . . . but you've got it. You've got *me*. I just wanna see you smile."

I blushed. "Well, mission accomplished."

He chuckled. "Have a good shift. A driver will be there to take you home when you get off."

"Thank you."

"Anytime, baby."

We disconnected the call. I rested my back against the wall, a huge smile on my face. As hard as I'd been trying to fight it, I had to accept that I liked this man. Maybe I didn't want to. Maybe I shouldn't have, but I did.

THE NEXT EVENING

I stood in front of my full-length mirror, turning from side to side, making sure that I looked okay. Callum told me to dress comfortably but still wouldn't indulge me in just what we were doing. I wasn't sure if I was too comfortable in the black cargo joggers, orange halter-styled body suit, and white canvas shoes.

"How long are we going to play this narrative?" Blake asked.

She, Avyn, and I were in my apartment as I got ready to go out with Callum. I think they loved being able to come here as much as I loved having a place of my own to come to. It felt like old times, back when I lived with my parents. They were always at my house.

I frowned as I stepped out of my closet. "What narrative?"

"That you're not dating the man you're dating?"

I sighed. "I've told y'all—"

"I know *what* you've told us. 'He's just a friend.' I call this bullshit. That man has been very, very intentional, okay? He's given you control of the narrative. He's been building your confidence.

He shows initiative, courtesy, and respect. You better snatch him up, Pasha."

"Y'all find it so hard to believe that maybe he just wants to be friends. I mean, I don't take him for shy. He wouldn't have any problems telling me he was into me if he really was."

"You better learn to read between the lines, girl." She rolled off my bed and stood before walking to the closet door. "I have to go to work, but please, send me pictures."

"I will."

She headed for the front door but called over her shoulder, "And take a shot for me!"

I nodded my head. "I will!"

Avyn appeared in the doorway with a bowl of Ramen. She stood against the wall with one leg crossed over the other, munching on the noodles. She shook her head at me.

"How many times are you going to look over yourself? You look fine, girl. Everything is sitting up, right and tight. The body is giving honey. Mr. Ellis is going to love you." She snapped her fingers.

I gave her a side eye. "I'm not about to play with you. Are you sure I look okay?"

She rolled he eyes. "Pasha, please don't make me smack you."

"I'm sorry! He refused to tell me what we were doing. All he said was to dress comfortably. I don't know if this is a good level of comfortable for me."

"Even if it isn't, you look cute. Didn't Beyoncé tell you that pretty hurts?"

I shook my head. "Somehow, I don't think this is what she meant. Anyway . . . do I look, you know . . . fat?"

She pushed off from the wall and placed her Ramen bowl on the dresser. She then turned and walked over to me. She turned me back to the mirror with her hands on my shoulders. Her arms came around me, and she hugged me tightly.

"You are absolutely beautiful, pooh. You deserve to embrace your body." Her hands went to my stomach. "You created and carried a life. You battled depression and anxiety along with losing a child and your parents. Nobody would look the same after the kinda trauma you had. You may have gained a little weight, but you are not fat. Most men, *real* men, appreciate a woman with meat on her bones. I've seen the way Callum looks at you. He likes *all* of this."

She playfully pretended to hump me from behind. I couldn't help but laugh as I pushed her off of me.

"My point is, fuck other people. My good sis Sheryl Lee Ralph said it best. People don't have to like you. They don't have to love you. They don't even have to respect you. But when you look in the mirror, you better love the person you see. Remember your affirmations."

I nodded. "I hear you."

Someone knocked on my door. I looked over at the clock on the wall.

"That's probably Callum. Would you mind getting the door? I need a minute."

"I've got you."

She left the space, and I took a few deep breaths. Grabbing my crossbody, I stuffed my phone, keys, wallet, and other essentials inside. I could hear Callum laughing with Avyn, and my heart began to race.

"Calm down, girl . . ." I told myself.

After strategically spraying on my perfume, I left the bedroom area and walked out into the living room. My breath hitched as my eyes landed on Callum. He wore black shorts, a short-sleeve white button-up, and a pair of black sneakers. A simple gold watch and chain were his jewelry of choice. His outfit was simple, but God, did he look delicious.

He looked up from his conversation with Avyn. I didn't miss how his eyes perused me from head to toe. He licked his lips, and a smile spread across his face. Stepping away from Avyn, he came into my space and pulled me into a hug. God, he smelled so good. I closed my eyes and allowed his scent to engulf me.

He kissed my forehead. "You look amazing. Orange is certainly your color."

I blushed. "Thank you."

"Are you ready?"

"Ready to see what you are about to get me into since you've been secretive."

He chuckled. "It wasn't a secret. I just want you to have fun without thinking about it. We are gonna relieve some stress."

"Mmm," Avyn moaned in the background. I shot her a look. "My bad, girl. I'm just gonna head upstairs. You two kids have fun and don't stay out too late. You have my girl in at a respectable hour, sir. Nothing is open late but legs."

"Avyn!" I exclaimed.

She laughed as she headed out my front door. I shook my head.

"I'm sorry about that. She has no filter."

"I promise, it's okay. I like her. She's unapologetically herself."

"Always."

He offered me his arm. "Shall we?"

I linked my arm through his. "We shall."

I wasn't sure what this "friend date" would entail, but I was ready for whatever it had in store.

CHAPTER
TWENTY-TWO

Callum

IT WAS BECOMING harder and harder to hide my attraction to this woman. I found her beautiful even when she wasn't at her best, but seeing her lately . . . that just did something to me. Growth and happiness were beautiful on her. I knew she was still dealing with a lot, but she had so much to be happy about these days. Seeing her genuinely smile did my heart all the good in the world.

The first stop of the night was a Riot Room. I knew she had stressors because I was dealing with stressors of my own. This was the perfect place for us to release some of that tension.

"Is this one of those smash rooms or whatever you call it?" she asked, looking around.

"Yes."

"God, I needed this. I can't tell you how many times I've just wanted to break some shit."

"Well, you can break all you want here."

I got us checked in, and we were led to our room. She didn't hesitate to suit up in the vest, gloves, and a face shield. After a brief rundown of rules and expectations, we were left alone. She eagerly grabbed a bat and went to work. When she smashed the first item, she took a deep breath. I could tell that felt good to her.

"Stay with it," I said. "You can fuck up as much shit in here as you want until you get it out."

"This is what I wanted to do the night you stopped for me."

She dragged the bat around the room until she found what she sought. It was a mirror. She raised the bat again.

"For all the times he called me fat."

Whack!

"For all the times he made me feel ugly and worthless."

Whack!

"For all the times he made me hate myself!"

Whack!

All the mirror pieces shattered and fell to the floor. She moved around the room, smashing the bat into various objects. She had stopped talking and was now channeling all of her anger. Her hits became harder and more forceful. I could only imagine that it was that man's image in her head every time that bat connected.

After a few minutes, she dropped the bat and leaned over, resting her hands on her knees, panting heavily.

"Feeling better?" I asked.

"That was liberating. I didn't realize I had that much rage built up."

"Look at how long you had to hold it in."

She stood upright and wiped the sweat from her brow. "I'm ready to go again. Are you going to join me? I know there has to be something you're angry about . . . something you want to get out."

I had enough to be upset about. After my uncle's funeral, my aunt Sheila and aunt Glenda popped up at my house to check me about coming and then leaving. They accused me of trying to start trouble, and that wasn't the case. I wouldn't have waited seventeen years if I wanted to start trouble. The whole visit started a big argument and a slew of unwanted pop-ups at my house.

One of the cousins who had been present during my parents' will reading showed up on some "putting me in my place" type of energy, and we almost came to blows. If it weren't for Martin stepping in, things could have gone completely left. One thing I didn't play about was disrupting my peace. Coming to the place where I lay my head and starting drama was a big *hell no*. Not only that, but this was also my parents' home, and *nobody* was going to disrespect that.

Picking up the sledgehammer I'd chosen as my weapon of choice, I crashed it into an old computer monitor. Pieces flew everywhere. Damn, that felt good. Pasha and I looked at each other and gave a simple nod before we tore that room apart. Nothing went untouched. By the time we finished, both of us were breathing heavily. She dropped the bat and came over to me.

Gentle brown eyes stared up at me. Slowly, she wrapped her arms around me and rested her head against my chest.

"Thank you, Callum. I didn't know how badly I needed that."

I embraced her warmly and kissed the top of her head. "I've got you. Whatever you need, I've got you."

We stood like that for a while until she pulled away.

"How about we go get something to eat?" I suggested. "I don't know about you, but I worked up an appetite."

"Me too."

"There's this food truck that has the best tacos you'll ever taste. It's down at the park. And there's this festival type of thing going on."

"I'm good with that."

"Well, let's get out of this stuff, and we can head on over."

"Okay."

We quickly left the space and undressed to head to the car. I was surprised when Pasha linked her fingers through mine for the short walk. She looked up at me with a smile, and I swear my heart swelled in its cavity. I lifted her fingers to my lips and kissed them. Maybe this wasn't a date date, but it sure as hell felt like one.

Pasha moaned, and her eyes closed as she took the first bit of the nachos I recommended. I looked up to see an almost euphoric expression on her beautiful face.

"Good?" I asked.

"That . . . Whew! That is amazing. I've never had nachos so flavorful."

"They are based in Charleston. I found them during a day trip with Bella and Precious. When I tell you I can taste this every time I think about it, I swear I'm not lying."

"They gave me so much! I don't know how I'm gonna eat this and the rest of this food!"

We had a spread of nachos, chicken on a stick, and loaded fries. I really hadn't eaten all day because I wanted to prepare my stomach for this.

I chuckled. "I know what you mean. Just make sure you save room for something sweet."

She stifled a laugh. "You sound like my late grandfather. It didn't matter what he ate. When he finished, it was always, '*Now I need something sweet*,' to follow."

"We are eating for the culture, baby."

She smiled. "I'm having a good time."

"That's all I wanted."

"You know . . ." She cleared her throat. "My girls seem to think something is going on between us."

"Do they now?"

"I've told them we are just friends, but they don't believe me." She looked up at me, her eyes piercing mine. "They seem to think you've been dating me, and I've just kinda been blind to it."

I swallowed my food and took a sip of my drink. After wiping my mouth, I leaned across the table a little, and she did the same.

"I will say this . . . I've been very intentional in my treatment of you. Make no mistake, I respect you as a woman. I value your friendship, but I believe that we were placed in each other's path for a reason. I don't know what it is, but I haven't been able to get you out of my head since the first time I met you. You are so beautiful to me, Pasha. Beneath the hurt and pain, I know there is an equally beautiful soul, and I just want to nurture it the way it deserves to be nurtured."

She blushed and covered her face. I slid closer to her and pulled her hands away.

"You don't have to be shy with me. You don't have to be afraid or worry. I'm not here to hurt you. I simply want to restore what was once broken by someone who never deserved you. I have to ask . . . Do *you* feel anything between us?"

"Yes," she whispered. "You just . . . You feel good to my spirit. I can't deny that."

"Then don't." I cupped her face. "Whenever you're ready to explore this, I'll be waiting for you."

A tear slipped from her eye, and I swiped it away.

I smiled softly. "Don't cry."

"I can't help it!" She fanned herself. "I wasn't looking for this, and now, here you are." She gripped my wrists as she gazed into my eyes. "I'm afraid to fall for you, but more than that, I'm afraid I won't be able to stop myself."

I wanted to reassure her. I wanted her to feel that everything I could put into this was genuine. I brought my face close to hers.

"Can I kiss you?" I asked.

Her breath hitched in her throat, and for a moment, she was still. Then slowly, she nodded her head. Gently, I pressed my lips to hers. I didn't grip or grope her. I wanted this kiss to be sweet, sensual, and comforting. She relaxed, and I felt her lips part. When her tongue slipped into my mouth, I swear it was the sweetest thing I'd ever tasted. A soft moan escaped her lips, and the sound caused her to pull back and place her hands on my chest. Her eyes remained closed.

"I could lose myself with you," she whispered.

I pressed my forehead to hers. "I'll never let you get lost."

She opened her eyes. Her hands slid up my chest to my face. She stared at me for a moment before wrapping them around my neck and pulling me into a tight hug.

"Just hold me for a little bit," she said softly.

I slid my arms around her waist and pulled her in closer. "As long as you need."

CHAPTER
TWENTY-THREE
Pasha

I COULDN'T BELIEVE I'D kissed this man.

More than that, I couldn't believe how much I liked it. His lips were so soft and sweet. When that moan escaped my lips, I had to end it. My mind told me to stop, but my body screamed to keep going. I felt a quiver in my lower region. I felt palpitations in my heart. I felt my nipples hardening against the pasties I wore beneath this strapless bra.

I hadn't been aroused in so long . . . touched in so long. My hormones went into an absolute frenzy. I'd never needed a cold shower so badly. How we could slip back into casual conversation after that was beyond me. One thing was for sure: I couldn't wait to get back to my girls and tell them everything.

The food truck festival was quite an experience. We'd eaten to our hearts' content, and now, we were talking around visiting other vendor tables. Like the farmers' market on Sundays, this one had a host of homemade goods. I picked up a few pairs of earrings and necklaces, a few scarves, and a handwoven purse that was too cute to pass up. Callum swooped in when I tried to pay for my items, telling me that as long as I was in his presence, I'd never have to go in my wallet.

The lady selling the purse smiled at that one. *"You better keep him, girl,"* she whispered to me. All I could do was blush. I'd been doing that all damn night. The man had me smiling so much that my cheeks hurt. I couldn't deny how happy I felt being with him. Raymond hadn't crossed my mind not one time, and the silence in that was so beautiful.

We'd been walking around for about an hour when we came upon a band playing island music. Couples had stopped to dance to it. When he pulled me toward the band, I started to protest.

"Callum! I can't dance!" I said, laughing.

"I got you. Just let me lead, and you follow."

I didn't have time to protest again before his arm snaked around my waist, and he pulled me into his chest. My body melted into his, immediately relinquishing all control. Slowly, he swayed, and I followed his movements. A smile spread across his face.

"There you go . . . move your hips a little."

I did as he said. It felt a little awkward at first, but I was soon able to catch the beat and keep up with him. Just as I caught a good rhythm, he spun me out and back in, pinning my back to his chest. His arms came around me once more. His head nestled against mine as he softly kissed my temple and cheeks.

"I could hold you like this all the time," he whispered in my ear.

"I might let you."

He chuckled. "You smell so good, Pasha. So sweet. So . . . delectable."

His hands gently caressed my midsection. For a moment, I felt self-conscious and tried to pull away.

"No," he said firmly. "I appreciate every inch of you, baby. Every single part of you is so beautiful to me." He dropped a kiss on my shoulder, causing me to expel a deep breath.

For the remainder of the song, I allowed him to hold me like that as he swayed me from side to side to the music. I felt so much comfort and peace in his arms. When this night came to an end, I was sure I'd be able to feel his body close to mine, even when we parted ways. The song ended, and he released me but grabbed my hand.

"How about that dessert?" he asked.

"I'm ready. I think I've walked that food down."

"It's a short trip around the corner. We can walk or drive."

"I'm okay with walking."

"Let's get to it then."

Hand in hand, we waded through the crowd. About ten minutes later, we came upon a bakery called Ms. Carol's.

"Is this the lady who made those cookies you inhaled at the farmers' market?" I asked, remembering the logo on the front.

He laughed. "First of all, don't come for me like that. Second, yes, this is her. She'll be closing soon, but I told her we were stopping by."

He pulled the door open and guided me inside. The bakery was small, but it was cute. It gave Grandma's Sweets vibes, and when Ms. Carol walked out to greet us, I understood why. She smiled wide as Callum pulled her in for a hug.

"There's my favorite customer," she said, patting his back.

"Hey, Ms. Carol. Thank you for staying open for us."

"Of course." She pulled back and cupped his face. "When you told me you were bringing a lady friend, I just had to meet her." She turned to me and reached for my hands. "Let me get a look at you . . . Ooooh, she's just as beautiful as you said she was, Callum."

I smiled. "Thank you, ma'am."

"And she has manners! I love her for you already. What's your name, baby?"

"Pasha."

"Pasha? Oh, that's pretty!" She patted my hand. "Come on, sugar. I've got something special just for y'all. Callum, lock that door."

He did as she requested as she led me to a table with three different desserts for us to sample. The first was a strawberry crunch cookie, then an Oreo cheesecake parfait, followed by what she called a cinnamon roll cake. The portions were big enough for us to share, but the way Callum was eyeballing that cake, I wasn't sure about that. Everything looked so good and smelled even better.

"You spoil me, Ms. Carol," Callum declared.

Ms. Carol grabbed two bottles of water and brought them to us. "Oh, hush. You know I love you." She kissed his cheek.

"You know I love you back."

"Has he shown you how hardheaded he is yet?" she asked me. "He has stopped in here faithfully twice a week for the last five years. Every time he comes to the farmers' market, I try to give him something on the house, and every time I turn my back, he slips me money anyway."

I giggled. "I think that's sweet."

She looked at him lovingly. "It is. He always says he won't take advantage of my kindness. He will make some woman a very lucky, happy spouse one day." She looked between the two of us. "You two make a beautiful pair. Are you from around here, honey?"

"Yes, ma'am. Born and raised."

"Who are your people?"

"Oh . . . Well, my parents were Virginia and Soloman Brooks. They passed away a few years ago."

"I'm so sorry! Please forgive me."

"It's okay," I assured her. "It's overwhelming at times, but I know that when I'm no longer here, I get to be with them again."

"To be absent from the body is to be present with the Lord. They are in good hands."

"Yes, ma'am."

We sat in the bakery chatting with Ms. Carol for a good hour. Once we finished with those delectable desserts, Callum offered to help her wipe down the front. It turned into him wiping down while she and I talked. He didn't complain. He simply smiled and went about his business. I thought the way she spoke about him was so sweet, and I could tell she cared for him.

"I have to ask," she said when he went to the back to grab a mop, "You really like my boy?"

I blushed. "Yes, ma'am. I wasn't expecting to, but he makes it hard not to like him with him being the person he is."

She smiled. "He's a good boy, and he has the purest heart. I know he'll be good to you, sugar. Promise me you'll be good to him too. He deserves all the love he pours into others. Promise me you'll treat him right."

"I promise."

She smiled as Callum came back out. "Okay, you've worked enough," she said, standing.

"I don't mind mopping for you," he protested.

"I mind. You're on a date, and I've stolen enough of your time. Take this pretty lady and get on out of here."

"Ms. Carol—"

"You heard what I said." She took the mop from him. "Go on. Enjoy the rest of your evening. I hope it's a good one."

Callum shook his head as he walked over to me. "You ready?"

"Yes. Thank you again, Ms. Carol. I'll be back to feed my sweet tooth."

She laughed. "I'll be waiting for you, baby. Y'all have a good night."

We said our goodbyes. Then Callum grabbed my hand and led me to the door and back out onto the street.

"I think it's safe to say she likes you," he commented.

"I like her too. She reminds me of my grandmother." I looked up at him. "She's very fond of you."

He smirked as he slipped his arms around my waist. "I'm a very likable guy."

"You are. Is that how you woo women, Mr. Ellis?"

"I don't know about wooing these women you speak of. I've been single for a few years now."

"So, there's never been a potential Mrs. Ellis?"

"Nope. Not even close. If there were a potential Mrs. Ellis, there'd be no potential for you and me. I like the possibility of there being a you and me."

He leaned in and kissed me. Once again, my body went on a rampage against me. I felt weak in the knees, and if he hadn't been holding me up, I was sure I would have fallen right to the ground. When he pulled away, he wiped the corners of my mouth.

"Yeah . . . I like that possibility a lot."

Jesus, be a fence!

Callum and I took the short stroll back to the food truck festival area. While the crowd had thinned out a little, there were still many people. The music was still going, and we couldn't walk past it without him pulling me into another dance. As awkward as I felt I looked, I'd quickly fallen in love with dancing with him. He was light on his feet but playful at the same time, and it made me laugh.

Before I knew it, we'd been out there for another hour. It was after midnight by the time we returned to his truck.

"You aren't as stiff as you said," he jested.

I playfully smacked his arm. "Whatever. I haven't had this much fun in a while," I said as he opened the passenger door.

"Don't go spoiling me with a good time, Mr. Ellis. I might get used to it."

"You should." He helped me into the truck and buckled me in. "Simple pleasures make me a happy man. And seeing that smile on your pretty face . . . that just makes my day."

He playfully planted several pecks all over my cheeks, causing me to giggle like a schoolgirl until that obnoxious snort came out. That made him laugh.

"Wait until I tell Bella you're a snorter too!"

"Get in the truck!" I exclaimed.

He snuck another kiss before closing the door and rounding the driver's side. I sat back with a smile on my face. When he climbed in, I looked at him admirably.

God . . . If you sent me this man, please don't let him break my heart, I prayed.

It was crazy. I'd never prayed about a man before, not even Raymond. Callum was nothing like I'd ever experienced. He did a number on my heart and mind. If he was for me, I needed the Big Guy to hear my prayers. I couldn't survive another heartbreak . . . I just couldn't.

Twelve thirty on the dot, we pulled into my building's parking lot. After finding a spot, he got out and came to my side to help me out. Hand in hand, we walked into the building. On the elevator, I stood in front of him with his hands resting on my shoulders.

"You know what?" he stated. "We didn't take a single photo to commemorate this evening."

"We didn't." I turned to face him. "I think your contact deserves a picture at the point."

I pulled out my phone and snapped a picture of him. When I showed it to him, he took the phone and pulled me close to him.

"Smile, baby."

I put on my best smile as he snapped a picture of both of us. I had to admit, it was cute. We did make a nice-looking pair.

"I think you should use that one," he said. "You make me look good, woman."

"Ooooh, you are laying it on thick, Mr. Ellis."

I laughed as the elevator stopped and the door dinged open. He grabbed my hand and pulled me out, leading me down the hallway toward my front door. When we reached it, I turned to him, pressing my back against the door.

"I guess this is good night." I looked up at him. "I had a really good time."

"Me too. Thank you for agreeing to my taking you out. Maybe next time, I can take you on a formal date."

"I'd like that . . . a lot."

I stepped closer to him, a bold move for me. My hands slid up his chest to his face, an even bolder move. The boldest move of all was me standing on my toes, wrapping my arms around his neck, and pressing my lips to his. I went as far as opening my mouth to receive his tongue to caress mine. My hands caressed the back of his head and neck as the kiss deepened.

It wasn't until the elevator dinged and the doors opened that we finally came up for air. Kelli, the neighbor I sometimes spoke to and had a casual conversation with, smirked as she walked past us to her door.

"Oh, please, don't let me stop you," she said, winking at me.

I knew my face was red. "Hey, Kelli," I mumbled, palming my forehead.

"Hey, girl . . . Bye, girl!" She disappeared into her apartment, her cackling echoing in the air.

"I should probably get going," Callum voiced. "Kissing you is dangerous for me." Even as he said it, he leaned in for another peck to my lips. "Sleep well, beautiful."

"You too."

I turned and slipped my key into the lock. Once it disengaged, I pushed the door open and stepped inside. When I turned back, I caught the tail end of a smile as Callum walked away. Closing the door, I leaned against it. My fingers went to my lips. I could still feel his against mine. I felt the gentle pulling as he sucked on the bottom one. He was right. Our kissing was dangerous for both of us.

I treaded into my bedroom and stripped down to get into the shower. Thirty minutes later, on my phone, I scrolled to the picture Callum and I had taken on the elevator. While I was smiling and looking at the camera, he was smiling and looking at me.

My nail glided over his handsome face. God did his big one with this man. I went through the motions of assigning the picture to his contact. His message thread popped up, and I found myself scrolling through it. There were countless words of affirmation and encouragement sprinkled throughout our messages. He was funny and loved to send me dad jokes. So much of him reminded me of my father, and I loved my daddy to pieces.

I ended up swiping the video call button. It rang three times before he answered shirtless and dripping in water droplets. For a moment, all I could do was stare at him.

"Pacha? You okay, love?"

The sound of his voice startled me. "Huh?"

"You froze up on me."

"I'm sorry. I got distracted. I just wanted to make sure you got home safe."

He smiled. "I'm home. Fresh out of the shower and getting ready for bed."

I lay back against the pillow. "Okay, well, I guess I'll let you go then. I'm about to lay it down myself."

"Wait. How would you feel about having dinner at my house on Sunday? I'll have Bella and the family come over. We can invite Malcolm and Avyn. I have another friend I can invite too. Just a family dinner, nothing big."

I was glad he suggested inviting more people. I wasn't sure I was ready to be alone with him in his home yet.

"That sounds nice."

"Great."

"Should I bring anything?"

"Just you, baby."

I smiled. "Okay. Well, I'll see you Sunday."

"See you then. Good night."

"Good night."

I ended the call and tossed the phone onto my dresser. My eyes closed, and all I could see was his face. I could feel his lips and hands all over me. My hands glided over my body, pretending that they were his. What was he doing to me? I knew what I *imagined* him doing to me. A moan slipped from my lips as my hands palmed my breasts. My nipples were already so sensitive that when I pinched them, I gasped.

"Ooooh . . ."

A hand slipped beneath my shirt and between my thighs. I found nothing but a slick center and a throbbing clit. It had been so long . . . too long. Using my middle and ring fingers, I massaged small circles around the sensitive bundle of nerves. The sensation caused my back to arch from the bed.

I hissed. "Shit . . ."

Blindly, I reached and felt around in my dresser with a free hand. When my fingers touched the items I was looking for, I pulled out the dildo and rose gifted to me by my girls. Neither had been put to use yet, but they'd been cleaned and ready to go. Slowly, I eased as much of the dildo into my wetness as I could handle.

Closing my eyes, I imagined that this was Callum. I imagined that he was slow stoking me while those beautiful brown eyes that made me swoon gazed into mine. I imagined my legs on his shoulders while he fed me inch after inch, forcing me to take all of him with every stroke.

"Oh . . . oh, my God . . ."

I panted heavily as I worked the dildo in and out of my wetness. My legs spread farther apart as I reached for the rose and turned it on to setting three, which Avyn told me was her favorite. The moment I placed it on my clit, my body violently began to jerk. I gasped as the powerful sensation forced my back to arch from the bed once again. Over and over, I filled my center with the beautiful, ten-inch monster. The more I stroked myself, the wetter I became.

"Shit!" I cried out, feeling my orgasm creeping up on me.

It hadn't even been five minutes, yet this little combo had me ready to tap out. Between the vibrations on my clit and the stretching of my tight walls, I couldn't hold back much longer. I closed my eyes and fully let the sensations flowing through my body engulf me. Audible cries filled the space as my body expelled one of the most powerful orgasms I'd ever had of my own doing.

Even as my body quaked and shook, I couldn't pull the rose away. When that second orgasm hit me, I felt like I lost all control of myself as I squirted, something I'd never done before. I fell back against the pillows, panting with tears streaming down my cheeks. Stars burst behind my eyes as I gazed up at the ceiling.

Damn it! Now I have to change my sheets.

CHAPTER TWENTY-FOUR
Callum

BELLA EYED ME as we moved about my kitchen. I knew she was wondering about the permanent smile on my face. When I told her to come over for a family dinner today, the first thing she asked was who all was coming. Once I ran the list to her, she was okay. She said she hoped I wasn't trying to play peacemaker in our current family drama. I assured her that dinner would be with the family we created, not the one we were born into.

"Why are you smiling so hard? Does this have anything to do with that date you won't tell me about?"

I chuckled. "You are so nosy."

"And you know this, so I don't know why you insist on torturing me. Give me the details. Did you and Pasha have a good time? What did you do?" She gasped. "Did you kiss her? Oh my God, you kissed her. That's why you're smiling so hard!"

I shook my head. "Yes, we had a good time. We went to a riot room to relieve some stress, then to a food truck festival, then to Miss Carol's for dessert—"

She smacked my arm. "You went there and didn't bring me anything back!"

"Bella, you were the last thing on my mind that night."

"I see how you do me. So . . . Did you kiss her?"

"Why are you in my business?"

"Again, you *are* my business."

I rolled my eyes. "Yes, we kissed. A couple of times, in fact."

She squealed in excitement. "She's comfortable with you. I love that for her."

I scoffed. "What about me?"

"Of course, I love that for you too. But after everything that she's gone through, I'm just happy that she's allowing herself to get close to someone again. I know that couldn't have been easy for her."

"It wasn't easy at all. But I knew that beforehand. I just remained consistent."

"Precious is so excited to see her today. She's been asking when she could come back over for dinner."

"Not my niece trying to steal my woman before I make her my woman."

"My baby says she wants an auntie and cousins. We've discussed this, Callum."

"Please don't make me put you out of my house before everyone else gets here."

"First of all, half of this house will always be mine. You can't get rid of me. Besides, what would you do without me?"

"Have a party."

I bent down to grab a pot from the cabinet, and she got me in a headlock. There we were in the middle of the kitchen, tussling. Now, I would never let her know she got the better of me, but she had a pretty good grip. Even the sounds of approaching footsteps did not make her let up.

Martin laughed as he stepped into the kitchen. "Children, children!" he said, clapping his hands. "No fighting in the kitchen. You're setting a bad example for the little one."

We looked up to see Precious grinning.

"I wanna play!" she squealed as she ran over, jumped on my back, and tickled my sides.

Even at my big age, I was ticklish, and baby girl loved to capitalize off that. I started laughing, and the three of us hit the floor. Bella pinned me down while Precious continued to tickle me. Martin just stood there, watching with a grin on his face. The man didn't make the first move to help me. When the doorbell rang, he walked off like he didn't witness me being assaulted.

"I concede!" I yelled.

"I don't know what that means!" Precious yelled back.

That only made my sister laugh harder. She used to do the same shit to me when we were kids. Sometimes, we got so loud that my parents would run in, thinking that we were trying to kill each other.

"What is going on?" Chris asked, appearing in the archway with Armani on his hip and Eva and their sons at his side.

Martin chuckled. "Please tell your friend that he is too big and too old to be ticklish."

Chris laughed. "Yeah, man. And how did you let Bella's little self pin you down?"

"She caught me off guard, man."

Martin shook his head. "Y'all are the two biggest kids when you get together."

"Well, I think it's sweet," Eva said. "My siblings that I would be fighting for real."

I scooped Precious up from the floor, then reached out a hand to help Bella up as well. "Why don't you and Eva take the kids and go find you something to do? The guys are going to cook tonight."

Eva laughed. "You know what that means, Bella. They're about to gossip. And you talk about women. Men gossip just as much, if not more, than we do. You just call it 'shooting the shit.'"

"Ooooh! Swear jar, Mommy!" Armani exclaimed.

"Ugh! I was doing so good! Remind me when we get home, baby girl. Come on, Bella boo. We can let the kids play outside while we sip wine and gossip ourselves."

"I think I like that idea. Nobody wants to hear their funky little gossip anyway."

She mushed my head before going into my fridge and grabbing a bottle. After getting two glasses, she and Eva took them out to the back patio with the girls. Just the other week, I bought a playground set for Precious to play on while she was here. She and Armani were sure to work up an appetite.

"Is Malcolm coming?" Chris asked, going into the fridge for a beer.

"He said he's on the way to pick up the girls now, and they'll be here shortly."

"So, did him and ol' girl make it official?"

I shrugged. "Man, I can't really tell you what's going on with that. All I know is he's waiting around for her to commit."

"More power to him." Chris popped the cap on his beer and took a long swig. "So you and Pasha? Is that a thing now?"

"It's . . . something I'm not quite sure what, but it's not what it used to be. She let me kiss her, so I think it's safe to assume we're moving in some kind of direction."

Both of their eyes widened, and Martin was the first to speak. "How did that even come about?"

"She told me that her friends are convinced that something more is happening between us. I let her know that I've been very intentional in the way that I handle her. I didn't just go for the kill. I asked her if I could kiss her."

I bit my lip, reminiscing about the number of kisses we shared Friday night. Every kiss was better than the last one, but the one in front of her door was the best. She initiated that one. She took charge and went after what she wanted. How could I not oblige her?

Chris smirked. "Look at him over there thinking about it now."

"He's been smiling since we got here," Martin revealed.

"You know, you are just like your wife . . . in my business."

He playfully slapped my back. "It's all love, bro. If you're happy, I'm happy. The only time I see you smile like this is with my baby. If someone else can make you feel like that, then I'm all for it."

"So when is this divorce gonna be final?" Chris asked. "Have you had any more run-ins with the soon-to-be ex-husband?"

"She told me it would be final thirty days after they last went to court. That was about a week and a half ago, so she will be a single woman in two and a half weeks. And, no, we have not had any run-ins with that bastard. Maybe it's the fact that she let him keep everything that keeps him from calling her on a blocked number like he had been."

"I don't even know that man, and I want to put hands on him," Chris stated. "If Eva and I ever broke up, she could have whatever she wanted. I may bring in the money, but she is the one that makes the household run as smoothly as it does. If something is off with her, something is off with me. You have to take care of your home first in marriage. That's the problem with a lot of unions. There's no communication, only expectations."

"You right about that," Martin agreed. "Bella and I share everything, no matter how ugly it is. It's always gonna be us against the world in our house. Ain't no divorce. You mad? Come talk this shit out, and let's see how we can work this out together."

I knew he wasn't just saying that for my benefit. He loved my sister differently than I did, but with the same intensity. Nobody could ever play in his face about her. I didn't have many married friends, but these two were the type I'd surround myself with. We shared like-minded views on marriage and relationships. I knew if I were ever on the wrong side of right, they would call me out on my shit and tell me to get myself together. Men held other men accountable for their actions. Clearly, nobody ever held Raymond Sinclaire accountable. But it was cool, though. I had plans to show his soon-to-be ex-wife everything she'd been missing, and then some.

Dinner was well underway with cooking when Malcolm finally showed up with Avyn and Pasha. From my kitchen window, I saw them pull up. Turning my pot down to simmer, I headed out to greet them. When I stepped onto the front porch and saw Pasha get out of the car in that floral jumpsuit, my heart began racing. Her hair was beautiful in its natural, curly state. Her face held a light beat of makeup, and she wore the same necklace and wristwatch I'd been seeing her in lately.

My baby was gorgeous.

When she saw me, she smiled. I made my way down the steps to greet them.

"Nice of you to join us," I jested with Malcolm.

"My bad, man. I got off work a little later than planned."

I nodded as I hugged Avyn. "Thank you for coming."

"Thank you for having me. I told Malcolm I could have driven us over here, but he insisted on picking us up."

Malcolm waved her off. "I told you I would, and I always keep my word."

I slid past them to Pasha and took her hands in mine. "You look amazing, love."

She blushed. "Thank you. You sure this isn't too much?"

"Nah, this . . ." I stepped back to get another good look at her, "This is perfection."

I pulled her into my arms and leaned in to kiss her. She didn't hesitate to kiss me back. For a moment, I forgot all about our friends standing right there.

"That's my girl," Avyn said, faking tears. "That's *my* girl!"

Pasha and I parted ways, both of us grinning at her.

"Don't start, Avyn," she warned her.

"What? I'm just here for this beautiful-ass couple. Thank you for making my boo smile like this."

"She deserves it," I said, looking back at Pasha. "She deserves everything." I pecked her lips again and grabbed her hand. "Come on, I want to introduce you two to everybody."

I led them inside. As soon as we walked into the house, everybody scrambled like they'd been doing something they had no business doing. I chuckled, knowing they had probably been watching us from the window. Precious ran right up to Pasha and jumped in her arms.

"Hey, friend!" she said, wrapping her little arms around Pasha's neck.

"Hey, friend. I missed you!"

She kissed her cheek before she placed her back on her feet. I smiled at their interaction.

"Y'all, this is Avyn and Pasha. Pasha, you already know Martin and Bella. But this is my friend, Chris, his wife, Eva, and their daughter, Armani, and their sons, CJ and Evan."

Both Pasha and Avyn offered warm smiles. "It's nice to meet you all."

"Yes," Avyn agreed. "Thank you for having us."

Bella clasped her hands. "Well! Since we were told to find something to do with ourselves while the men cook, ladies, why don't you join Eva and me out back for some wine?"

"Say less!" Avyn held up a bag. "We brought wine too."

Bella giggled. "I like you already. Come on."

She, Eva, Armani, and Precious all walked off toward the back. Pasha tried to follow, but I held her back.

"Wait a minute," I said, pulling her into my chest. "Can I get a moment alone with you?"

She blushed. "Okay."

The fellas grinned and shook their heads as I led her to my bedroom. Closing the door, I motioned for her to sit on the bed. She took a seat and crossed her legs. I took notice of the new polish on her fingers and toes. Today, she was sporting hot pink on both.

"I like this color on you," I said, picking up her hand.

"You noticed?"

"I notice everything about you, baby. I'm paying attention even when you think I'm not."

She smiled as she palmed my cheek. "I . . . I missed you. Is that weird?"

"Nah. I missed you too. I've been anxious for you to get here, and now I don't wanna share you."

She giggled. "You have a houseful of guests."

"I can send them home with to-go plates."

"Callum!"

I chuckled. "I'm playing. Can you stay a little longer tonight? I'll take you home."

"I can. I'm off tomorrow. I don't have any plans other than car shopping."

"You're finally ready?"

"I am. I have enough for a down payment or something I can pay cash for. I was going to ask you to come with me if you weren't busy. I don't know much about cars and don't want to get swindled because of that."

"Of course. I got you."

"Thank—"

I gave her a look that cut her off. She giggled as she shook her head.

"I appreciate you."

She leaned in and cupped my face, softly kissing my lips. I pulled her into my lap, and my arms went around her waist, pulling her closer. I captured her lips once more as my hands roamed her body respectfully. When she started grinding on me, I couldn't will my dick not to brick up in response.

"Pasha . . . baby . . . You are gonna start some trouble if you keep doing that."

She giggled as she wrapped her arms around my neck and kissed me deeper. The grinding hadn't stopped, and now my dick was straining against my pants. My hands migrated to her ass, giving it a gentle squeeze, followed by a hard slap. She moaned against my mouth, and that shit turned me on so damn bad.

"I know y'all better get out here!" Bella called from the door, forcing us to break apart. Pasha looked at me, and I looked at her before we both burst into laughter.

"We're coming. Damn!" I hollered at the door.

"Figuratively or—"

"Bella Jane!"

She cackled as I heard her footsteps trail off. I shook my head.

"Let's get back out there before the rest of them start coming looking for us."

I sat up and stood with her in my arms. She clung to me as though she thought I would drop her.

"Don't worry . . . I can hold you just fine, baby."

Kissing her lips, I placed her on her feet. We headed back out front with everybody, only to be greeted with grins and shakes of the head. I guess I really had been single for a while. I never brought women around that I wasn't serious about. I was serious about Pasha. The more time I spent with her, the more I wanted to spend with her.

I cared for her.

Dare I say . . . I was falling for her?

CHAPTER TWENTY-FIVE

Pasha

I HEADED OUT TO the patio area where the women were gathered, sipping wine and watching the girls play. When I stepped outside, they all turned to look at me with grins on their faces.

"What?" I asked, taking a seat and crossing my legs.

"Oh, nothing," Avyn looked me over. "Nothing looks out of place."

"That's because nothing happened!" I exclaimed. "We just talked . . . and kissed a little."

She squealed. "Kelli told me that man was slobbering you down in the hallway after your date. You should have let him in."

Bella pretended to gag. "Um, hello? That's my brother, and that's nasty. Pasha, I like you, boo, but I don't want to think about Callum getting busy with anybody. That man raised me, for goodness' sake."

"I get it. Don't discuss my nonexistent sex life with your brother with you."

"Thank you! However . . . on a related note, you deserve to get some, girl."

"Hell yeah, she does," Avyn agreed. "Allow that man to pop that proverbial cherry again. You know you want him."

Bella giggled. "Besides, I heard that moan when you were in his bedroom. Unless my ears were mistaken, I heard an ass slap too. I know those anywhere!"

I palmed my forehead. I was going to die of embarrassment before I got a chance to devour whatever the guys were cooking.

"Bella, don't embarrass her," Eva said, coming to my defense. She offered me a smile. "You look like a good girl. Don't follow this heathen."

Avyn laughed. "She has her own personal heathen right here."

Eva shrugged. "I tried, girl."

If they knew about my solo sessions with Callum in mind for the past two nights, they would absolutely think that I was a heathen too. The suction cup bottom on that dildo had really come in handy. Masturbation had been foreign to me for years now. I wasn't in a headspace to be aroused. I didn't want Raymond to touch me, but I couldn't say no, and it was so unenjoyable for me.

Sometimes, I would fake it, and when I couldn't force myself to do that, I just lay there. He didn't care enough to get up, so why would I care enough to pretend for his ego? My mental health caused my sex drive to suffer. Being in that house day in and day out, all alone or with him, feeling alone, did a number on me. It took me awhile to realize it because I was so hurt, but leaving me was the best thing Raymond could have done for me.

Being without him healed so much of what was broken inside of me. I woke up to peace these days. I went to bed with a clear mind most nights. I didn't have to deal with constant belittling or degrading comments. Maybe I had a ways to go with fully accepting myself, but I was slowly falling in love with this version of me. This version breathed easier. She walked lighter. She showed confidence on the outside, even if the inside didn't quite match yet. She was growing and doing more for herself, by herself, and I was so damn proud of her.

I picked up an empty wineglass and grabbed the bottle that was chilling.

"I'm not that innocent," I finally responded, pouring myself a serving.

They all looked at me with smirks. I was thankful that Eva changed the subject.

"So, how long have you two been friends?" she asked.

"Since we were kids," Avyn answered. "She's more than a friend. She's my sister." She reached out and grabbed my hand to kiss it.

"I love that," Eva said. "You two are lucky to have each other. I can barely stand my biological sister." We shared a laugh. "So, Avyn . . . How long have you and Malcolm been a thing?"

"Oh, we aren't really a thing. Our relationship is one of convenience and has been for about a year now. I mean, I like him, and he likes me, but we aren't a couple."

"But he wants to be," I added. "She wants to be too, but she's scared."

"Throw me under the bus, why don't you!" Avyn exclaimed.

I laughed. "I'm not throwing you under the bus. I gently placed it on top of you. You've encouraged me to explore things with Callum for a while, and now I'm returning the sentiment."

"Malcolm is a good guy," Bella stated. "My brother has good taste in friends. They don't lie. They don't cheat. They don't put their hands on you. They are all about their families and their careers, just like him. That could be your husband, girl."

Eva's eyes glistened as she spoke. "Ooooh, you two would have the cutest babies!"

"Babies?" Avyn shook her head. "You're sipping a little too much over there."

Eva laughed. "I'm sorry. I have baby fever. Armani is getting older, and Chris and I have been trying again. Pasha, do you want kids?"

The space fell silent. I swallowed hard.

"I, um . . . I had a son. He passed away before birth."

Her hand flew to her mouth. "Oh my God! I'm so sorry! I didn't know!"

"It's okay," I assured her. "Yes, I want children. It just has to be with the right man, this time. I can't take another man like my husband."

Her eyes widened. "You're married?"

"I assumed Callum told your husband everything. But yes. I'm about two weeks shy of being officially divorced."

"And we are going to celebrate!" Avyn said, pouring another glass of wine. "For everything you've endured, you deserve this freedom . . . well, at least until you and lover boy make things officially official." She tapped my glass and then took her drink to the head. "Damn, that's good. What is that?"

"It's called Celestial Rose," Bella answered. "My mother used to drink this all the time, and I'd always beg her to let me have a sip. Callum let me taste it for my eighteenth birthday, and I've been in love ever since. He always has a bottle here for me."

"You two seem so close," Avyn commented.

Eva giggled. "You two missed them tussling in the kitchen earlier. She had him in a hell of a headlock while Precious tickled him."

Avyn laughed. "That big ol' man is ticklish?"

"Is he!" Bella exclaimed. "He used to take me to the nail shop. With our mom passing, he always tried to do things with me that our parents would have done. Anyway, one time, he decided to get a pedicure with me, and he damn near kicked that lady in the face."

I stifled a laugh as I reminded myself to keep that tidbit of information to test out. We continued talking until the patio door opened, and Callum stuck out his head.

"Dinner is ready."

We all climbed to our feet and gathered the multiple bottles of wine from the table. Bella and Eva called the girls in to wash their hands. After washing my own, Callum motioned me over to where he stood with a plate in his hands.

"What can I serve you?" he asked, motioning to the spread on the counter.

My mouth watered at the sight of the rice, collard greens, fried chicken, honey-baked ham, macaroni and cheese, yams, and corn bread.

"Y'all made all of this?" I asked.

"Yes, ma'am," he said proudly.

"Everything looks so good!"

"Are you shocked I can cook? Look at me. I don't miss a meal, baby."

I giggled. "I'll take a little of everything. This feels like a holiday meal."

"Well, it's a special occasion. The woman I care about is meeting the people I love most. Hopefully, we can do this more often."

"I'd like that."

"Then it's done."

He started fixing my plate, and all I could do was watch him. I could get used to being served. I was always the one cooking and serving Raymond. He never lifted a finger to serve me first. When Callum was done, he grabbed my hand and led me into the dining room, where he pulled out my chair and placed the food in front of me as I sat.

"Tea, lemonade, or water?" he asked.

"Can I have tea and water?"

"Sure thing."

He tried to walk away, but I grabbed his hand.

"Hey . . . Thank you."

He smiled as he leaned in and pressed his lips to mine. "You're welcome, baby."

I settled in my seat as he walked away and waited for everyone else. The dining room table could comfortably fit eight people. A little table with chairs was set up off to the side for the kids. As they sat waiting patiently, Precious smiled at me before coming over.

"Miss Pasha?"

"Yes, baby."

"Do you like Uncle Cay now?"

"Would that be a problem?"

She shook her head. "No, ma'am. He told my mommy he really likes you."

"Oh, he did, did he?"

She grinned and nodded. "You look so pretty today! Uncle Cay keeps watching you."

I looked back to find Callum's eyes on me. He smiled as he continued to fix his own plate. I smiled and turned back to Precious.

"Well, I think your uncle is a very handsome man, and I can't stop looking at him either. But don't tell him I said that," I added in a whisper.

She covered her mouth and giggled. "Okay."

"What are you two whispering about?" Callum asked, placing both plates and the drinks down.

"Nothing!" Precious said, grinning. "Miss Pasha, did you know Uncle Cay was ticklish?"

"A little birdie might have mentioned it."

"Don't you dare, Precious Gisselle," Callum warned her.

Precious crept around my chair to her uncle. Before she could pounce on him for another tickle attack, he grabbed her up and tickled her instead. She erupted in a fit of giggles. Armani decided she didn't want to be left out and came running over. Callum grabbed her up with a free hand and began smothering their faces with kisses. It was so adorable the way he was so playful with them.

"Tickle him, Ms. Pasha!" Precious squealed.

"Baby, don't you—"

My fingers were in his sides before he could get the words out. He couldn't stop me because that could result in him dropping both girls. A loud laugh erupted from his throat as he tried to wiggle away. Everybody else trickled into the dining room, shaking their heads and laughing.

"All right, girls," Bella said. "You can torture your uncle later. It's time to eat."

I stopped tickling him, and Callum placed them back on their feet. They both kissed his cheek before going to their table.

"You know I'm gonna have to get my lick back for that, right?" he asked, smirking.

"I'm not ticklish, sir."

"I'll figure out something."

A devilish grin appeared on his face, and I felt my flesh heat up. Suddenly, I was a little nervous to be alone with him tonight after everybody left. Did I want to be? Yes. Would I be able to control myself? That I wasn't sure of.

Dinner was excellent, and time seemed to fly by. Before I knew it, everyone was packing up to leave, seeing how they all had to work the next day. I had such a great time with everybody. They welcomed Avyn and me with open arms. We'd even exchanged numbers with Eva and Bella, who were actively planning a kid-free girls' night. My social life was vastly improving. Avyn and I had agreed to come to game night at Chris and Eva's the following weekend. Judging by this group, I knew things would get loud and possibly competitive.

"Alone at last," Callum said, closing the front door.

He ventured over to the couch where I was laid out, nursing a full stomach. The itis was kicking in, and my eyes were getting heavy. I felt the couch dip under his weight as he slid behind me. A strong arm wrapped around my midsection, and soft lips kissed my temple.

"Did you have a good time?" he asked.

"I had a great time. Your friends are hilarious and down to earth."

"They're okay."

I giggled as I turned over to face him. Propping my head up on my hand, I traced his eyebrows with my nail.

"I'm jealous," I said, admiring his features.

"Of?"

"The fact that you were blessed with perfect eyebrows and full lashes."

He chuckled. "I got it from my father."

"Do you look like him or your mother?"

"I'm his twin. I never had to wonder what I'd look like when I got older. Bella looks like both of them."

"I look like my mom. I banned her from coming to my school. The boys gawked at her. So did the male staff."

He chuckled. "So your mom was a MILF?"

I frowned. "That's nasty. I guess I see how Bella feels thinking about you being with women."

He chuckled. "She said that? What were y'all talking about?"

"I'd rather not repeat it."

"Mmm-hmm."

His hold on me tightened, and the next thing I knew, he rolled onto his back and pulled me on top of him.

"Callum! I'm too heavy for this!"

"Woman, if you don't lay your ass down and get comfortable. I told you, I can handle you. All of you. Every inch, every curve, every pound. None of what you're thinking fazes me. You could smother me, and I promise, I'd be okay." He cupped my face. "Let me make this clear. I love a thick woman. Your body is beautiful to me, baby. I won't have you feeling self-conscious about it around me."

He pecked my lips and then rested my head on his chest. My body finally relaxed against his. Before long, I heard the soft sounds of him snoring lightly. My eyelids were so heavy, and I was so comfortable that, eventually, I drifted off to sleep right along with him.

CHAPTER TWENTY-SIX
Callum

MY EYES OPENED, and it was pitch black in my house.

Looking down at my smartwatch, I saw that it was almost eleven. Pasha was still resting comfortably on my chest. It hadn't been my intention to fall asleep, but that I kicked in and took me out. Grabbing my phone, I went to the app that controlled the lights and turned the one on in the hallway. A dim glow illuminated the space. Angling my head, I looked at Pasha while she slept.

God, she was beautiful.

I couldn't help but touch her. My hands gently caressed her arms and back before my fingers threaded through her curls, massaging her scalp. A soft moan escaped her throat as she slightly stirred.

"Baby . . ." I called softly. "Baby?"

She moaned again, and I swear it was the sexiest thing I'd ever heard. My dick twitched in my pants. Her eyes fluttered open, and she looked down at me.

"You let me fall asleep," she mumbled.

"I fell asleep before you, so who let who fall asleep? Come on. Let me get you home."

She pushed herself up and into her straddling position, grazing my hardness in the process. She sat back in my lap, staring down at me. Her hands fingered the hem of my shirt, and she bit her lip, seemingly contemplating her next moves. Slowly, she pushed my shirt up, revealing my tattooed chest. The entire piece was a dedication to my parents.

"This is a different view other than video calls," she said softly. Her nails trailed along the ink etched into my skin. "They're beautiful."

"Thank you."

"Are these your parents?" she asked, tracing their names.

"Yes."

"Does it still hurt? Wait, that was stupid. I meant, does it get easier . . . to lose them? It's been much longer for you than it has for me."

"It never really gets any easier. I miss them every day. I've just learned to live without them."

Her eyes met mine. Crooking her finger, she leaned in and beckoned me to meet her. I partially sat up, and the moment I was within reach, her lips found mine. Our kiss was soft and sensual but soon turned lustful. She slipped her tongue into my mouth and caressed mine with it. As the kiss deepened, she started grinding against me, just like she had earlier in my bedroom. My dick was painfully erect within a minute or two.

"Pash . . ." I mumbled against her lips.

"Yes . . ."

"Baby, you have to stop."

"I don't want to stop. I . . . I want you, Callum. I want you so badly."

She sat back on my lap. Then she slowly pulled the sleeves of her jumper down and slipped her arms out. Beneath the top portion was a sexy, black lace bra. Her nipples were hard and straining against the fabric. My eyes trailed her top half. Unlike me, she was free of tattoos. Her smooth cocoa skin was flawless. Reaching behind her, she unhooked the bra and pulled it from her shoulders.

I could tell she was nervous by the way she covered herself. She had to know she didn't have to do this. As bad as I wanted to do it, I wouldn't if it meant she'd be uncomfortable later. Temporary pleasures would always be fleeting.

"Please?" she whispered, barely audible.

"There's no going back after this, Pasha."

"I know. . . . I want to move forward. My body craves you, Callum. There is only so much I can do to help myself before I need the real thing." She leaned in and kissed my neck. "I need the real thing . . . please. Make love to me."

I answered her by removing her hands from her breasts. Two perfectly kissed chocolate nipples stared back at me. I licked my lips as I dipped my head and kissed them, one, then the other. She shuddered as I took the first one between my lips, suckling it. Her hands went to the back of my head as mine went to her ass. She moaned softly as I gripped it and slowly grinded her against me.

"Callum, . . ." she whimpered. "That feels so good."

My dick was fighting to free itself from these pants. The friction of her warm mound grinding against it was pure torture. Securing her in my arms, I stood from the couch and carried her to my bedroom. Inside, I placed her in the center of my bed. Her top half was exposed, but I needed to see all of her, . . . touch all of her.

"Turn over for me, baby," I instructed.

She rolled onto her stomach, and I located the zipper holding the fabric together. I pulled it down slowly, planting kisses on her exposed flesh. Her skin was so soft and supple. She smelled so damn good that it was intoxicating. I maneuvered the jumpsuit down over her hips, with her lifting up slightly to assist me. When that black lace thong made an appearance, I bit my lip. Her ass was perfect and round, swallowing up the flimsy fabric.

"Mmm . . ." I moaned as I caressed the soft mounds. "Shit."

I gave her cheeks a hard slap before smoothing the sting over with my hand. She whimpered slightly as I stooped to kiss the red-tinted areas. When I pulled off the jumper the rest of the way, I found the seat of her panties soaked.

"Look at you," I mumbled, pulling the fabric to the side. Her lips glistened with her essence. "Damn, baby."

When I ran my finger through her slit, she gasped. "Callum . . . please!"

Sucking her juices from my fingers, I allowed the taste and her smell to linger on my palate so I could commit them to memory. Eagerly, I removed the thong and tossed it aside. Rolling her over onto her back, I gazed down at her with admiration.

"God, you're so beautiful," I whispered, pulling my shirt over my head. "So perfect."

She watched intently as I unbuckled my belt and unbuttoned my pants. Her hands roamed the softness of her body, gripping and groping various areas of flesh. Her pretty brown eyes trailed my six-foot-two frame as I pushed my pants down over my hips. They pooled at my ankles, and I kicked them off.

As I advanced toward the bed, she backed toward the headboard and lay flat on her back, spread eagle. I climbed on the bed and made my way between her legs and up to her lips.

"Can I taste you, Pasha?" I asked, kissing her neck. "Can I offer you everything I have to pleasure you?"

As I spoke, my hand slipped between her legs to cup her mound. The heat radiating from her center was calling me. Her chest heaved as she nodded. Using my ring and middle fingers. I parted her lower lips and stroked her clit.

"Callum!" she whined.

"I need to hear you say it, baby. Tell me that I can taste you."

She gasped. "You can . . . You can taste me!"

I wasted no time, leaving a trail of wet kisses from her neck to her breasts, down her stomach, and against her inner thigh. She writhed beneath me. Her breathing was labored, and her body trembled slightly.

"Relax," I coaxed as I came face-to-face with her sweet-smelling, clean-shaven, juicy honeypot. Closing my eyes, I dove in headfirst. Slowly, my tongue licked and lapped at every ounce of natural nectar that was expelled from her.

"Callum . . ."

Her back arched from the bed, and her hand found its way to the back of my head. I locked my arms around her thighs to hold her in place as I feasted on her.

"Oh God!" she cried out. "You feel . . . Oh God, you feel so good!"

My taste buds were having a party. She was so sweet. . . . So delectable. . . . So fucking insatiable. I found solace between her thighs, so much that I wanted to pack up and take residence there. I just knew that once I buried myself within her walls, that was it.

I slid my middle and ring finger into her wetness as I made love to her swollen clit with my mouth. Every time my fingers retreated, they were soaked even more. My slow thrusting increased to the point where every stroke was audible. They weren't to be drowned out by the sounds of her moans or cries of pleasure, however.

"I'm coming . . . shit! I'm gonna come!"

Crooking my fingers, I tapped against her G-spot. If she was going to come, I wanted her first orgasm to be worth it. Again, her back arched. Her legs trembled. Her mouth opened, and out poured the most beautiful cry of pleasure as she came hard. She lay before me, panting heavily. I climbed to my feet and removed my boxers, allowing my dick to spring forward. Moving to the nightstand, I plucked a condom from the box.

She turned her head slightly to look at me. Her eyes dropped, then widened. She bit her lip as she watched me rip the condom open and roll it down over my length. Joining her in bed, once again, I hovered over her. Her hands came to my face, and her eyes searched mine. She looked like she wanted to say something.

"Talk to me, Pasha. What's on your mind?"

Tears brimmed in her eyes as she spoke. "Promise me. . . . Promise me you won't hurt me, . . . that you won't break my heart."

I swiped at the tear that slipped down her face. Taking her hand, I placed it over my heart.

"I will never hurt you or break your heart, Pasha. I'm falling for you. I want to love you. . . . How can I ever hurt you?"

She pulled my head to hers and kissed me passionately. I pulled her legs around my waist, and the head of my dick lined up perfectly with her entrance. I teased her a little by rubbing it up and down her slit.

"Put it in," she begged. "Please, put it in."

She didn't have to ask again. I slid into her tight, wet walls, causing her to gasp and sink her nails into my flesh.

"Ooooh . . ." She moaned, and she took every inch.

I fed her long, deep, and powerful strokes. Every thrust caused her to gasp as she clung to me. Dropping the bends of her knees into the crooks of my arms, I pushed them forward, spreading her wide and sinking deeper into her. My strokes remained slow and steady. She asked me to make love to her, so I wouldn't rush it. I wanted her to experience every intricate moment of pleasure. She buried her face in the crook of my neck. The sweet sounds of her moans propelled the thrusting of my hips.

"Ca-Callum . . . right there. . . ."

"Right here, baby?" I thrust upward, stroking her G-spot. Her nails sank into my flesh.

"Yes! Yes! Ooooh! . . ."

"Can I have you, Pasha? Tell me you'll be mine."

"I'm yours. . . . God, I'm yours!"

"Mmmm. I love the sound of that. You know how much you deserve the love I want to give you? How much you deserve to be worshiped like the queen you are? If you let me, I can give you the world. Can I give that to you?"

"Yes! Ooooh shit! I feel it coming! I'm gonna cum!"

She spiraled into a fit of heavy pants as she clung to me for dear life. Her walls contracted around my shaft, forcing my eyes to close. I could feel my nut rising to meet hers. With a final thrust, her walls contracted, squeezing me to the point of eruption. My seeds spilled into the condom at the same time that her juices overflowed. She fell still and silent, and when I looked down at her, her beautiful face was contorted in pleasure.

Finally, she expelled a breathy gasp. Tears spilled from her eyes and down her cheeks. Before I knew it, she was in full-blown tears. I rested the weight of my body on top of her and wrapped my arms around her. I wasn't sure why she was crying, but I knew that pressure had a calming effect. Within a few minutes, her cries turned to whimpers, then to sniffles. Then there was nothing.

Lifting my head, I looked down at her. "Are you okay?" I asked softly.

"Yes. That was just intense. It's been a long time since I've enjoyed someone making love to me. I'd gotten used to just lying there and taking it that I forgot what real pleasure felt like."

"You will always experience real pleasure with me. Even if I don't get mine, you'll always get yours."

She traced my bottom lip with her thumb. "How would that be fair?"

"I'm not a selfish lover. I'm gonna take care of you in every capacity." I pressed my lips to hers, kissing her softly. When she slipped her tongue into my mouth, my dick hardened inside her.

She moaned softly. "Can we go again?"

I smirked. "We can go as long as you can stand it, baby."

Though this was unexpected, it was damn sure a hell of a ride.

CHAPTER
TWENTY-SEVEN
Pasha

THE BRIGHT MORNING sun beat down on the side of my face. I slowly opened my eyes and quickly realized I was not in my own bed. A quick glance around told me that I was in a man's bed. Not just any man, though. Callum Ellis. Panic might have set in any other time, but today, I simply relaxed into the comfort of this king-size mattress and stared at the ceiling with a smile.

Last night had been everything.

He had been everything. The way my body responded to him was insane. After years of feeling like a cum rag because I was having sex when I didn't have the desire, it felt so good to have my needs taken care of for once. He was intentional. He was gentle. He was simply . . . perfect.

The sound of my phone ringing broke my thoughts. Callum must have plugged it up last night because I don't remember ever leaving his bedroom once we got in here. Sitting up, I grabbed the phone from the charger. Not so much to my surprise, it was Avyn.

"Hello?"

"Um . . . Miss Ma'am? Where are you?"

"What do you mean?"

"Well, I'm standing in your apartment, and you are nowhere to be found."

"Well . . ."

"Oop! Bitch! . . . Did you not come home last night?"

"Well—"

She screamed in my ear. "I *knew* it!"

I giggled. "What do you know because you haven't let me answer, Avyn?"

"Answer this video call. I need to look at your face."

She didn't allow me to protest before the video call came through. I answered after two rings.

"Yes?"

She squinted at me, moving her head around like she was looking at something. When a smile spread across her face, I prepared myself for her foolishness.

"You got some," she stated. "And don't act slow. You know *precisely* what I'm talking about. You let that man have his way with you, didn't you?"

I couldn't hide the redness in my face from blushing so hard.

"Would you be surprised if I said I initiated it?"

"No, I wouldn't. That's what he wanted, for you to come to him when you were ready. I need details—every single, intricate, nasty detail."

"It wasn't nasty, Avyn. It was beautiful . . . so damn beautiful."

"Aww, pooh! I love that for you. I really do. You two look so good together. I watched the way he looked at you and loved on you yesterday. That man is smitten."

"He told me he wants to love me, and because of that, he could never hurt me."

"Girl, you're gonna make me cry. When you two get married, just remember, I look good in nude colors."

I shook my head. "I'm two weeks shy of being divorced. I'm not thinking about being a wife again so soon."

"Maybe not yet. But you will. You talked about being somebody's wife our entire lives."

"I know. But circumstances have changed. I don't want to be just a wife. I'm a woman. I want something of my own. I want my own accomplishments, and I want to keep making my own money. I like that. It feels too good to make my own money to ever return to anything else."

"I hear that. I wouldn't mind a little sugar daddy that doesn't want any sugar, though."

I kissed my teeth. "You need to go on and give Malcolm the chance he deserves. I've watched you with that man, Avyn. He adores you. I'd even go as far as saying that he loves you."

She huffed. "I'm gonna talk to him."

"When?"

"Soon."

"Before game night."

She huffed. "Okay, fine."

"Don't sound like that. Stop playing hard to get and claim your man. That's what you would tell me."

She rolled her eyes. "You know, sometimes, I hate that you know me so well."

"To know you is to love you."

The door to the bedroom opened, and Callum stepped in dressed in nothing but his boxers and carrying a tray of food in his hands. A smile spread across my face as he approached me and set the tray across my lap.

"Good morning, baby," he said, leaning in.

"Good morning."

I forgot all about Avyn being on the phone when he leaned in and captured my lips. The kiss he gave me was soft and sweet but still laced with so much lust.

"Well, damn!" Avyn exclaimed. "Are y'all trying to entice me?"

Callum and I looked at the phone and grinned.

"My bad," he said, wiping my lip with his thumb.

"Don't mind me. I'm gonna let you two go. Let me know how the car search goes, Pash. If you get one, you better roll by and let me see it."

I giggled. "I will. Love you."

"I love you too. Bye, Callum."

"Bye, Avyn."

I disconnected the call and set the phone back on the dresser. My mouth watered as I looked down at the spread of sausage omelets, toast, fresh fruit, apple juice, and coffee. My stomach was definitely empty right now.

"This looks so good. Thank you."

"You're welcome."

He unrolled the silverware and proceeded to feed me. There was something so intimate about a gesture like this. This man had a way of giving me all types of butterflies.

"How did you sleep?" he asked.

"Very peacefully. I'm well rested for today."

"Do you know what kind of car you're looking for?"

"Something good on gas, not too many miles, no accidents or body damage. I'm okay with a midsized car or small SUV. Honestly, I just want to get from point A to point B."

He chuckled. "I get it. If you want, I can take you to the dealership where I purchase the cars for my car service. We have a good relationship."

"Okay. We definitely have to stop by my place first. I wasn't anticipating sleeping over last night."

"I know. I don't regret it, though."

"Me either." I blushed as I avoided his eyes. "Last night was amazing. The second time around . . . Whew!"

The second round had me acting out of character. Round one was sweet and sensual lovemaking. Round two brought out the rough, nasty version of him. He took me from behind with my face in the mattress and my ass in the air. I was sure his nearest neighbor could hear me screaming in the wee hours of the morning.

Callum chuckled. "Well, I'm glad I could be of service. Eat up, and I can serve you in the shower before we leave."

I blushed as he held a piece of the omelet to my lips. Part of me wanted to say forget the food and take me now. But I didn't say that. Instead, I continued to allow him to feed me, all while imagining this shower session in my head.

That round in the shower almost made me want to stay in today.

However, I was determined to get this car. So, after we got out, Callum gave me one of his shirts and a pair of sweats to wear so I didn't have to do the walk of shame back into my apartment. It didn't matter because we ran into Kelli as we stepped off the elevator. She looked between us and smiled.

"Well, at least I didn't have to hear you through the wall last night," she said. When Callum frowned in confusion, she added, *"Don't worry, she was alone."*

I was mortified. Callum thought it was hilarious. When we got into my apartment, he insisted I show him what had me cumming and crying loud enough for my neighbor to hear it. I wasn't doing that. I made him wait in the living room while I got dressed. I felt terrible because I still hadn't gotten a couch yet. Well, I'd purchased one, but it was on back order.

He sat patiently while I found something to put on. Thirty minutes later, we pulled up to Platinum City Car Sales. His guy met us at the door and introduced himself as Ryan. He took us straight to the lot to look around. He asked me the typical questions like what I was looking for, how much I was hoping to pay a month, and what kind of down payment I had. I would have loved to find something I could pay cash for, but looking around this lot, I knew I wouldn't find it here.

"What's wrong?" Callum asked, noticing the look on my face.

I sighed. "I don't think this will be the place. Everything here is nice, but I'm sure it will be more than I can afford. Can we look somewhere else?"

He was quiet for a moment, seemingly thinking about his next words.

"What is it?" I asked.

"What if I just bought you the car?"

"No. This has to be something I do on my own. And we don't know each other well enough for me to agree to that, Callum. Thank you, but no."

"I knew you'd say no, but it was worth a shot." Again, he was quiet, and then a smile spread across his face. "Can I take you somewhere?" he asked. "I wanna show you something."

"What is it?"

"Just trust me, okay?"

I sighed again. "Okay."

He thanked Ryan for his help before taking my hand and leading me back to his truck. I sat in the passenger seat, quietly watching the scenery as he drove. We ended up back at his house. When we pulled into the driveway, my brows furrowed in confusion.

"Why are we here?" I asked.

"This."

He pressed the button for the garage, and it opened. Sitting inside was a black SUV.

"What's this?" I asked curiously.

"This was the first car I bought myself when the business started picking up. I've kept up the maintenance on it. All the tires are good. I drive it once a week to keep it up. It's paid for. The taxes are up to date, and the title is clean."

"Are you . . . Are you offering to sell me your car?"

"Yes." He opened the glove compartment and pulled out a set of keys. "Sit in it. Take a look around, take it for a test drive, and let me know what you think."

I hesitated for a moment before taking the keys from his hand. Getting out of the car, I walked into the garage and looked over the vehicle. It was in perfect condition. The tires looked almost brand new. It was shiny, like it had recently been washed and waxed. When I opened the door, I was greeted with that fresh car scent. It was free of dirt or debris and looked like it had been thoroughly detailed.

There was a touch screen panel, a sunroof, and leather seats. When I switched it on, it ran so smoothly. I turned on the air and was immediately greeted by a cool breeze. I put it in reverse and carefully backed out of the garage. Callum stood behind his truck, hands shoved in his pocket. He nodded, motioning for me to take the car for a spin. Carefully, I backed out of the driveway and onto the road. As soon as I was far enough away from the house, I called Avyn and placed the phone in the cup holder.

"Hey, pooh," she answered. "How's the car search going?"

"The dealership we visited was expensive, so that was a no. Avyn. . . . This man offered to buy me a car."

"Aww, shit, now! You must have put that thing on him heavy, girl!"

I shook my head. "I said no. I want to buy this car myself."

"I know, I know. You want your independence."

"He brought me back to his house. The man wants to sell me his car."

"The one he drives?"

"No. It was one in his garage. He said it was the first one he bought when business took off."

"Well, what's wrong with that? Is it a nice car?"

"It is. It's perfect."

"I'm not seeing the problem then, Pash."

I sighed. "What if he changes his mind about me? What if he decides he really doesn't want to be with me and wants it back?"

"Pasha, don't do this to yourself. That man cares for you. I see it in his eyes, baby. He's not Raymond. Just from being around him a few times, I can see he's good people. I'm positive that he only wants to help you. Go through the legal channels today and take the car. He said he would sell it, not give it to you. You're still doing this yourself. He's just offering you an option."

"I'm afraid of this relationship, Avyn. He asked me to be his last night. Granted, he was inside me when he asked, but I think he meant it."

"I know he did."

"How?"

"Because I heard him tell the guys that he was falling for you last night. You were outside with the girls, sipping the second round of wine. I went to the bathroom, and as I was coming around the corner, he looked at you with so much adoration. They were joking, telling him he looked like he was in love, and he openly admitted that he was falling for you. He didn't even know I was standing there."

I knew she was telling the truth. He spoke those exact words to me last night.

"This is crazy, Avyn," I said as I drove into a parking lot to turn around. I briefly stopped the car. "I wasn't supposed to fall for this man."

"Maybe not. But sometimes, God puts the people we need right in our path. We don't have to search for them. Sometimes, it's just that easy. Wait! . . . Did you say you were falling for him?"

Tears stung my eyes as I answered. "Yes."

"Awww, baby. That's beautiful, Pash. You deserve that."

"It hasn't been long enough—"

"My daddy fell for my mama the moment he saw her in those bell bottoms, crop top, and those two Afro puffs. He asked her to marry him a month after they met, and they have been together for thirty-five years. It happens. You met him when you needed more than what the girls or I could give you. Just let him be that for you, and don't question it, boo."

I swiped at the tears streaming down my face. I was so afraid to fall for Callum, and he gave me every reason to do so,—no helmet, no safety net required. He was a good man. He was patient, caring, and kind. He was selfless and encouraging. He made me laugh and smile, and, God, did he do wonders for my mind and body. I was the only thing standing in the way of fully embracing what was growing between us.

I sniffled. "You're right."

"I know I am. Now, dry your pretty eyes. Put on a smile, and go handle your business. I love you."

"I love you too."

I disconnected the call and took a few minutes to gather myself before heading back to Callum's. When I got there, he was sitting on the bed of his truck, waiting patiently. As I stopped beside the truck, he hopped down and came over to open the door.

"Well, . . . What do you think?"

"I love it. You've kept it up very well. How much do you want for it? I have six thousand left over from selling my ring."

"Let's say two, and we call it even."

I hesitated. That wasn't much for a whole car in this condition.

"That feels like robbery, Callum."

"If you would *take* the car, I would just give it to you, Pasha. I have no use for it. And I honestly don't want your money. I'm sure there are better things you can do with it. This is me compromising and respecting your wishes to purchase a car for yourself." He grabbed my hands, gently massaging them with his thumbs. "Please. . . . Let me help you, baby."

I closed my eyes and took a deep breath. He was throwing me a lifeline, and I would swallow my pride and accept it.

"Okay," I whispered, tears streaming down my face. "Okay."

He pulled me into his arms and held me tightly. All I could do was sob against his chest. He'd been so good to me, and part of me felt like it was so unreal to have him in my life. He didn't want anything from me. He did nothing with expectations of something in return.

"I'm sorry I'm such a mess!" I wailed.

He chuckled. "You aren't a mess. And even if you were, I'd still be right here." He lifted my head and wiped away my tears. When he was done, he kissed my lips. "I see you, Pasha—all of you. You've got me, baby. Whatever you need from me, it's yours. Until you are comfortable accepting it, I'll work within your limits. You never have to be uncomfortable taking anything from me that I willingly give because it comes from my heart."

He pressed his forehead to mine. For a moment, we stood there, eyes closed, simply basking in each other. God, I was going to fall head over heels in love with this man. I knew it, I felt it, and I had to accept it.

"Thank you," I whispered.

"What have I told you about thanking me, woman?"

I couldn't help but laugh. "If I have to get used to this, you have to get used to me expressing gratitude. I don't know any other way to be."

"I understand. Come on. Let's go take care of this, and then I'm taking my girl out to lunch. I'm sure you'll want to personalize your car too. Just . . . none of those big-ass eyelashes, okay?"

I laughed. "What do you have against the lashes?"

"On people? Nothing. I take that back. I feel the same way about lashes on cars as I do about excessive lashes on people. They look silly."

"I agree with you there." I looked back at the car. "I probably won't do too much to it."

"Well, it's yours."

"It's not mine until I hand over the funds and you hand over the title and bill of sale."

"Let's get to it then."

He went into the glove compartment and grabbed the title and registration. After that, we climbed into the truck, headed to the bank, and then the DMV. I was sure we would be there for a while, but I would have officially bought my first car once we walked out!

CHAPTER
TWENTY-EIGHT
Callum

THE SMILE ON Pasha's face when we walked out of the DMV with the title to my SUV officially in her name was priceless. She smiled all through our lunch date, and she was still smiling when we got back to my house. When we stepped over the threshold, she led me to my bedroom, stripped both of us down, and gave me the ride of my life. Gone was the shy, timid woman. Present was this strong, confident sexual prowess.

I loved seeing her genuinely happy. She deserved so much more, and I wanted to give it to her. The $2,000 she gave me for the car would sit in my safe until I could find a way to sneak it back to her. I didn't want the money. I didn't need it, and I was sure she could use it for something.

A few days had passed since the exchange. I'd seen her every day since then. Whether it was me taking to her lunch or seeing her after work, every day we were together. I loved being in her presence. I loved how comfortable she'd become, curling up in my lap while we watched TV or simply held a conversation. The side of her I'd been waiting to see was shining through.

Today was Friday, the day of the dinner at the mayor's mansion. Whenever there was an event involving city officials who booked my car service, I always included armed security for an additional fee. I met with the drivers and the security team to discuss the protocol for tonight's event.

I'd just finished and was gathering my things to leave when someone knocked on my office door. I looked up to see William standing there. I hadn't seen him since the funeral and hadn't spoken to him since he called, apologizing for his mother showing up at my house.

"What can I help you with?" I asked, motioning for him to sit.

"I wanted to speak with you."

"About?"

He sighed as he sat while I continued to stand. "I know we can't just put everything that happened behind us, but I'd like to try to work through it."

"I don't think that's going to happen. I made peace with that at your father's funeral. It's definitely not going to happen after our family members collectively decided to come to my house and show their asses. I don't want or need that type of negativity in my life. I said I was okay with possibly building a relationship with you, Mo, and Jess again, but after that, I think it's best if we keep things as they are."

"I just feel like family should be better than this, man."

"William, Bella and I have spent seventeen years isolated from '*the family*.' You know what we've done in that time? We built a family of our own. They may not be blood, but they have been solid."

"I understand that. And I'm sorry it had to come to that."

"That's the thing. It didn't *have* to come to that. A bunch of greedy people decided that a dollar was more important than family. My father warned me long ago that I had to watch out for certain people in our family. He always told me that he prayed every night for God to allow him and my mother to live to see

Bella and me reach adulthood. I always wondered why he said that."

I took a seat across from him and laced my fingers.

"You want to know an interesting piece of information I learned about five years ago, William?"

He looked curious. He didn't say anything, but he nodded his head.

"When our grandmother died, she left her children quite a bit of money. Now, Aunt Glenda and Uncle James blew through theirs. She spent hers tricking off on men who wanted nothing more than her generous hand. Your mother helped your father spend his living lavishly, and now they have nothing to show for it. My mother put hers into a trust for Bella and me.

"Not even my father knew about this, but her siblings and your mother did. You see, when I overheard them talking about the money they all thought they should get to share, I assumed that it was the insurance money. But, no. It was the trust. A trust I didn't know about until I found the paperwork when I remodeled the house a few years back. It was under a loose board in the back of their master bedroom closet."

My grandmother died when I was thirteen. The trust was opened when I turned fourteen. That paperwork sat in a box under the floorboards for an additional fourteen years because the only person who knew it was there was gone. When I found it, the first person I called was Bella. She verified everything with the bank. We went through the legal channels and came out with several hundred thousand dollars apiece. We invested it over the years, and it blessed us tenfold.

I sat back in my chair. "You know what your mother said to me when she came over spewing all that animosity? She said it was too bad that I wasn't on that boat with my parents."

His eyes widened, and it caused me to chuckle, though nothing was funny.

"Imagine that," I continued. "My own aunt wishing death upon me over money. Now, *that* shit hurt."

"Callum . . . I'm . . . I'm sorry, man."

"Don't be. She said what she said, and I fully believe she meant it. I would never ask you to go against your mother. Regardless of what I think of her, she's the only parent you have left, and I know you love her. You won't be jeopardizing your relationship on my behalf. There's no love lost between us, but I'm standing firm in protecting my peace."

He looked hurt by my rejection. I hated to have to do it because, once upon a time, he and his siblings were my favorite cousins. Sheila was his mother. As spiteful as she was, I believed she would cut him off for having anything to do with me. I knew what it was like to be without my parents. Having someone be dead to you without them actually being dead can hurt about as bad as if they were already gone.

William stood and extended his hand. "I'm sorry, I truly am. I hate that this is your decision, but I'll respect it. For what it's worth, I've always wished things were different."

"Yeah, . . . me too."

No other words were spoken between us. He dropped my hand and left the office. I sat back in my chair, covering my face with my hands. I thought back to that conversation with my aunt that day.

I'd been sitting in my living room watching TV when I heard a car door close outside. I walked over to the window to see Sheila and Glenda marching up the front steps. I sighed heavily as I unlocked and opened the door.

"Can I help you?" I asked.

They barged right past me and into the house.

"Why, yes, won't you come in?" I said sarcastically as I closed the door.

"We won't be long," Sheila said, glaring at me. "I just want to know what made you think it was okay to come to my husband's funeral, starting trouble?"

"I didn't come to start trouble. I came to pay my respects."

She scoffed. "Pay your respects? After the way that you disrespected all of us?"

"You mean after the way that all of you stood in my parents' house two weeks after their death, fighting over who should get their money? Or after I caught you in my parents' bedroom going through their things? Or after all of you flat-out said you wouldn't take us in without compensation? If I disrespected anybody, I promise it was warranted."

Sheila rolled her eyes. "We all had children of our own. Did you really think we could take you in without some kind of payment? Raising kids ain't cheap."

"And I completely understand that. I would have gladly given you money to make sure that my sister was okay while I was in school. None of you talked to me. None of you asked how we could make this work. None of you asked anything. And after hearing what was said, do you honestly think I would leave my only sister in the hands of people who didn't give a fuck about her? Sheila, you were my uncle's wife, not even my blood, so you had no say-so at all. That's why I cursed you out. You spoke for you and your husband, and he allowed that shit. All you wanted was the money.

"Glenda, not only did you want the money, but you also wanted my parents' house. You were already prepared to kick me out and move in here. Where was I supposed to go when I came home from school? Did you expect me to sleep on the couch when I had a whole bedroom?"

Glenda shook her head. "Sacrifices had to be made if you wanted your sister to be taken care of—"

"Sacrifices?" I yelled. "My parents sacrificed their lives! That's the only way anybody would have gotten that insurance money!"

Sheila laughed. "It wasn't just insurance money. You think we didn't know about the trust fund?"

My brows furrowed.

"Oh, you're confused now?" Glenda asked. "You were willing to throw us a few dollars to care for Bella while you blew through your trust fund? You wanted to saddle us with the responsibility of raising a kid for five years while you went off and lived your best life."

I laughed. When I say laughed, it was a good, hearty laugh. They looked angry at my reaction. Sheila raised a hand to slap me, but I grabbed it.

"Don't even think about putting your damn hands on me. My parents didn't hit me, and I'll be damned if you start."

She glared at me and snatched her arm away.

"According to my mother's letter, my grandmother left all three of her children money. Sheila, you and your husband ran through his trying to keep up with the Joneses. Glenda, you decided to be a damn sugar mama to men who dropped you as soon as they got all they could get out of you. My mother, being the smart woman she was, invested hers in her children. You were gagging on audacity and entitlement if you thought for a second that either of you would capitalize off that money."

I walked over to my front door and opened it.

"James is dead. I'm sure he had a nice insurance policy, so, Sheila, you'll be okay. Glenda, . . . you like to trick. Maybe you'll find a man who's willing to trick off on you one day. Now, get out of my house."

They stood there for a moment, stewing in anger.

"Get out!"

Slowly, they walked toward the door. Sheila stopped in front of me. Her evil eyes trailed me from head to toe.

"Your mother always thought she was better than the rest of us. I never liked her. It's too bad you weren't on the damn boat."

That stung. It didn't have to come to that.

"I'm sorry you feel that way," I said, not showing any emotion.

"Stay away from my children."

"Well, you made sure they stayed away this long so . . . I have no problem with that."

When they were good and gone, I sat on my couch and had a long cry about that shit. It was the moment I knew I could never have a relationship with my family again. I accepted it. It is what it is at this point.

I arrived at Pasha's around seven to pick her up for game night.

After that visit from William, I just wanted to see her face. I'd already called and spoken to Bella about it, but somehow, seeing Pasha always put me in a good headspace. I lightly tapped on her front door. A few seconds passed before she opened it with a smile.

"Hey, you."

"Hey, baby."

I stepped in and pecked her lips before I pulled her into my arms for a hug. When she tried to pull away, I held her tighter.

"Not yet," I said softly.

She didn't question me. She simply wrapped her arms tighter around my frame and stroked my back. She didn't know how much I needed this hug.

"I got you," she whispered, kissing my cheek.

For a while, she held me while I worked through the flight of emotions surging through me. When my nerves finally calmed, I pulled back and looked down at her. She cupped my face, gently stroking my cheeks.

"Better?" she asked.

"Much better."

"Do you want to talk about it?"

I nodded. She led me over to her new couch, and we sat down. After a heavy sigh, I gave her the rundown of everything that had transpired after the funeral. She listened attentively as she held my hand.

"I'm so sorry they treated you like that, Callum. You didn't deserve that at all."

"It's fine. It hurts, but I'll be okay. I created a family with people who show me nothing but love and no expectations in return."

"You're blessed to have them."

"I'm blessed to have you as a part of that." I leaned in and softly kissed her lips. "You make me happy, Pasha."

She smiled softly. "You make me happy too . . . very happy. You know, this whole thing makes me want to reach back out to some of my family. When my depression settled in after my parents died, I withdrew from so much of the world. They understood, and for a long time, they continued to reach out to me. But over time, it stopped. I've always felt bad about that. I didn't want to project the way I was feeling onto anybody. I just wonder if they'd be open to a relationship now that I'm getting it together."

"If you want to try, I will support you. Don't let my situation deter that."

"I know there's a family reunion coming up. They host one at the same time every year. Maybe I'll go."

"Maybe you should. If it's on your heart to restore your relationships, I say it's worth a try. You never know until you put yourself back out there."

"You're right." She sighed. "I'm ready to get going. Malcolm is picking Avyn up since she had to work a little later."

"I heard she finally gave my boy a chance."

She giggled. "She did. It's about time. I told her to stop playing with that man."

"Between you and me, I think he shed a tear or two."

"Awww! That's so sweet!"

"It's something. Come on, let's go. Chris already texted me asking if we were on the way when I arrived."

"Well, let's not keep them waiting."

"Bookend!" Avyn yelled.

"That's it!" Pasha confirmed.

"Wait a minute!" Bella exclaimed. "How the hell were we supposed to guess that?"

We were playing Pictionary. It was Pasha, Avyn, Malcolm, and I versus Martin, Bella, Chris, and Eva. So far, our team was up by five points.

I chuckled. "It was easy, Bella. There's the bookcase, the books, and the bookends holding them up."

"Who uses bookends? You don't just line the shelf from corner to corner? That's that fancy shit."

"Don't be a sore loser."

She frowned as she stuck her middle finger up at me. I laughed it off as I stood to grab the marker for my turn.

"Good one, baby," I said, pecking Pasha's lips.

"I guessed the word," Avyn reminded me.

"You did good, love." Malcolm kissed her cheek, and it made her smile.

I shook my head as I plucked a card from the stack. The word was spaghetti. I was a horrible artist, so I prayed that somebody on my team could see through the less-than-stellar drawing I was about to make.

"*Bowl!*"

"*Food!*"

"*Uh . . . uh . . . dammit . . .*"

There was the snapping of fingers as Martin tried to get his words together. My team sat quietly, watching while the others were yelling out answers.

"Pasta!" Eva yelled.

"Pasta?" Chris questioned. "That looks like a pile of hair."

"Why would he draw a pile of hair, Christopher?"

While they went back and forth, I drew the meatballs and a horribly constructed fork.

"Spaghetti!" Pasha yelled.

"That's it!"

The other team groaned.

"I'm tired of this game," Bella declared. "Pick something else. Y'all are working up my blood pressure, and I need a drink."

She stood, and the rest of the women rose and followed her to the kitchen, cracking jokes along the way. Chris and Martin turned to Malcolm and me.

"Y'all are on your way to being banned from Game Night," Martin informed us. "How do you both bring newbies in and they whip our ass? I don't like that."

"Well, look who you have on your team," I retorted. "A pile of hair, Chris?"

He laughed. "In my defense, you draw like a three-year-old."

"That's okay. My baby knew what it was."

They all grinned at me.

"This man." Martin shook his head. "You've been waiting to claim that title. Look at that smile on his face."

"I'm happy for you, man." Chris reached out and slapped my hand. "You two do look good together. And she's almost completely single."

"Yeah, man. Only a little while longer. I want to do something special for her. Maybe take her away for a weekend or something. She's done a lot of growing in the last couple of months. I wanna celebrate that with her. I want to celebrate *her*."

Malcolm raised an eyebrow. "If I didn't know any better, I'd say you were in love."

I smirked. "I might be inclined to say you're right . . . almost. I care deeply about her. My feelings are strong as hell. I'm not sure if it's love yet, but it's the closest thing to it."

Martin chuckled. "He's being modest. Looking at you two, I can see it won't last long. Seriously, man. I wish you the best of luck. I've been around a long time. I've witnessed you love and care for your sister like she was your own child. You pour into her and my daughter, and I have so much respect for you, man. You deserve to get a happy ending, finally. Pasha too. If you can find that with each other, I'm all for it."

Malcolm and Chris nodded in agreeance.

I pinched the bridge of my nose, fighting back tears. "I appreciate that, man."

The girls returned with drinks for all of us. I noticed that Eva had been sipping on water and juice all night. She was sitting next to Chris at this moment, talking softly with smiles on their faces. I wasn't the only one who noticed.

"What are y'all whispering about?" Bella asked. "There's been a lot of these lovey-dovey moments tonight."

They looked at each other, and he nodded.

Eva surveyed the room. "Well . . . We were going to wait a little while before we announced it, but . . . We're having a baby!"

I felt Pasha tense, then relax next to me. I looked over, and she held a smile on her face, but there was sadness in her eyes. She offered congratulations along with everyone else, but I could tell that the news was a gut punch. It was nothing personal against Chris and Eva. It was simply a reminder. I reached out and grabbed her hand. Pulling it to my lips, I kissed it.

She offered me a timid smile, but I could tell she was breaking inside.

CHAPTER
TWENTY-NINE
Pasha

I FELT SICK TO my stomach.

I didn't want to ruin our fun, but the news of Chris and Eva expecting was like a low blow. It had nothing to do with them. I was happy for them. The ability to bring life into the world was a joyous occasion and deserved to be celebrated. I sat there and toasted them with everyone else, but I couldn't take it when the conversation shifted to baby talk. I excused myself to the kitchen to grab another drink.

Callum and Avyn followed shortly. When they found me, I was struggling to open a bottle of wine. Tears were stinging my eyes as I tried to pry the cork out. Avyn took the bottle from my hands and set it aside while Callum wrapped his arm around me and led me outside. The moment the cool air hit my face, I felt a wave of nausea hit the pit of my stomach and quickly made its way up through my esophagus.

I sprinted away from them and over to some bushes, where I spewed out my guts.

"Get her some water and a towel," I heard Avyn say to Callum.

In an instant, she was at my side, holding my hair back. She gently rubbed my back until I was at the point of dry heaving.

Callum was standing with a cold towel to wipe my mouth and face when I stood. I tried to hold back the tears as they tended to me, but they just kept coming. Before I knew it, I was on the ground with my knees in my chest, bawling like a baby.

"I'm sorry . . . I-I tried to hold it in!"

"It's okay," they both said, hovering beside me.

I didn't know why this pregnancy announcement hit me like this. I'd been around Precious and Armani. I'd spoken about wanting to try again in the future. Why did the announcement do me like this?

"It's okay, Pash," Avyn whispered, kissing my temple. "We've got you."

"We're right here," Callum assured me. He sat on the ground behind me, wrapped his arms around my waist, and gently rocked me.

The harder I tried to calm down, the worse it felt.

"I . . . I can't . . . I can't breathe. I can't breathe . . ."

"You're having a panic attack," Avyn informed me. "Look at me, Pasha."

I tried to focus on her face, but my body wouldn't cooperate.

"Listen to the sound of my voice," she said softly. "Tell me three things you see."

I panted heavily as I looked around, trying to focus my attention elsewhere. "Um . . . trees . . . f-flowers . . . a p-playground s-set."

"Good, good. . . . Close your eyes for me."

I did as she said and closed my eyes.

"Tell me three things you can hear."

I listened. "C-cars on the road. . . . Crickets. . . . An owl."

"You're doing so good, pooh. Keep your eyes closed and focus on your breathing. I need you to move three parts of your body for me."

I focused my attention again. First, I stretched and flexed my fingers. Then my toes, followed by my neck. Slowly, my body began to relax. Calm settled, and embarrassment set in. I hadn't had a panic attack in so long that I almost forgot what it felt like. Avyn had seen me at my worst with those, but this was new for Callum. I wasn't sure what he thought of it, and I couldn't bring myself to look at him right now. Looking past Avyn, I could see everybody standing on the back deck, looking out with concerned faces.

"I want to go home, Avyn . . ." I said quietly. "I can't go back in there after this."

Callum gently rubbed my arms. "Baby, nobody is going to judge you."

I ignored him. "Please," I begged her.

"Okay. I'm sure Malcolm will let me borrow his car."

She stood and beckoned him over. They spoke quietly for a moment before he handed over his keys. She came back over and helped me to my feet.

"Just give her some time," she said to Callum, who I was sure was confused. "I'll let you know when we make it back."

She led me away from him. Eva stepped forward in front of me when we got closer to the group.

"I'm so sorry, Pasha. . . . I wasn't thinking."

I shook my head. "No. No, this was good news, and I'm so happy for you. It's just me. It's nothing to do with you. Thank you for having me tonight, but I think it's best if I leave."

She didn't try to protest, and it wouldn't have done her any good. She simply pulled me in for a hug and kissed my cheek before allowing Avyn to lead me inside. Avyn grabbed her purse and mine, and we headed out to Malcolm's car. As we settled in, I saw Callum standing in the doorway. He looked hurt, and I hated that. I knew he wanted to console me, but I just needed to go home and gather myself right now.

Back in my apartment, I sat in the tub in the bubble bath Avyn had ready for me. She stepped out to call Callum and let him know that we were here, and I was okay. Only I was far from okay. My heart was aching in its cavity, and the drive back was filled with loud and deafening silence. I cried the entire ride. I cried in the elevator. I cried for twenty minutes in my bed while Avyn lay there with me, gently rocking me and wiping my tears. Eva's announcement did a number on me.

It made me sad because I knew that being with Callum meant I would be around everybody in attendance tonight. I'd have to watch her belly grow. I'd probably find myself touching it. I'd have to listen to her picking out baby names or talk about her pregnancy journey, all while I sat there, childless . . . a childless mother, mourning the loss of three pregnancies and the death of a child.

The realization was too much for me. I might have held it together if Callum hadn't grabbed my hand. It was like a knee-jerk reaction for him when the words left Eva's mouth. It was as though he felt the shift in my spirit when the feeling hit me. I was so embarrassed about breaking down like that in front of everyone.

I never wanted Eva or Chris to feel like I made their moment about me. That wasn't my intention. Their baby was a beautiful blessing, and I wish them a happy and healthy pregnancy. I just couldn't wholeheartedly share in their moment.

A knock at the door interrupted my thoughts. It crept open, and Avyn stepped in with a coffee mug.

"I made you some tea," she said softly. She placed it on the edge of the tub and sat on my countertop. "Talk to me, Pash."

"I want my baby, Avyn."

"I know, pooh."

"I don't understand how I can be blessed with something so beautiful, and he be snatched away from me before I could really love him. I know they say God doesn't make mistakes, but I can't believe he would want this. There had to have been something I could've done, Avyn. There had to be. I refuse to believe that God wanted me to lose three babies and then turn around and give birth to a stillborn. I refuse to believe that I deserve this type of pain. It had to have been me."

My tears started up again. Avyn began to get down from the counter and approach me, but I stopped her. I had to get it out of my system.

"Pash. . . . None of those losses were because of anything you did. The doctors all said that."

"Then somebody is lying!" I screamed. "*Something's wrong with you. You're sabotaging these pregnancies. You didn't eat right! You didn't take care of yourself.* It was me, Avyn! *Me!*"

"Did *he* say that to you?"

"Yes! Over and over and over again!"

She hopped down from the counter and came over to me against my protesting. I tried to push her away, but she kept coming to the point where she climbed into the tub with me, clothes and all, and wrapped me up in a hug that I so desperately needed. I cried profusely against her, letting out anguished cry after anguished cry. I cried for me. I cried for the babies I'd lost. I cried for my son. I needed to purge because it was eating me alive.

Avyn pulled back and cupped my face.

"You listen to me. Raymond was a narcissistic, evil, selfish son of a bitch. He manipulated you for years, Pasha. You were good to him until you could no longer fulfill his desires. *That* is not on you. The loss of those innocent babies is *not* on you. I was with you through every single pregnancy. You did everything you were supposed to do, baby.—Everything. Losing them was *not* your fault. Your miscarriages were developmental. Your stillborn was . . . was an accident, something completely out of your control. It wasn't you, and you have to stop believing that. Do you hear me?"

I nodded with tears streaming down my face. I heard her. It didn't make it any easier to accept. Not when I had my own husband in my ear, blaming me every chance he got.

"I'd like to be alone," I whispered.

"Pash—"

"Please. I just want to shower and go to bed, Avyn. I promise I'm okay."

"You are shutting me out again. I won't let you do that. I love you, and I'm gonna be right here whether or not you like it. I don't care if I have to camp out in your living room. You are not getting rid of me tonight."

She stood from the tub and stepped out. After grabbing a towel and wrapping it around herself, she left the bathroom. I sighed as I sank under the water. This was going to be a long night.

⌒⌒

By the time I got out of the shower, I wasn't feeling any better. I actually felt worse. On top of my grief, I felt deep, immense anger. I wanted to break something . . . hit something . . . fuck up something. I knew exactly *who* I wanted to direct that anger toward, but there was no chance of me getting out of my apartment tonight.

I heard voices in my living room when I walked out of the bathroom. Peeking around the corner, I saw Blake and Tia. They were all dressed in their pajamas and had made themselves comfortable on my couch. I remained quiet as I went into my closet to change into a pair of leggings and an oversized T-shirt.

Back in my bedroom, I plugged my phone into the charger and placed it on the dresser before turning back the covers and climbing into bed. Just as my head hit the pillow, my phone gave a notification. I saw it as I picked it up to see a message from Callum.

Callum: Avyn already assured me that you were safe and going to bed, but I needed to reach out to you. I care for you,

Pasha. I know you know that. I know you may need some
time, but I'm right here, baby. Please don't shut me out.

I wanted to respond, but I couldn't. My heart wasn't in the
right place right now. I knew that it was all in my head. Sleep was
the last thing on my mind. I rolled onto my side and stared out the
window at the lights from the city surrounding me.

Every so often, one of the girls came to check on me. When
I heard their footsteps, I pretended to be asleep. As soon as they
were gone, my eyes flew open. This went on for two hours until
they finally all fell asleep. The apartment was quiet and dark aside
from the light above the stove.

Easing out of bed, I went into my closet and closed the door.
I got my keepsake box down and sat in the middle of the floor.
Lifting the lid, I pulled out the blanket my son had been swaddled
in. Holding it up, I buried my face in it. It no longer smelled like
him, but I could never forget his scent.

I set it aside and picked up the small container that housed
his umbilical cord and wristband. Jordan Michael Sinclair . . . my
little sunshine. I picked up the photos the hospital so graciously
provided me with as part of their bereavement program. Tears
whirled in my eyes as I looked at his handsome little face. He
looked so much like my father. Even in his cold state, he simply
looked like he was sleeping peacefully. Only it wasn't a peaceful
sleep. It was an endless slumber.

I put the items on the floor and picked up the final object,
his little urn of ashes. Lifting it to my lips, I kissed the cold metal.

"My sweet baby boy . . . Mommy misses you so much. It's so
unfair that you can't be here."

Again, I felt the tears streaming down my face. They weren't
just tears of sadness. I felt so much anger and rage thinking about
the way Raymond left me to grieve by myself. He didn't leave
physically, but mentally and emotionally, he abandoned me. In

front of other people, he was the most loving and doting husband in the world. Alone, he was cruel and standoffish. For weeks after our son passed, he looked at me in disgust.

Every time I cried, he'd make me feel worse by telling me I should have done this or that, and our child would be here. When he decided he wanted to try again, I was barely six weeks postdelivery. I wasn't sexually or mentally ready to try to have another baby, and I adamantly refused him. He cursed me from here to hell and called me everything but a child of God. How could he think I'd be ready after the loss I experienced?

As I sat there stewing in my anger, I thought of all the things I wanted to say to him that I never said. I thought of all the pain I wanted to inflict upon him. He was basking in the joy of another woman carrying his child while mine was sitting here with his ashes in an urn.

I placed the items back in the box and put it on the top shelf. After slipping on a hoodie and my sneakers, I left the closet. I walked carefully to the front door so I wouldn't wake the girls and grabbed my keys. After quietly unlocking the door, I slipped into the hallway, took the elevator down, and quickly went to my car.

My mind raced as I drove through the semiquiet city streets to the place that was once my home. It was after midnight when I arrived. The light in the living room was on, and Raymond's car was in the driveway. Memories of coming home to my things sitting on the front lawn filled my head. I saw Adora proudly standing in my doorway, laughing at me. I felt embarrassed knowing my neighbors could probably hear and see everything. Anger coursed through my veins as I climbed out of the car and stormed up to the front door, banging on it.

I could hear movement on the other side before it swung open. There stood my soon-to-be ex-husband, his mistress . . . and their baby. She'd given birth. I stared at the beautiful, curly-haired little girl swaddled in a pink blanket. For a moment, I was stunned.

"What the hell are you doing here this time of night?" Raymond snapped, breaking my stare.

I blinked and refocused my gaze on his angry face. "I have something to say to you."

Adora scoffed. "You show up here after midnight, banging on our door while my child is sleeping, and you think you're gonna talk to him? I get that you don't have any children, but please, consider those of us who do."

"The only thing saving you from my fist meeting your face is the fact that you are holding that baby. Consider *that*, bitch."

"Adora, take my daughter upstairs and wait for me, baby," Raymond instructed.

She frowned.

"You should listen like you've been trained to do," I said, folding my arms.

"Bitch—"

"Adora!" Raymond raised his voice. "Go—now."

He leaned in and kissed her, then motioned for her to leave. Reluctantly, she backed away and took the stairs. Raymond stepped out onto the front porch and closed the door.

"What, Pasha? What did you have to say that was so important it could—"

I hauled off and slapped the shit out of him will all my might. He stumbled backward, his body hitting the door with a thud. When he realized what had transpired, he tried to come at me, but I raised my foot and kicked him as hard as I could in the groin. *That* took him to his knees.

"You bitch . . ." He seethed through gritted teeth.

I stood over him and bent down. Grabbing his face, I forced his eyes to meet mine.

"I . . . fucking . . . hate you. I hate you for all the mean and nasty things you said to me. I hate you for making me hate myself. I hate you for making me grieve the loss of our son alone! I gave you the best of me, and when my best wasn't up to your standards, you discarded me like trash. You used me until you couldn't use me anymore. I was your wife, . . . your *wife*, Raymond. Through sickness and health, until death do us part. *That's* what you promised me! Where were you when I needed you? Where were you when I needed a shoulder to cry on? A listening ear? Comfort from my fucking husband? I was dying inside, and you were out here sticking your dick in other women and getting them pregnant!"

I slapped him again.

"Do you know how many times I wanted to take my life and end it all? *That's* how bad my depression was, and you did nothing to make things better for me! I catered to you day and night for years. I fed you, cleaned your house, and washed your dirty drawers. I gave you my body when I didn't even feel like it, and you, in turn, made me feel like my body was disgusting. This is the same body that tried to carry four of your children! This is the same body that was poked and prodded with needles for fertility treatments to bear *you* a child. How *dare* you shame me. How *dare* you disrespect me!"

"You were weak!" he spat, shoving me away. He climbed to his feet and towered over me as he glared at me. "I knew it from the moment I laid eyes on you. You were nothing but a young girl trying to play a woman's game with an older man. You were the perfect submissive, and it was so easy to make you one."

I shoved him, but it did nothing but cause him to laugh.

"You want the truth, right? That's what you came here for, right? You want to get some shit off your chest. Don't grow a backbone now, Pasha. That man has you feeling yourself. He gave you a little bit of confidence, and you thought it would be a good idea to come over to *my* house!"

He backed me down the steps.

"Look at you. You're nothing. You don't have shit, and you will *never* be shit. As soon as he leaves you, you'll be back to your same old, tired, depressed self. I'm sure you'll find something to eat your way through it like you always do. Who knows, maybe this time, you'll actually have the nerve to take the coward's way out. You cut off your family. Your parents are dead, and so is your son. Who would really miss you?"

I saw red. . . . Burning, hot, fire red. If I could get away with murdering him where he stood, I would gladly do it. The smirk on his face as the last words left his mouth made my blood boil. I looked down at the bricks lining the driveway. It would be so easy to pick up one and smash it into his head over and over until there was nothing but bloody brain matter splattered across the lawn.

But I couldn't do that. He'd already stripped me of so much. I wouldn't allow him to rob me of my freedom too. I stepped toe-to-toe with him.

"The hell you wished for me is the one you will burn in, Raymond. I promise you that. You can tear me down and try to hurt me with your words, but that says more about you than it ever will about me. You are insecure. You get off on being a narcissistic son of a bitch because it somehow makes up for what you lack. You are selfish and heartless, and you will never be deserving of real love or happiness. One of these days, you'll get what's coming to you. You'll reap what you sow."

I backed away from him and returned to my car with his laughter and obscenities ringing in my ears. I fought back the tears stinging my eyes. He wouldn't be the cause of another tear—not from me. I almost let the devil use me to do his dirty bidding. My mother always told me that injustice never profited. Raymond may have won this battle, but he was waging a war against his own karma.

When I got back to my apartment, I walked in to the girls sitting on my couch, worried looks on their faces. The moment the door opened, they all jumped to their feet.

"Where have you been!" Avyn yelled at me. "You just left! No note, no text,—no nothing! You left your phone here. Anything could have happened to you, Pasha."

"I want to be alone," I stated, hanging up my keys.

"No, you don't need—"

"I want to be alone!" I screamed. "I love y'all, but I need peace and quiet and time to myself right now! Please, get out!"

They looked at me like I was crazy, and maybe I was crazy. But I needed this. I needed time to process the surge of emotions flowing through me. I didn't want to blow up at them. I didn't want to be comforted. I just needed to feel it. I spent too much time burying my feelings deep inside myself. If I didn't feel every bit of this starting right now, I was going to fall right back into my depressive state. I couldn't afford that.

I cleared my throat. "I apologize for yelling. I promise, on my son, I will text you and let you know I'm okay. I just . . . I need to be alone. Please, understand that."

A look of reluctance filled their faces. Quietly, they gathered their things and headed for the door.

"I'll put in some vacation time for you at work," Avyn said. She turned back once she was on the other side. "We love you, Pasch. Remember that."

She didn't give me a chance to respond before she closed the door. I looked around the now-empty apartment. I was alone, . . . just like I was used to being.

CHAPTER THIRTY
Callum

TWO WEEKS LATER

IT HAD BEEN two weeks since I'd last seen Pasha, and I felt the void. I missed her terribly. She'd only texted me that she needed some time to deal with a few things and that she was sorry. She wouldn't answer my calls. She wouldn't open the door when I showed up at her apartment. I'd gone over the day after game night, pleading with her to at least lay eyes on her. She never responded.

Defeated, I'd gone upstairs to Avyn's apartment to talk to her. She gave me the spill on what happened after they left. I understood why she chose to remove herself from the space. What I didn't understand was why she was adamant about doing this alone.

"Callum, you have to snap out of this," Bella said, turning off my television. "You've been moping around here for two weeks. I know you miss her—"

"I don't just miss her."

She placed her hands on her hips. "You love her, don't you?"

"Yes, I love her. I got to watch her grow into her own woman. I witnessed her confidence expand. I watched her go from being homeless and helpless to taking care of herself. How could I not fall in love with the growth in her?"

"I knew this was coming. I should have put money on it."

"Very funny, Bella."

"I'm just kidding. I need to see you smile. You haven't been roasting me like usual. Precious misses her favorite uncle. You haven't picked her up early as much, and she's noticed."

"I'm sorry, Bell. I'll get her tomorrow. I miss my baby."

"I think you should continue to let her know you're here, but give her some space. Sometimes, we want to deal with hurt alone to feel it fully. Feeling is healing, Callum. Deciding to heal is a personal journey. When you deep dive into your feelings, it can take you to dark places. You don't want to pull people down with you. You don't want anybody distracting you in doing the work you need to do."

"Are you an accountant or a psychologist?"

She giggled. "I took a few psych classes, and I read. My point is you have to give her time to do what she needs to do for herself. Sometimes, the most important part of healing has to be done alone. I know she cares for you. I might even go as far as saying she loves you. If fate can put you in each other's paths twice already, the third time has got to be the charm."

Sitting there, I wondered if I had pursued her too soon. Did I do too much too soon? Every part of me that I'd given her was genuine. Every word was true. Every hug, kiss, or lovemaking session was from my heart. I sighed, praying my sister was right. Maybe she needed something that only she could give herself. I was patient. I had faith that what we were building was solid enough to hold up while she got herself together.

⁓

I turned into the parking lot of the hotel where Pasha worked. While I was sure she wouldn't be here, I prayed that Avyn was. She told me Pasha had promised to let her know she was alive and well while she took the time to herself. I just wanted to know if she was okay. I hadn't seen Avyn since the Sunday after game night. She told me the same thing Bella had . . . give her some time.

I headed inside to the front desk.

"Hi, is Avyn here?" I asked the receptionist.

"Um, . . . sure. Give me a second."

She disappeared into the back and returned shortly with Avyn in tow.

"Callum? Hey, how are you?" She rounded the counter and gave me a warm hug.

"I've seen better days," I answered.

"You look like shit."

"Then I look like I feel. Do you have a minute?"

"Yeah." She led me into the same space where we first talked about Pasha. After closing the door, she motioned for me to sit down.

"You want to know about Pasha?"

"I do. Damn, this feels like déjà vu all over again."

"I know." She sighed. "I haven't laid eyes on her in two weeks. She took a personal leave of absence from here and the grocery store. She's not at her apartment, and I don't know where she is, but she assured me she's alive and well."

I shook my head. "This is crazy."

"She reached a breaking point, Callum. I honestly feel like this would be good for her. She's never had time to just work on healing alone. It's been circumstance after circumstance. Now, she's free of that bastard." A look of disgust presented on her face. "She went to confront Raymond."

"What? When?"

"Game night. Remember I told you she left the apartment, and we didn't know where she went?"

"Yeah, but how do you know she confronted him?"

"Because I ran into him at the gas station, and he all but cursed me out about it. He told me I needed to keep my bitch on a leash because next time, he was pressing charges. Malcolm had to put me into the car because I was about to tag his ass."

My brows furrowed. I was upset that she went over there and did God knows what. She was lucky she'd gotten away with throwing bricks through that man's windows. Going back there was pushing it.

"Did she say anything about it?" I asked.

Avyn shook her head. "She refused to talk about it. The only thing she responded with was she said what she needed to say, and she was done with him."

"Good."

"You know their divorce was finalized."

I ran my hand over my head. "I know. I've texted and called her, but she won't respond. I miss her, Avyn. I feel like my heart just upped and walked away from me."

She looked at me curiously. "You love her, don't you?"

I chuckled lightly. "Is it obvious?"

"Is fat meat greasy? I knew this was bound to happen. From the night I found her reservation in your name, I knew you'd be someone special to her. God broke the mold when he made you, Mr. Ellis. . . . Just don't tell Malcolm I said that."

I chuckled. "I won't."

She stood. "I promise, I'll try to get her to call you when I talk to her."

"Thank you, Avyn."

"It's nothing. You brought my bestie back to me. It's the least I can do."

She pulled me in for a hug before we exited the room and went our separate ways. Back in my car, I settled into the driver's seat and pulled out my phone. Going to Pasha's and my text thread,

I hit the button to send her a voice message like I'd been doing for fourteen days now.

"Hey, baby. . . . It's day fourteen. I miss you, Pasha. My days and nights have all seemed to run together at this point. . . . I'm worried about you, baby. I know you told Avyn that you're okay, but I can't believe that until I lay eyes on you or at least hear your voice. Just please . . . Call me or come home."

I gripped the phone as I swallowed the lump in my throat.

"I love you, Pasha. That's not how I wanted to tell you, but I love and miss you. Come home."

I sent the message and placed my phone in the cupholder. Silently, I said a prayer. I hoped wherever she was, she was safe and taking care of herself.

CHAPTER
THIRTY-ONE
Pasha

I STOOD ON THE balcony of my hotel, sipping a glass of wine as I looked out at the ocean. The cool breeze and sunshine felt wonderful against my skin. For the last week and a half, I'd been down in Charleston, South Carolina, clearing my head and my heart. After signing my divorce papers, I immediately packed a bag and left the city. I desperately needed a getaway, even if it was only an hour from home.

I had planned to come here and release my son's ashes into the ocean. I walked along the beach the night I arrived to find a good spot. I'd said a prayer and tried to free his little soul, but I'd only been able to dump a small amount of his ashes. If I'd released all of him, that was it. I'd never have him close again, and I didn't want that. That night, I sat along the shore and cried my eyes out.

I knew letting go was hard. I knew it would be impossible to let go completely. But I didn't think saying goodbye would cause me so much distress. Since that night, I'd mostly been in my room. I practiced yoga and meditation. I prayed for strength and healing. My son's ashes sat in the urn on the desk next to my journal. I'd been writing in it every day. I wrote to my parents, my son, my girls, Callum, and myself.

Callum. . . . I missed him terribly, but I couldn't talk to him right now. I missed being in his arms. I missed his hugs and kisses. I missed his comfort. Every day since that night, he'd sent me messages telling me how much he missed me. He sent beautiful affirmations and words of encouragement. He pleaded with me just to hear my voice. It was hard ignoring him, but I needed my space.

Avyn only heard from me because I promised her I'd be in touch. I sent an "I'm alive, and I'm fine" message every three days. She has slipped in a few other messages, and I'd respond to what was necessary, but that was it. I needed to grant myself the peace by any means that had been disrupted the last few years of my life.

I left the balcony and headed back inside to the desk. After sitting, I went to my contact information and sent Dr. Thomas a video request. It was time for my therapy session, and she graciously agreed to do a virtual chat. The screen populated, and her face suddenly appeared. She held a warm smile.

"Good morning, Pasha."

"Good morning."

"How are you feeling this morning?"

"I feel okay. I was up at sunrise to meditate and do some reflective journaling."

"Meditation? That's new for you. How is that going?"

"Well. It's peaceful and helps to clear my mind, if only for a little while."

"How are you feeling after finalizing your divorce?"

I smiled softly. "Free. I know I shouldn't have confronted Raymond the other week, but I needed to get that off my chest. Even if he didn't care, it was important to me that he knew what he did to me and how he made me feel. Being free of him lifted a world of weight off my shoulders."

"I imagine so. Have you accomplished anything you wanted to do since being away?"

I sighed. "I'm becoming more in tune with myself, slowly but surely. I haven't cried in four days, so that's a plus. Um . . . I still haven't been able to let go of all of my son's ashes. I released a little, but I can't bring myself to do the rest."

She offered a sympathetic smile. "That's okay, Pasha."

"It haunted me for days, Dr. Thomas. I saw him in my dreams, and even there, he was dead. I touched him and held him. I cried for him the same as I did when they placed him in my arms in the hospital."

"Dreams like that have several meanings. I'm no expert in dream interpretation, but in your case, I think it means you have yet to let go of your grief. You have to find a healthy way to let go so that you can heal, Pasha."

I shook my head. "I can't let him go. He'll think I forgot about him. I could never forget him, Dr. Thomas."

"You don't have to forget him. But I can't imagine he would want his mommy to continue to blame herself. He wouldn't want you to walk around carrying all of this guilt. His death was not your fault, Pasha. I saw you throughout your pregnancy. You told me how careful you were about what you ate, how you exercised regularly, took your vitamins, and went to all your appointments. You were careful. What happened to him was a horrible accident, and there was nothing you could do."

Tears stung my eyes. "How do I tell my brain that? How do I let him go when I have nothing left of him but a few items from the hospital and his ashes? I wanted to bury him. I wanted a place where I could go visit him and sit with him like I do my parents."

"It's not too late to do that."

I shook my head. "I don't have the money for that. There's the plot, the headstone, fees . . . I can't afford it. I told Raymond I wanted a burial, and he told me it would be too much for me. It was what I needed, and he just ignored it because he didn't want to deal with me and my emotions. . . . He controlled everything. I was so stupid to stay with him for so long."

"You were dependent on him, and he knew that. Narcissists have a way of making you feel like you'll have nothing without them. But you are not under him anymore. You have your own now, and *you* did that. If you want to bury your son, you can do that now. Many funeral homes do this free of charge."

"They do? I didn't know that."

"I can give you a list of places I know that do the service. You may have to pay a small plot fee depending on where you want him to be, but you can bury your son in peace."

I began to cry. Had I known this information, I would have done it alone. My baby deserved to be laid to rest. I wanted him with my parents. I wanted him where the three people I loved most could all be together until I joined them in the afterlife. Dr. Thomas and I spoke for another thirty minutes before I got off the phone. After talking to her, I felt I needed to nap.

Getting up from the chair, I walked over to the bed and climbed under the covers. As soon as my head hit the pillow, I got a text notification. Picking up the phone, I saw that it was Callum. When I opened the thread, a voice message populated. I hovered over the play button for a moment before pressing it. His deep voice came through, and I could hear its sadness.

"Hey, baby. . . . It's day fourteen. I miss you, Pasha. My days and nights have all seemed to run together at this point. . . . I'm worried about you, baby. I know you told Avyn that you're okay, but I can't believe that until I lay eyes on you or at least hear your voice. Just please . . . Call me or come home."

There was a slight pause, and I thought the message was done until he said something I wasn't expecting.

"I love you, Pasha. That's not how I wanted to tell you, but I love and miss you. Come home."

My body shot up from the bed. I stared at the phone. Did he just say that? I pressed play again, listening carefully to the message.

"*I love you, Pasha . . .*"

"He loves me," I parroted.

My heart fluttered. I hadn't imagined hearing those words would make me feel so good. He told me he wanted to love me. If I was honest with myself, I was a little afraid of loving him. I was afraid to give my heart to another man and have him do what Raymond did . . . or worse. But Callum was different. His spirit felt different with mine. He was sweet, caring, loving, gentle, and so intentional.

I hated being away from him. It killed me not to speak with him. So many times, I wanted to pick up the phone when he called me. I knew I was wrong for shutting him out, but I needed this. If I knew his heart the way I felt it did, he would understand, and he wouldn't hold it against me. Still, hearing him tell me he loved me made me vulnerable.

I looked back down at the phone. With trembling fingers, I picked it up and pressed the call button. He answered on the first ring.

"Baby."

"Callum . . ."

"Baby, where are you? Are you okay? God, it's good to hear your voice, Pasha. I've been so worried about you."

"I'm okay. I just needed to get away and clear my head. I'm sorry I abandoned you—"

"No, don't apologize. You know what you need better than anybody. I can't hold that against you. I just . . . I miss you."

"I miss you too." Tears spilled down my cheeks. "Did you . . . Did you mean it? When you said you love me."

"Of course I meant it."

"Say it."

He didn't hesitate. "I love you, Pasha. I love your smile. I love your voice and the way you say my name. I love your eyes and the way you look at me so innocently. They make me want to protect you from all the bad in the world. I love the way your body feels in my arms when I hold you. I love kissing you, making love to you. I love your strength and resilience. With all that life has thrown at you, you're still here, and I'm *so* proud of you for still being here. I love your friendship with Avyn and how she's willing to go to bat for you every time. She's a little crazy, but they make the best friends."

I giggled when he said that. My girl had a few loose screws, but they were the reason I loved her so much.

"I'm in love with every part of you, baby," Callum said. "You never have to wonder about that."

". . . Can you come to me?" I asked through my tears.

"All I need is an address, and I'll be there."

I quickly rattled off the name and address of the hotel along with my room number. The overwhelming need to be in his arms overtook me. How was I supposed to go about my day after he told me something like this?

∽

An hour and forty-five minutes later, someone knocked on my door. After getting off the phone, I'd showered and washed my hair and was now dressed in biker shorts and an oversized T-shirt. I'd flat-twisted my hair and pinned it in a low bun. After checking myself in the mirror, I headed to the door. My hand lingered on the knob for a moment. With a deep breath, I opened it.

There stood Callum dressed in a pair of shorts, a T-shirt, and slides with a duffle bag in his hand. When his eyes landed on mine, he dropped the bag and pulled me into his arms. My hands went to his face, gently stroking his cheeks. I searched his eyes for any signs of anger or disgust. The only thing I saw in them was love.

"I love you too," I whispered. I pecked his lips. "I love you too."

I did love him. I loved him for everything he was and everything I was when I was with him. He'd been so good to me. He'd been patient, kind, and understanding. He's been a source of strength, a listening ear, and a shoulder to cry on. How could I not love him?

We shared a sensual kiss before I pulled him inside. He grabbed his bag and followed me into the bedroom. After dropping it next to the bed, he took my hand and pulled me out onto the balcony. Taking a seat on the chaise, he pulled me down between his legs. His arms came around my waist as he kissed my temple.

"I've missed you, love," he said.

"I've missed you too."

"How's your mental, baby?"

"I'm getting there, Callum. I've been allowing myself to just feel every emotion without fighting it. I think I've stifled a lot of my pain because I was made to feel ashamed of how I responded to it. The hardest part has been dealing with the grief of losing my son. When Eva revealed she was pregnant, it was like he grabbed ahold of me and wouldn't let go. All I have left of him are a few things from the hospital, a few pictures, and his ashes."

I paused for a moment and closed my eyes. I could feel myself becoming emotional. After a deep breath, I continued.

"I've gone through that box so many times. I've touched and smelled his things, and it never had a hold on me like it did this time. It haunted me for days. I couldn't eat; I couldn't sleep. Every time I closed my eyes, I saw my baby's face. I see my parents, and they're both telling me I need to release them all so that I can really start to heal."

I sat up and turned to face him. He grabbed my hands and kissed them.

"I want to bury my son properly. I think if I give him a proper homegoing service, it will give me closure. Dr. Thomas, my therapist, said many funeral homes will do it free of charge."

"Really? I didn't know that."

"Me either. She said there may only be a small fee for the plot."

"I'll take care of whatever the cost is."

"I can't ask you to do that—"

"You didn't ask. I told you, whatever you need from me, it's yours. I don't wanna hear any protests. Please. . . . Let me do this for you. You want him next to your parents, right?"

"Yes," I whispered.

"I'll make it happen."

I looked up at him. Where had this man been eight years ago? Why couldn't he have been the man I ran into instead of Raymond? I might have saved myself from so much heartbreak. I often wondered where my life would have taken me if I'd never met Raymond. But on the other hand, I could have met someone worse instead of better. I could have been dealing with physical or sexual abuse on top of mental and emotional. Whatever the reason for Callum and me meeting later in life, I was grateful to have him now.

CHAPTER
THIRTY-TWO
Callum

I STAYED WITH PASHA for three days before she decided she was ready to come home. During that time, I sat back and watched her during the early morning hours when she thought I was asleep. Frequently, she'd sit out on the balcony and meditate or pray. I wondered what was going through her head during those times. I didn't ask, and she didn't elaborate. I figured her talks with God were personal and something she needed for herself.

While she prayed for herself, I prayed for her. I asked God to touch her, heal her heart, and protect her mind. It's hell trying to leave past trauma behind. Some things aren't easy to let go of, her son being one of them. When I told her I'd pay for the costs of the funeral, I didn't think twice about that. I thought about my parents and how I wouldn't have had any peace if their bodies hadn't been recovered after their accident.

I couldn't imagine not being able to give them a proper burial or being able to visit them. While cemetery visits could be emotional, they gave me comfort. Sometimes, sitting out there with my parents granted me peace. I knew they were watching over Bella and me and were proud of what they saw. We'd lived up to everything they'd hoped and dreamed for us, or at least I hoped we had.

"All right, Mr. Ellis, this is the final total."

Today was Thursday, and I was meeting with the advisor for the cemetery. Yesterday, Pasha and I visited the funeral home to inquire about a small service. The whole ordeal took a lot out of her, so I told her I would handle everything else. I roped in Avyn to get flowers and their friends together. My friends would be here to support her on Saturday as well. They were all on board to be there for her when I told them what we were doing.

Whipping out the envelope with the cash Pasha had given me for the car, I paid for the plot. I couldn't think of a better way to return it to her. When I told Mr. Smart the story, he was generous enough to knock a substantial amount off the price. He told me that he would have just given it to us for free if he could have. I appreciated that.

"Thank you, Mr. Smart. You don't know how much this means to my girlfriend."

"I can only imagine. I pray that this brings her the peace she's looking for."

"Thank you."

I stood and shook his hand, then left the building. I climbed in my car and headed to Pasha's. For some odd reason, traffic was backed up for at least a mile. When I'd finally made it past all the hangups, I saw that there had been an accident. A car had slammed into the back of an eighteen-wheeler. It was a mangled mess. The streets were lined with fire trucks and police cars. The sight of the coroner van alerted me that someone hadn't made it. I said a silent prayer as I drove past.

The ten-minute drive turned into at least forty-five. It was nearing twelve when I made it to Pasha's. While she'd come home, she was still on a leave of absence from work until the following week. Pulling into the parking lot, I grabbed a spot and headed inside, up to her floor. Stepping off the elevator, I went to her door and lightly knocked. She opened it a few seconds later.

"Hey, come on in."

She left the door open and hurried off. When I stepped in, she was at the stove cooking. The small space smelled terrific. After hanging up my keys, I headed to where she stood at the stove. Wrapping my arms around her waist, I kissed her temple. She tilted her head up and offered me her lips.

"I missed you," she said softly.

"I missed you too. What are you cooking?"

"Pepper steak and rice. You hungry?"

"I'm starving. I didn't eat breakfast."

"Well, it's almost ready. I just need the sauce to thicken up a little."

She turned the eye down to simmer and covered the pot with a lid. Turning in my arms, she wrapped her arms around my neck and hugged me tightly. Bending my knees a little, I stooped to pick her up. With her legs around my waist, I turned and placed her on the counter. She continued to hug me as I placed kisses on the side of her face.

"Where's your mental today?" I asked, gliding my hands up and down her back.

"A seven."

"That's better than yesterday."

"I had a good cry this morning. I journaled about it, and I felt a little better." She pulled back, looking at me with sad eyes. "How did everything go?"

"Everything is paid for and set for Saturday. How are you feeling about it?"

She sighed. "It's long overdue. He'll be with my parents, and that's how I want it."

"I'm sure they are taking great care of him. He's probably the most spoiled little boy running around the pearly gates."

She smiled softly. "They would have spoiled him rotten, especially my father."

I chuckled. "My parents would have loved Precious. Spoiled wouldn't have been the word."

"Like *you* don't spoil her?"

"I'm guilty. She's the closest thing I have to a kid of my own. She can get whatever she wants out of me, and she knows that."

"The perks of being an uncle. My aunts and uncles were the same way when I was growing up. Mama and Daddy may say no, but TiTi and Unc always came through."

"Have you given more thought to this family reunion?"

She sighed. "I'm gonna go. I logged into FlexSpace for the first time in years. We have this group where they drop all the information, so I know where it will be." She smiled a little. "I went scrolling through my profile, and so many family members have tagged me in old memories or written on my wall expressing how much they missed me or my parents."

"They never forgot about you. I think this will be good for you. A found family is great, but blood will always feel different."

"Are you regretting cutting off yours?"

I shook my head. "I did what was best for Bella and me. My father told me a long time ago that there were snakes in my mother's family. I learned that the hard way. Nobody will ever get the chance to burn me once, let alone twice. I've got my tribe, and I've got you."

I leaned in and pecked her lips.

"I love you," she whispered.

"Say that again."

She giggled. "I said, I love you, Mr. Ellis."

"I love you too, Ms. Brooks."

She revealed that with her divorce, she decided to go back to her maiden name. She said the decision gave her part of her identity back, a part of her that she'd lost a long time ago. I loved that for her.

Settled in the living room, Pasha and I enjoyed the food she made. It was so good that I went back for a second helping. Then the itis kicked in. I found myself stretched out on the couch between her legs with my head resting on her breasts. We'd started off watching a movie before I drifted off to sleep. I wasn't sure how long I'd been out, but I was awakened by Pasha tapping me.

"Callum. . . . Callum!"

My eyes slowly opened, and I looked around. "What's up?"

"Look!"

She pointed at the television. A news report about the accident I'd passed earlier was on the screen.

"That's him," she whispered.

"Who?"

"Raymond."

"Wait . . . You serious? I passed this on my way here earlier."

I sat up, and so did she. Grabbing the remote, she turned up the volume.

"In other news, a horrific scene from the sight of a crash downtown. An accident took place around nine thirty this morning, leaving one dead. Thirty-eight-year-old Dr. Raymond Sinclair, a surgeon at Baptist Hospital, tragically lost his life when he crashed head-on into the back of this eighteen-wheeler—"

Pasha swallowed hard. " . . . He's dead."

I could tell she wasn't sure how to feel about the news. He was horrible to her, but I couldn't picture her wishing death on him. She didn't have that kind of hate in her heart.

"Are you okay?" I asked, grabbing her hand.

"I'm . . . I'm fine. Just in shock." She swallowed hard again. "This is crazy."

"It is."

She reached for the remote and turned off the television. "I don't even have words right now. I mean . . . When I told him he'd reap what he'd sown, I didn't mean this. He's really dead."

"What's going through your mind right now?"

She shrugged. "Is it bad that I don't feel remorse?"

"Given what you've been through with him, no. I mean, it's sad he lost his life, but I don't think I'd be able to shed a tear."

"The only person I feel even the slightest bit of remorse for is the baby. She's the innocent party in all of this, and now, she has to grow up without a father." She shook her head as she rested against me. I wrapped an arm around her, gently stroking her arm.

"All you can do is say a prayer for her."

"You're right. God have mercy on her."

We sat in silence for the longest time. I wasn't sure what was running through Pasha's head, but the news was a lot to swallow. Their divorce was fresh, and now the man who contributed to a lot of her pain was dead. I could only imagine that it was a bittersweet feeling. On one hand, she couldn't celebrate his death. On the other hand, she had no reason to be sad that he was gone.

CHAPTER
THIRTY-THREE
Pasha

Raymond's untimely demise came as a shocker. I felt for his daughter, who had lost her father, and his parents, who had lost their son. But I couldn't find it in my heart to feel any remorse for him. I also didn't have the energy to focus on him at all. Today was Saturday, the day of my baby's funeral. All of my focus and energy had to pour into that.

When I went to bed last night, I was unsure how I would feel in the morning. I thought I would be overcome with emotion. I thought I would wake up in tears and not even want to go to the ceremony. However, what I woke up with was peace. There was comfort in knowing that my son was finally going to be laid to rest. There was comfort in knowing I had a place to visit him with my parents.

I spent the night at Callum's. The morning was a quiet one. I was sure he didn't know what to say to me, but he expressed his love in subtle ways. There were the forehead kisses, the gentle hand squeezes, and light hugs from behind as I got ready. Currently, I was in his bathroom, putting the finishing touches on my makeup.

When I finished, I closed my eyes and said a quick prayer. I asked God to continue to give me the strength to make it through today. I was thankful for Callum and his initiative in this process. The trip to the funeral home to inquire about an urn vault took a lot out of me. When he volunteered to take over the rest of the planning, I didn't stop him. I needed him, and he unselfishly provided me with his time.

The funeral home had provided a beautiful powder-blue marble vault for my baby. Inside, his remains would be safe from moisture or any disturbances in the ground once he was laid to rest. As Dr. Thomas said, they offered me the service for free, expressing their deepest sympathy for my loss.

Opening my eyes, I looked at myself in the mirror. It was time. After taking a deep breath, I left the bathroom and walked into the bedroom. As I made my way into the living room, I could hear voices. When I rounded the corner, I was surprised to see all of Callum's friends, Bella, Martin, and Precious, all dressed in black. When they noticed me, everyone stood. Callum came to me and reached for my hands.

"I hope you don't mind, but they all wanted to support you."

I looked around at everyone. I didn't mind them being here at all. Their support touched my heart.

"Thank you," I said softly.

Precious, Armani, CJ, and Evan approached me with flowers. I stooped down to take them and hugged and kissed them on their cheeks.

"Thank you."

They all kissed my cheek before returning to their parents. I made my rounds, greeting and hugging everyone.

"Are you ready?" Callum asked.

I nodded. We all left the house and dispersed into our respective vehicles. Avyn and the girls were meeting us at the cemetery. I settled into the soft leather seat and closed my eyes. For the duration of the fifteen-minute drive, I stayed like that. I just needed a moment to myself to mentally prepare for what I was about to do.

Callum alerted me when we pulled up to the cemetery. He got out of the car and walked around to my side to let me out. The funeral home director was already waiting for us. I watched as he opened the trunk of his SUV and pulled out the vault housing my son. My heart fluttered. This will be the last time I ever got to hold him.

"I need a minute," I said, looking up at Callum.

He nodded and let go of my hand. I made my way over to the director. He offered me a warm and sympathetic smile.

"Good morning, Ms. Brooks. It's an honor to be able to do this for you."

"Thank you." I hesitated for a moment. "Can I hold him?"

"Of course."

He gently placed the vault into my hands. The moment I held it, I felt a heavy weight in the pit of my stomach. Tears sprang forward to my eyes. Bending down, I pressed a kiss on top of the vault.

"I'm not ready to say goodbye to you, but I know this is something I have to do. You have your grandma and grandpa, and there's no need to be afraid. I know they're gonna take good care of you. I know they'll shower you with all the love I wish I could've given you. . . . I need you to know that I love you and am sorry you couldn't be here. You can finally rest now."

Again, I kissed the vault before placing it back into the director's hands. Walking back over to Callum, he received me with open arms. For a few moments, he held me and gently rubbed my back.

"Are you ready?" he asked softly.

I nodded. He grabbed my hand, and all of us followed behind the director. As we neared the plot where he would be buried, I noticed a group had gathered. Not only had my girls shown up, but their families had shown up as well. All of them held roses in their hands. Pastor Richards, who'd given my parents' eulogy, stood in front of the plot. My heart swelled once again. The love being shown today was unmatched. When we came to a stop, Pastor Richards came to hug me.

"I'm so sorry for your loss, Pasha. I had no idea."

"Thank you, Pastor."

He kissed my cheek before reclaiming his spot. The funeral director placed the vault on the small table. Everyone grabbed a spot in the available seating. Once we were all settled, Pastor Richards began. He spoke about God's love for us and the love we should have for each other as his children. He talked about grief and how we couldn't allow it to consume us. Then he said something that made perfect sense.

"Grief is a form of love. It is the pent-up love you can no longer give or share; it is the loss of the love you can no longer receive."

That summed up exactly how I felt. It was devastating carrying around love for someone who wasn't here to receive it. Of course, there were ways to express that love in other ways, but it would never feel as good as it would if that person were physically here. I listened with an open heart and tried to soak up the words. I knew I'd forever feel this pain, but if I could leave here feeling a little lighter today, that meant progress.

When it came time to place the vault in the ground, I held my head high. I wouldn't cry at this moment because this was what I'd wanted for my baby. Callum squeezed my hand as he'd been doing every so often throughout the service. Pastor Richards asked us to bow our heads as he led us in prayer.

"Lord, I ask for comfort in this young mother's pain. Bring her an abundance of your healing mercies. She may grieve because she cannot see him any longer, but we know to be absent from the body is to be present with the Lord. We rejoice, knowing that little Jordan feels no pain and bears no sickness. He is at peace with his Heavenly Father. I ask that you cover Pasha in your love. Let her know that your grace and mercy are everlasting. In Jesus' name, we pray. Amen."

"Amen."

Everyone stood while I remained seated beside Callum, who held a protective arm around me. One by one, they greeted me with love and condolences. Avyn's parents were the last to come to me. They had been like my second family practically my whole life. Mrs. Timmons reached for me, pulling me into her arms. She embraced me in a motherly hug. I hadn't had one in so long, and to receive it from a woman who had been like a second mother to me was overwhelming.

That was the moment I broke. My tears and cries came in full force. My knees felt weak, but she held me up like only a mother could.

"It's okay, baby. I've got you, and God's got you."

For the longest time, she held me, whispering prayers over me. Mr. Timmons gently rubbed my back in a soothing manner. When I finally composed myself, his wife held me away from her.

"We love you, Pasha. We've always loved you, and you will always have a family with us."

"Thank you," I whispered.

"We have something for you," Mr. Timmons said.

He stepped behind my parents' graves and stooped down. When he came back, in his hand was a beautiful marble slab with my son's name, sunrise, and sunset engraved on it. There was also a little teddy bear etched into it. Mr. Timmons was a mason. The fact that he did this meant so much to me.

"This is . . . beautiful," I whispered.

"We wanted you to have something to mark his burial plot," he explained. "I wasn't sure if you would get a headstone, and I know those things take time. So I got right to work when Avyn told us about the service."

"Thank you. You don't know how much this means to me."

He placed the slab in a chair and pulled me into a warm hug.

"I'm so sorry, baby girl," he stated. "I know you would have made an excellent mother. You had to parent my hellraiser throughout your friendship."

That made me laugh a little. "She's not so bad."

He pulled away and kissed my forehead. "Everybody is welcome to come to our house for the repast. We've taken care of food and everything."

"Thank you both. You didn't have to do that."

"No, baby." He cupped my face. "You should be around people who care about you today. Your mother and father would have done the same if it were Avyn in your shoes."

I nodded. "They would have. They loved her."

"And we love you." Mrs. Timmons gently rubbed my arm. "I'll let everyone know. You take as much time here as you need."

"Yes, ma'am."

They both hugged and kissed me once again before leaving me. I reclaimed my seat next to Callum. I rested my head against his shoulder, and his arm immediately came around me.

"Thank you for all you've done," I said softly as I watched the digger fill the small hole.

"There is no need to thank me. I love you. There's nothing I wouldn't do for you." He kissed my temple.

"Can we stay here for a little while?"

"As long as you need."

I rested against him. We stayed until the last dirt was placed on the plot and smoothed over. The director picked up the marble slab and put it on the grave. I stood and walked in front of all three plots. Three-fourths of my heart was buried here. I would never understand why it had to be them. I'd never understand why they had to go, and I was left here to fend without them . . . but I was still here.

I had to live for them if I couldn't live with them.

I still had life. I had love in abundance. I may have been bruised. I may have bent, but I wasn't as broken as I once thought. The good Lord had kept me for a reason. It was my time to make the most of this life I had left.

More people than I expected were at the Timmons' home.

In addition to the family that came to the service, many of Avyn's aunts and cousins were at the house preparing food before we arrived. They all greeted me with open arms and warm hugs. I was taken care of from the moment I stepped into the house. I couldn't move unless someone were there to ensure I didn't need anything.

"Everyone is so nice," Callum commented.

"They are. It's been like this since I met them. When my parents passed away, Avyn's family was right there to help me grieve." I looked around at all the people. "This is what I miss. To be surrounded with unconditional love and support."

"Well, you have a chance to have that back," he stated, kissing my forehead.

"I have to get it back. You know what I realized while I was away? I needed to do part of this journey on my own to prove to myself that I was strong enough. But just like it takes a village to raise a child, it also takes a village to heal. I don't want to be broken, Callum. My grief and depression took over so much of my life. I don't want it to have that kind of power over me moving forward."

"I have faith in you, baby. Where you fall, I'll be right there to pick you up. You have me for as long as you want me."

"I don't think I could ever *not* want you, Callum. You've been a blessing since day one. I don't know if we were meant to cross paths, but I'm so grateful that you were the one to rescue me that night. You are the best type of unexpected gift, and I love you so much."

I pulled his head to mine and kissed him passionately. It was a brief kiss because the sound of someone clearing their throat interrupted us. We looked up to see Mr. and Mrs. Timmons. They took a seat across from us.

"Pasha, . . . I don't believe you introduced us to your friend here," Mrs. Timmons said with a smile.

"Oh! I'm so sorry. Mr. and Mrs. Timmons, this is Callum Ellis, my boyfriend."

Callum extended his hand. "It's very nice to meet you. We didn't get a chance to be formally introduced earlier."

"It's nice to meet you," Mrs. Timmons said. "My daughter told me what you did for Pasha. Thank you for being here for her."

"No thanks are necessary."

"I guess I don't need to ask if he's good to you," Mr. Timmons said.

"He's very good to me," I confirmed with a light smile.

"Then he's okay with us." The smile slowly faded from his face. "We, um . . . We heard about Raymond. How are you handling that?"

"Honestly, it's sad that he lost his life, but I don't feel any type of way about it. It might sound horrible to say, but I dealt with enough from that man. He made life so much harder for me this last year and a half. I can't say I'm sad he's gone, but I can't give any of my focus to that. I'll pray for his family, but I left all of him behind the day I signed those divorce papers. He was dead to me long before now."

Mrs. Timmons nodded. "Well . . . I'm glad you're okay in that department." She reached for my hand. "Again, I'm so sorry about the loss of your son. You held it together gracefully today. It takes strength and courage to bury a child. No mother should ever have to do that. I'm so happy you finally got to lay him to rest."

"Me too. He's right where he should be . . . next to his grandma and grandpa. I felt so much peace this morning, knowing that they would be rightfully reunited. I couldn't have done this without Avyn and this beautiful man right here."

I grabbed Callum's hand and squeezed it. He blushed at me calling him beautiful, but it was true. He was a beautiful soul inside and out. I would always stand on the fact that God broke the mold when he created this man. I never expected to find love like this. . . . Not this soon and maybe not ever. He was everything I could ever want, but more than that, he was exactly what I needed, and to think I was afraid to let him pursue me. He gave me the courage to love him with how he treated me.

I wasn't sure how long I would have him, but as long as he was mine, I would love him fiercely, unselfishly, and with my entire heart.

CHAPTER
THIRTY-FOUR
Callum

TWO MONTHS LATER

I SAT ON THE edge of her bed, watching Pasha get ready.

It was Saturday and the day of her family reunion. My baby was so nervous. I'd convinced her to reach out before the event so she wouldn't go in blind. It took some persuasion, but I finally got her to agree to post in the group on FlexSpace. She was transparent in telling them her story from beginning to end. In the message, she detailed her struggles with her mental health, the demise of her marriage, as well as her divorce and journey to starting over.

It was no surprise to me that they responded with love and support. Family, *real* family, would never hold her response to grief against her. They showered her with words of encouragement and condolences. Their response was a little overwhelming, but it was precisely what she needed.

Since then, she'd seen a few of her cousins and two of her aunts. The smile on her face when she returned from her lunch dates with them was beautiful. She was glowing, and I loved that for her. I was glad at least one of us got to mend our familial relationships.

"Do I look okay?" she asked again.

"Baby . . . I'm gonna tell you the same thing I told you five outfits ago. You look beautiful."

She looked back at me. "You didn't have to do me like that."

"You did it to yourself, woman." I stood and stepped behind her in the mirror, wrapping my arms around her. "You are perfect and look perfect in whatever you put on."

She looked up at me with a smirk. "You're just saying that because you're ready to go," she jested.

"I *am* ready to go because we have an hour and a half drive. But I also mean it. You look amazing."

She'd lost about twenty pounds in the last two months. She still had her thickness, but it was more toned. She'd lost her stomach, but her breasts, hips, and ass all remained the same. I wasn't mad at that. I loved her body before, and I still love it now. The high-waisted shorts she wore stopped midthigh and showed off their thickness. The crop top showed off a sliver of stomach flesh.

She completed the outfit with sneakers, a simple pair of studs, her mother's necklace, and her father's wristwatch, which I'd since gotten repaired for her. Since it was a little hot out, she pulled her curly mane into a sleek puffball. I loved that style on her. It always presented the perfect, unobstructed opportunity to kiss her neck.

"I do look cute, don't I?" she asked.

I shook my head. Her confidence was growing, and I loved it. I loved that she was beginning to see herself as the beautiful woman we all knew she was, inside and out.

"Come on, woman," I said, patting her thigh. "You know I like to be on time."

"And you know a Black event never starts on time. You're only on time if you're late to these things."

I shook my head as I headed out of the bedroom area to the front door. A few seconds later, she joined me. For a moment, I just admired her. She'd come such a long way. She'd upped her therapy sessions for a while. She was journaling more. She'd be active with her yoga, exercise, and meditation. I was so proud of her will to live and be better.

"What?" she asked, looking up and catching me.

"What do you mean 'what'? I can't admire you?"

She smiled. "Of course, you can." She stood on her toes and pressed her lips to mine. "Come on, let's go."

"After you, my love."

After stopping for gas, our total trip time ended up being two hours.

This year, the family reunion was being held on a yacht. It wasn't a small one either. I was sure her family paid a pretty penny to rent this big baby out for the day. There were three levels and a pool on board. Pasha told me we would be on the water all day. I wouldn't object to that. The weather was beautiful, the perfect day to be outside.

I climbed out of my truck and went to the passenger side to let her out. Hand in hand, we walked toward the boat.

"Pasha!" came a loud squeal from in front of us.

We looked up to see a young woman, probably Pasha's age, running toward us. She damn near knocked her down as she ran into her arms for a hug. They were both squealing and talking over each other. When they finally parted, the woman looked up at me.

"Who's this?"

"Journey, this is my boyfriend, Callum. Callum, this is my cousin, Journey."

"Her once-favorite cousin," Journey stressed, elbowing her. She extended her hand to me. "It's nice to meet you. You did good, girl. Where did you find him, and does he have a brother?"

I chuckled. "It's nice to meet you, Journey. Unfortunately, I don't have a brother."

"A friend?"

"None that are single."

"Well, damn." She shook her head and blew out a heavy breath. "Anyway! It's so good to see you, Pasha. We've really missed you. Family reunions aren't the same without Uncle Solomon and Aunt Virginia cutting up on the dance floor."

"Wait," I interrupted. "So, your parents could dance, but all you have is your two-step?"

She playfully shoved me. "Don't come for my two-step! And, yes, my parents had serious moves. They just didn't pass their rhythm down to me."

Journey laughed. "They sure didn't. But don't worry. I'm gonna loosen her up a bit. Wait until you see her hit this cupid shuffle."

"Y'all still play that?" Pasha asked.

"Every year, boo."

Journey linked her arm through Pasha's and pulled her ahead as they continued to chat. I trailed behind. I came for moral support, so I didn't feel any type of way about that. She was with her family, the people who loved her as much as I did. I'd never stop her from enjoying this reunion with them.

As I boarded the boat, I was greeted with more squealing women. It was clear this was a family thing amongst the women.

Pasha was swarmed with a mixture of younger and older women, all smothering her with hugs and kisses. Her smile was bright and wide. I could feel the joy radiating through her.

"Oh!" Journey exclaimed, looking back at me. She came over and grabbed my hand, pulling me over to the group. "This handsome specimen is Pasha's boyfriend, Callum."

She began rattling off everybody's names, and it was hard to keep up. At least ten women surrounded us.

I smiled and extended my hand to each of them. "Good morning, ladies. It's very nice to meet you all."

They all smiled and said hello.

"Well, he is quite the looker," said the woman I remembered as Aunty Trudy. "I see you, niece. You better hold on tight to this one."

Pasha slipped her arms around my waist. "Trust me, I am. He's not going anywhere, and neither am I."

She tilted her head up, and I pressed my lips to hers. The women giggled and whistled.

Aunt Trudy clapped her hands. "All right now, let's get this party started. Callum, I hope you can hang. Things might get a little wild on this boat. We don't know how to act when we get together."

I chuckled. "I'm ready for whatever, Ms. Trudy."

"Don't say I didn't warn you, handsome."

She playfully winked at me. The group turned to walk ahead, with Pasha and me trailing behind.

"I feel at home," she said, looking over at me. "I needed that push to do this. I won't say the words you've banned me from saying, but you already know what I want to say."

I'd put her on a ban from saying *thank you* to me so much. I didn't need thanks. Anything I did for her was out of love or necessity, never for recognition. It was hard for her, but she'd been doing better by simply accepting it and moving on.

"Anytime, baby."

"When we get back, I have something special for you."

"Something special?"

"Mmm-hmm. Something lacy, black, and very sexy."

"Three of my favorite words. I'll be patiently waiting."

I was lying. I had the image in my head already. As soon as we hit the door, those clothes were coming off.

Ms. Trudy wasn't lying when she said her family didn't know how to act when they got together. By the time I was introduced to everybody, most of them were already a few drinks in, and it wasn't even noon. I wasn't mad, though. They were funny and entertaining. She introduced me to her uncle Peter, and the man practically took me under his wing. I knew he was good and tipsy when he started calling me "nephew" and slapping my back as he talked to me.

He'd taken me around the men in the family, and, of course, they had a lot of questions for me. I didn't mind. Now that they were privy to Raymond's treatment of Pasha, I understood the vetting process they put me through. Nobody was disrespectful; they were simply concerned, and I respected that.

Around one, we settled in the dining area to eat lunch. There was a mouthwatering buffet spread of everything you could think of. Pasha and I sat with Journey and a few of her other cousins. The only sound that could be heard was smacking and moaning at the taste of the food. Whoever prepared the meal did a hell of a job.

"I'm not gonna be any good after this," Pasha commented, rubbing her stomach.

Journey giggled. "Dancing is up next. You'll work that off. Callum, can you dance?"

"I can. I've been trying to teach your cousin here a few moves. She's not so stiff anymore."

Pasha poked me in the ribs. "You've been coming for me since before we left, you know that?"

"It's all love, baby."

I leaned in and pecked her lips, causing her to smile.

"Y'all are just too cute," Journey commented. "It's so good to see you smile again, Pash. I can tell he makes you happy."

She looked at me. "He makes me very happy. You have no idea."

"I see it on you, girl. You're glowing."

She did have this glow about her. It was the glow of a woman who'd gone through tragedy and was finally finding her happiness again. It was the most beautiful thing I'd ever seen. Words couldn't express how much I loved this for her, . . . how much I loved *her*. Life was changing for her, and it was only up from here.

CHAPTER THIRTY-FIVE
Pasha

TODAY OWED ME absolutely nothing.

Spending time with my family was fun, refreshing, and so very needed. I thought things would be awkward, but once Callum and I got there, it felt as natural as if I'd been around all along. We quickly fell back into the flow of old relationships as though no time had passed. The only thing missing was my parents. Much to my surprise, there was a memorial service to honor the family members we'd lost over the years. My parents and my son were both included.

That made me tear up a little.

All in all, I had a great time. Journey was already planning a cousins' gathering. She said she wanted to get drunk and act up without the watchful eyes of our elders. I probably wouldn't get too drunk, but I told her to let me know the details, and I would be there.

Callum and I arrived back at my apartment around midnight. The moment we stepped inside, I began stripping out of my clothes. I wanted to give him a proper thank-you for pushing me to go to this reunion. He eagerly followed the trail of clothes I left behind on my way to the shower. As he undressed, I hopped in and turned on the water to the perfect temperature for both of us. He always complained that I liked that water set on hell, so I had to find a happy medium.

The shower door opened, and he stepped in behind me. I felt his eyes on me as I lathered my body. His hands came to my waist, and he pulled me against him, planting my ass against his hardness. I moaned softly as he cupped my breasts and teased my nipples.

"We can skip the lingerie," he whispered in my ear. "It will only be in my way. I prefer you just like this. . . . Easy access."

"Well then . . ." I turned around in his arms, pressing my front to his. "Allow me to clean you up so I can get you dirty."

He smirked as I grabbed his body wash and the second loofah to bathe him. Slowly, I sensually cleansed every part of him, paying particular attention to his dick. He looked at me lustfully as I stroked it.

"Pash . . ." He groaned as my grip tightened. "Don't tease me, woman."

"You want me?" I asked, stroking faster.

"So . . . fucking bad."

"Then come and get me."

I released him, then opened the shower door and stepped out. He still had to rinse off, and it gave me just enough time to towel dry and head into my bedroom. By the time I was climbing into bed, he stepped into the room, naked as when I'd left him in the shower. He licked his lips as he approached where I lay waiting for him.

"What am I gonna do with your beautiful ass?" he questioned, running a finger between my breasts.

"I can think of a few things."

His lips crashed into mine as he climbed into bed and made himself comfortable between my legs. I rolled him over onto his back and straddled him.

"That's what we're doing tonight?" he smirked. "This is exactly what we're doing."

He pulled me close to him and kissed me again, this time slowly and sensually. I began to grind against him, causing his dick to harden beneath me. Within seconds, he was at full attention. I was already so wet for him that his length was saturated with my juices. As I kissed him, I reached between us and guided him into me. Mutual moans of satisfaction passed between us as he sank into my walls.

I gasped as they expanded to accommodate him. "Shit!"

I hovered slightly as I worked him in and out of my wetness. His hands gripped my ass, spreading my cheeks apart to allow him to go deeper.

"You're so wet . . ." He mumbled, kissing the tops of my breasts.

"All for you, baby. You see what you do to me?"

"Mmm . . . I feel that shit."

He gave my ass a hefty slap, causing me to gasp. His lips latched onto my nipples, forcing whimpers from my throat.

"Ooooh, that feels so good! . . ."

I settled into a slow, sensual ride. My walls contracted around his length with every rise and fall of my hips. Bending his knees, he thrust upward to meet me. With each stroke, the tip of his glorious dick kissed my cervix.

"Callum . . ." I whispered. "You feel so good, baby. . ."

"Take it," he commanded, thrusting harder. "You can take it, can't you?"

"Yes . . . aaaah, . . . fuck!"

"You're wetting me up, baby."

"Ooooh . . . You're so deep!"

Gripping my cheeks, he pounded me from below. My ass clapped and slapped against his thighs, creating a rhythm all its own.

"Don't stop! God, don't stop!"

He flipped me over onto my back and draped my legs over his shoulders. Without missing a beat, he continued thrusting, forcing me to take those glorious strokes.

"Oh God!" I cried out, pressing my head into the pillow.

My chest heaved as tears sprang from my eyes and fell down the sides of my face.

"Shit! Ooooh . . . I'm gonna cum . . . I'm gonna cum!"

He chuckled. "You tapping out on me, love? You said you could take it."

"I can take it. I can—"

He began thrusting wildly into me, stroking my G-spot as he did. My body was riddled with pleasure. I felt him in my stomach. I felt him in the curling of my toes. When he hit that one spot, I cried out so loud that I knew Kelli heard me through the walls. At that point, I was done for. I felt my orgasm building, and when he gave the final death stroke, I released a waterfall, drenching his stomach. That didn't stop him. He continued to stroke me through my orgasm until his collided with mine. His seed shot deep inside of me as his body stiffened on top of mine.

"Fuck!"

A deep, guttural growl emitted from his throat before his body relaxed. He looked down at me. Grabbing his face, I pulled him into the sexiest kiss while his manhood throbbed inside me.

"I love you," I whispered to him.

"I love you too."

Callum and I lay intertwined in my covers two rounds later, with my arm and leg tossed over him. He gently stroked my back as I rested my head on his chest.

"I never want this to end," I said softly, looking up at him. "Being with you, I mean."

"It never has to end," he said, meeting my gaze. "As long as you want me, I'll be here, no ifs, ands, or buts about it. I want you forever, Pasha. It doesn't have to be right now; it doesn't even have to be within the next year, but one day, you will be my wife and the mother of my children."

I sat up and looked at him. "What if . . . What if I can't give you children?"

"I have faith that when the time is right, the good Lord will bless your womb and cover you to carry my child. Even if that isn't the case, there is more than one way to become a parent. No matter how it happens, you and I will raise a beautiful family together. We'll have a beautiful life together, filled with so much love and happiness. Can you see that, baby?"

I nodded. I could see it, but more than that, I *wanted* it. I had enough heartbreak and was ready for my happy ending. Maybe it wouldn't be painted the way I envisioned, but as long as I ended up happy, I would take that. I believed I could have endless happy endings and beautiful beginnings with this man. He'd proven that real love existed.

Love that was rooted in mutual respect.

Love that was patient and kind.

Love that wasn't prideful.

Love that was, above all else, unconditional.

EPILOGUE

TEN MONTHS LATER

*"P*ASHA LEANN BROOKS."

"That's my best friend!" Avyn screamed.

"Go, Pash!" That was Blake.

"That's my girl!" That was Tia.

"Go, Auntie P!" Of course, that was Precious.

We were rolling deep today. Not only were both of our friends in attendance but so were many of Pasha's family members. We were in the auditorium of South Tech. Today, my baby was graduating with her certificate in phlebotomy. She'd completed her coursework. She'd done her internship and passed her boards. Today, she was walking across the stage as a certified phlebotomy tech, and in two weeks, she'd be starting her first official job at an oncology center.

We'd braved long study sessions and sleepless nights. We'd braved the stress of school, work, and maintaining our relationship with each other, family, and friends. It wasn't an easy journey for her. At times, she wanted to give up, but we were all right there to give her that extra push she needed. Now, here she was.

My heart swelled with pride as our eyes connected in the crowd. She smiled and blew me a kiss, which I didn't hesitate to return. I snapped as many pictures as possible of her receiving her certificate before returning to her seat. Anxiously, we sat through the remainder of the program. Pasha wasted no time finding us when it was over. I spotted her coming toward us and quickly made my way through the crowd to her. When I reached her, I scooped her up in my arms and spun her around.

"I'm so proud of you, baby," I said, kissing all over her face.

"Thank you. You know, this certificate is just as much yours as it is mine. You pushed me when I needed it most. I couldn't have done this without you." She pressed her lips to mine. "Oh!"

I took a step back. "What's wrong."

She unzipped her robe and placed my hand on her slowly protruding stomach. I felt a slight movement, and a smile spread across my face.

"She's moving . . ."

"She was so active throughout the entire program. I guess she wanted me to know she was proud of me too."

We were currently twenty weeks pregnant with a healthy baby girl. It came as a shock when we first found out Pasha was expecting. She cried. She said she wasn't ready. She was terrified of losing another child. But as her belly began to grow, she fell in love. She forced the feelings of fear and doubt away and embraced the blessing growing inside her. We were having a baby, and we couldn't be any more excited about that.

"Congratulations, Mommy," I said, pecking her lips.

"Thank you, Daddy."

We shared a passionate kiss right in the middle of the hustle and bustle of the crowd. It wasn't until our families made their way over that our lips parted.

"All right now," Bella said, smirking. "That's how we got this one. Hey, TiTi's sugar pie!" She stooped to kiss Pasha's belly before pulling her into a hug. "I'm so proud of you!"

"Thank you."

Everybody else made their rounds, hugging, kissing, and congratulating my baby. I gripped the box in my pocket, waiting for the moment they were all done. I'd been waiting so long to ask her this question, and I prayed she was ready to say yes. She'd been a free woman for less than a year, but I knew in my heart that she was meant to be mine. I couldn't let another moment pass without asking her officially to do so.

"Baby?" I said softly.

She turned to me, studying my face. "Is everything okay?"

I smiled. "Everything is perfect. I wanted to ask you something."

Pulling the ring from my pocket, I dropped down on one knee. Her eyes widened, and her hand flew to her chest.

"Callum . . ."

I took her free hand in mine.

"Pasha LeAnn Brooks. . . . I love you. I think I was destined to love you from the moment I laid eyes on you. You are the embodiment of strength, resilience, and perseverance. Life took so much from you, yet you are still here, standing tall. I've watched you overcome every obstacle and jump over every hurdle. When people tried to count you out, you made a liar out of them. I'm so, so proud of the woman you've become and so in love with the woman and mother you will be. I know it hasn't been long, but, baby, I can't see me being with anybody but you. I love you with all my heart and soul. If you do me the honor of becoming my wife, I promise to spend the rest of my life making you and our daughter as happy as possible. Will you marry me, Pasha?"

I opened the ring box and presented her with the three-carat, princess-cut diamond ring. Again, her eyes widened. She looked around at our family and friends, who eagerly nodded. A crowd of spectators watched in adoration.

"Yes, . . ." she whispered, nodding. "Yes."

I slipped the ring from the box and onto her finger. The moment I stood, she threw herself into my arms and crashed her lips into mine. Cheers and claps erupted around us. When she pulled away, she playfully slapped my chest.

I chuckled. "What was that for?"

"You couldn't let me make it through the day before you made me mess up my makeup!"

I laughed out loud as I pulled her in close and whispered in her ear. "By the end of the night, it was going to be ruined anyway."

"All right, nasty!" Avyn said with her bionic ears.

We shared a laugh. Pasha and I shared yet another kiss. "How about we go grab something to eat? I'm sure both of my babies are hungry."

She smiled. "You read our mind."

Hand in hand, we left the building with our family in tow. This was the end of yet another journey, but the beginning of something beautiful.

EPILOGUE
Pasha

FIVE MONTHS LATER

Mikalya Jordan Ellis.

My beautiful baby girl came into the world screaming at eight pounds, seven ounces. She was named after her father and her big brother. The moment the doctor placed her in my arms was the second time I knew real, unconditional love. The chubby, brown-eyed baby with a headful of jet-black curls was the spitting image of her daddy.

I would have laughed if someone had told me a year and a half ago that I would be where I am today. I'd come out of a bad marriage. I was drowning in grief and depression. I had nothing to live for. Then God sent me an angel named Callum. He healed my broken heart. He restored my belief in love and gave me the courage to love again after being so broken.

It had been a long road. The work I'd done on myself was far from over. I was still seeing Dr. Thomas, though I'd dropped my visits down to once every other week. I still journaled every morning. I still meditated and did yoga. I found that both brought me peace and tranquility. Callum had even taken to practicing with me; strangely enough, it brought us closer as a couple.

I was active in my healing journey. I had the love of my friends and family. I was a mother, and my angel was now my husband. Callum and I got married at a small ceremony a month after he proposed. There was no need to wait. I knew I wanted to be with him, and he'd proven time and time again that he wanted to be with me too. The love we shared was beautiful and healing all on its own. How lucky was I to be able to call him my husband?

I looked at him, pacing the room as he held our daughter. My heart swelled with pride.

"She's so perfect," he said in utter amazement. "I can't believe we made her."

I smiled. "You're going to spoil her."

"Damn right, I am." He grinned as he fingered her curls. "Daddy's baby can have whatever she wants. Ain't that right, princess?"

He walked over and placed her in my arms. I looked down at her with those big, bright eyes. I was surprised she was awake. Then again, as much as Callum had talked to her in the womb, she was probably trying to look at him like, *"There's that motormouth."*

"Hi, Princess," I said softly, fingering her chubby cheek. "You are a miracle, you know that? You're named after two of the greatest loves of my life, and you will be nothing but great."

I kissed her forehead. "God, . . . I never know how strong this love could be so soon."

With my son, I had to bottle up all the love I wanted to give him that I never could. Mikayla was my blessing, my rainbow baby. This was my chance to shower her with every ounce of love, attention, and affection she so rightfully deserved. I would pour into her. I would honor and protect her. She would know love because of her father and me. She would be respected. She would be celebrated because life was a gift. Every day we got to live was a day we would never have again.

"Who couldn't love this face?" Callum asked, sliding into the hospital bed with me.

"You only say that because she looks just like you," I jested.

He grinned. "Well, *you* love my face."

"I love everything about you, Mr. Ellis."

"And I love everything about you, Mrs. Ellis." He looked down at Mikayla. "I guess we better soak up as much of her as possible. Everybody is on the way to meet her. You've got quite the family, MJ."

"Quite the family, indeed."

If I've learned nothing else, I've learned that love and family are two of the most important things anyone could possess. I thought I lost both of those things when I lost my parents and my son. Life and time have given me both back tenfold. My daughter had an amazing biological family and an equally amazing extended family. She was surrounded by love. She was the embodiment of the courage to love.

THE END

AFTERWORD

Thank you for reading *Courage To Love Again*. I hope you enjoyed Pasha and Callum's story as much as I enjoyed writing it! Please leave a review if you enjoyed this novel. Feel free to connect with me on Facebook, Twitter, and Instagram! Don't forget to sign up for my mailing list for sneak peeks, giveaways, and more!

Much love,
Kimberly Brown

AMAZON AUTHOR PAGE:
www.amazon.com/stores/author/B09CLQDDYG/about
FACEBOOK & INSTAGRAM: @authorkimberlybrown
FACEBOOK READERS GROUP:kimberlyscozycorner
X: @AuthorKBrown
WEBSITE: www.authorkimberlybrown.com

DEDICATION

To B.Love, my publisher and mentor, thank you for being the blessing that God put in my life. You are gifted and anointed in your purpose. I appreciate your hard work and your dedication. You inspire me to be a better writer and pursue my dreams. Thank you for making my dream of becoming a published author a reality.

To my BLP sisters, past and present, you all are such a fantastic group of women. Thank you for your unwavering love, support, and prayers. You are the best publishing family that anyone could ask for.

To LaSheera Lee, thank you for every opportunity you have worked in my favor. You do so much behind the scenes, and your hard work and advocacy are unmatched.

To my readers, I love y'all! You all show up and show out for me every single time. You have made my author journey so enjoyable. I appreciate every page read, every recommendation, every like, share, or message in my inbox. Thank you for your unwavering support and for allowing me to share my gift with you.

To Black Odyssey Media, thank you for the opportunity to share this story with the world.

Last but not least, to my love, thank you for sticking out this journey with me and being my support system. You've dealt with the long nights, back-to-back deadlines, traveling for book events, and hustling my paperbacks at work, LOL. I love you, and I appreciate your patience so that I can live out my dream.